AURORA

ALSO BY DAVID KOEPP

Cold Storage

AURORA

A NOVEL

DAVID KOEPP

HARPER

An Imprint of HarperCollinsPublishers

AURORA. Copyright © 2022 by David Koepp. All rights reserved. Printed in the United States of America. No part of this book may be used or reproduced in any manner whatsoever without written permission except in the case of brief quotations embodied in critical articles and reviews. For information, address HarperCollins Publishers, 195 Broadway, New York, NY 10007.

HarperCollins books may be purchased for educational, business, or sales promotional use. For information, please email the Special Markets Department at SPsales@harpercollins.com.

FIRST EDITION

Library of Congress Cataloging-in-Publication Data has been applied for.

ISBN 978-0-06-291647-1

22 23 24 25 26   LSC   10 9 8 7 6 5 4 3 2 1

For Melissa,
around whom I am in orbit

We are here to help each other get through this thing, whatever it is.

—Mark Vonnegut, MD, in a letter to Kurt Vonnegut,
as quoted in *Bluebeard*

AURORA

THE CARRINGTON EVENT

On September 1, 1859, a giant cloud of solar plasma drenched with magnetic field lines, brewed deep inside the sun's convective zone, erupted from the corona and burst free of the star's gravitational pull. A coronal mass ejection (CME) is in itself no big solar news—typically, the sun belches out three or four of them per earth day at the peak of its activity cycle. But on that day in 1859, the dense gaseous cloud of the CME was significantly greater than usual, about the total mass of Mount Everest, and the angle of its inflection happened to target it perfectly toward the earth. The resulting electromagnetic chaos would come to be known as the Carrington Event, named after the British astronomer who witnessed it.

Traveling at six million miles per hour, the solar energy breached the earth's magnetosphere seventeen hours after eruption, enveloping the planet in electrical current. Telegraph operators across the globe reported streams of fire bursting from their signal boards, platinum relay switches melted, and, around the world, there were reports that the night skies lit up as in daytime. The swirling magnetic displays of the northern lights were visible as far south as Cuba and Jamaica, the southern lights as far north as Colombia.

Thankfully, in 1859, telegraph systems were the only significant electrical networks in operation anywhere and could be repaired within a few days. For the vast majority of the earth's inhabitants, life immediately went back to normal, and the Carrington Event did little more than enliven the last few humdrum days of summer.

Twenty-three years later, on September 4, 1882, Thomas Edison would turn on the generators at Pearl Street Station, in Lower Manhattan, activating America's first power grid. Human beings were on the path to total electrical addiction.

A major CME hits the earth full force, on average, every hundred and fifty years.

We are overdue.

PART I
ONSET

1.

The thing about Norman Levy was that everyone knew Norman Levy. As a college professor at the University of Chicago, he'd been a magnetic force for talented and curious people and could always spot a kindred spirit when he saw one. Students who'd never quite fit in anywhere felt utterly at home in the professor's cramped college office, or over dinners and coffees and drinks at his wood-frame house near the end of Cayuga Lane, in nearby Aurora. Norman, a solar scientist, had dedicated his entire professional life to the study of the sun, but his real and abiding interest was in people. A childless widower, he collected friends the way some people collect butterflies, but not to press them into a book; no, he wanted to prod and question and provoke them, to *talk* to them. There was, he was certain, absolutely nothing more worth doing than talking to people.

But not at 6:32 a.m. Central Standard Time, which was the exact moment when the phone on the wall in his kitchen rang on Tuesday, April 14. Norman, standing at the sink and staring out the window while the coffee brewed, stirred himself from his pre-caffeine reverie and scowled at the phone. A line from a movie ran uselessly through his head—"None of my friends would call at this hour"—which was a lie. His friends called all the time, it was the curse of knowing people in myriad time zones. Norman shuffled over to the phone, tilted his glasses up so he could read the caller ID, and saw SILVER SPRING, MARYLAND. He picked up the handset.

"We've talked about this," Norman said.

The voice from the other end was tense and excited. "Did you see any imaging from GOES-16 in the past twenty-four hours?"

"It's six-thirty in the morning here, kiddo."

"And I'm calling you anyway, Norman. So, imagine."

Norman could hear the urgency in Perry St. John's voice, and he cleared his throat, pulling himself to attention. He liked Perry and had since the moment the kid walked into his Introduction to Astrophysics class, listened to one lecture, then went right up to the revered professor and announced that he was looking for a mentor and had just settled on Norman. Who could resist that kind of chutzpah? Twenty years of dinners and phone calls and e-mails after that first day in class, Perry was one of the lead researchers at NOAA's main observation station monitoring solar events. He put up with the lily-white astronomic industry giving him second looks and suspicious glances and, boy, did he get tired of saying, "Yes, Neil deGrasse Tyson *is* a great inspiration to me." But he stayed with it, even when they started pushing him into media interviews just so they could have a Black face out there, because it was the job he was born to do. He liked to tell people he was a weatherman, which was technically true, but the kind of storms he monitored made category 5 earth hurricanes look like spring showers.

He repeated his question to Norman. "Have you seen imaging from the past cycle?"

"Last night," Norman said, "and thank you again for the login. Hours of fun. *Hours*, Perry."

"Did you see the flare?"

"Yes. Two of 'em, big ones. SUVI picked it up. They saturated the X-ray irradiance sensors, so I haven't checked back. Why?"

Perry paused on the other end, thinking. "Is it possible they masked a secondary burst? Or tertiary?"

Norman furrowed his brow. "I suppose. Did the radiation hit DSCOVR yet?"

DSCOVR, the Deep Space Climate Observatory satellite, had been a crucial tool in the monitoring of space weather in general and solar activity in particular since late 2015, when after its successful launch it took up its orbit at Lagrange point 1, a neutral gravity sweet spot about a million miles from the earth. From there, DSCOVR essentially hovered in place between the earth and sun, the array of sensors in its nose beaming near-to-real-time information back to NOAA.

"Yes," Perry answered, "they'll miss earth by seven degrees in about forty-five minutes. It's what's behind them I'm talking about."

"What's behind them?"

"There was a third flare, zero degrees of inflection, and it's moving through cleared space. New images are posted in the nowcasting. Take a look. I'll wait."

Ignoring the coffee, Norman took the cordless phone into his study and sat at the big oak dining table he used for a desk. He flipped open his laptop, cradled the phone on his shoulder, and went directly to the NOAA site that featured integrated images from GOES-16 and NASA's orbiting Solar Dynamics Observatory. To the untrained eye, the sets of solar images and strings of data on Norman's screen would have been meaningless, but to a mind that had been assimilating data both in visual and quantitative form like this for sixty-five years, the coronal captures and strings of numeric data he saw were the astronomical equivalent of a guy standing on the edge of a cliff, waving a lantern, and screaming, "The bridge is out!"

"Angle of inflection was what now?" Norman asked.

"Zero," Perry repeated, though he was sure Norman had heard him.

Norman blinked. He absorbed the data. Twice.

"This can't be right," he said.

"Let's assume it is," Perry said. "Do you have time to run a few models?"

"I'm eighty-eight fucking years old, Perry. Of course I have time."

"Model out the particle radiation at geostationary orbit," Perry said.

"No kidding." Norman was fully alert and on it now. He opened up a second laptop, logged in to the CME public monitoring dashboard run by the Goddard Space Flight Center, and began to pull data from the hundreds of amateur enthusiasts all over the world who kept an unofficial eye on sunspot activity. Perry wasn't the only one who'd noticed the unusual amounts of proton and X-ray flux that had erupted in the past eighteen hours. The sun-watching community was recording, posting, and interpreting like mad. What Norman saw confirmed what Perry had suggested: there had been not one but a series of three flares, each bigger than the last, and the sheer luminosity of the first two had, in effect, blinded the array of monitoring equipment to the massive third flare, which had released a CME that was now surfing through space in the relatively clear solar wake of the previous disruptions.

The information Norman began loading into his self-designed modeling software was complex and wide-ranging, covering physical and technological risk factors to the earth's power supply based on the potential impact of a plasma field of the size and intensity they'd just recorded. When he hit enter and the final result displayed in a small flashing box on his screen, Norman felt the floor sinking away from him.

"Shit," he said.

"What'd you get?"

"My model's no good. Running another. Hang on." He cleared the field and started over, pulling data from different collection sites around the world, running an alternate scenario, varying the electrical-field amplitudes and direction as widely as he could imagine. He wanted a different outcome.

He wanted to be wrong.

At NOAA, Perry sat at his monitoring station and listened to Norman's frantic typing on the other end of the phone. Norman had been one of the foremost solar researchers of his era for a reason: his models were never wrong. Perry knew whatever Norman's first result had been, it would prove accurate. But he also knew better than to interrupt the old man while he was working. Impatient, Perry pulled data and ran his own models while he waited.

Behind him, his colleagues looked up from their early-morning fogs, wondering what he was up to. Ken Murtagh, an IT IS WHAT IT IS coffee mug in hand, peered over Perry's shoulder while the young maestro banged away at a series of computers. Terry Fitzpatrick, who'd been up with a grandbaby all night and was too tired to get out of his chair, just tiny-stepped it over across the floor, rolling up on Perry's other side and squinting down at his screens.

Murtagh saw the various images and data streams playing past and regarded Perry suspiciously. "What is this? You playing a game?" Because the numbers couldn't be right.

Fitzpatrick looked at the data, then at Perry. He pushed his glasses up on top of his head and asked a question.

"Glancing blow?"

"Doesn't look like it."

Fitz just stared at the screen, absorbing the information as Perry loaded it into the simulations. "How long?"

Perry, who'd been cradling his cell phone to his shoulder, realized his neck was killing him and lifted his head, letting the phone drop to the desktop with a clatter while he inputted. From the other end of the call, the others could hear Norman's agitated voice calling out, "Hey! Hey, you still there?!" But Perry kept typing, running one model after another, and each time one of them pinged with its COMPLETE message, the result was the same, or similar.

"Perry," Fitz said with rising urgency, "how long do we have?"

From the phone, Norman's voice was squawking, distorting the speaker. Murtagh reached down, turned the phone over, and hit the speaker button. Norman's voice burst out, too loud.

"—not wrong! This shit is *not* wrong!"

Heads turned all over the room. Others started to filter over, and Norman's voice distorted through the speaker. Perry held up a hand, silencing the argument behind him for a moment while he hit enter, telling the computer to run his final simulation. They all shut up, waiting for it. The computer pinged with a conclusion.

Perry looked down at his cell phone, on the desktop. "Norman? You still there?"

"Yeah."

"You ran it?"

"Three times, with Convac's new transformer specs. You?"

"Same." Perry cleared his throat. "It's Carrington-level, isn't it?" The seven men and women who were now assembled behind him stared down at the phone, waiting for a response from someone on the other end whom none of them knew. But for some reason, everything relied on that unknown man's reply.

From the speaker, Norman's voice was raspy. "In the thirtieth year, in the fifth day of the fourth month, as I was among the exiles on the banks of the river Chebar—"

Murtagh interrupted, like a man who suddenly realizes he is the butt of a joke. "Excuse me, who the hell are you and what exactly are we doing here?"

Undeterred, Norman finished the quote. "—heaven opened and I saw visions from God."

Perry looked up at Murtagh. "It's the Bible."

"No shit it's the Bible. Why is that old man quoting the Bible?"

"Ezekiel's vision, 593 B.C.," Perry said. "Some people think it was earth's first recorded auroral event."

Fitz put a hand on Perry's shoulder. "How long 'til it hits, Perry?"

"Between seven and twelve hours. Give or take. Solar winds are highly variable."

Fitz stood up and looked at Murtagh, whose already pale face was several shades whiter than it had been a few minutes ago.

"So we're islanding?" Fitz asked.

"I'm not calling that. Are you calling that?"

"Ken, it's a worldwide black-sky event."

"I'll call a stepdown," Murtagh said.

"A *stepdown*? Why not just put on a pair of *sunglasses*? How many plus-1,000 amps on the grid are pre-1972?"

"Top of my head? At least two thousand."

Fitz nodded, thinking. "Start with those. I'll call around and try to get a handle on how many of the other ten thousand have winding hot spots likely to blow with thirty DC amps per phase."

Perry shook his head. "You'd better figure fifty."

"OK, fifty." Fitz was activated now, his fatigue forgotten.

But Murtagh was frozen in place. "I don't even know where to start."

Fitz looked at him. "Start?" he asked. "We gotta silo the whole fucking country."

In Aurora, Norman put the cordless phone down on his desk and let their argument play out over the tinny speaker. He pushed himself up out of his chair, regarding for a moment the complex home radio setup that crowded the far end of his desk. Soon enough, he thought, that's going to be the only way to communicate.

He went to the window, the big one that looked out over the cul-de-sac on which he lived. The sun was just breaking up the pre-dawn sky but hadn't come over the horizon. Nearly all the houses were dark, except for the occasional porch light still on from the night before. As Norman watched, the mercury-vapor streetlights winked out as they did every morning, their sensors picking up that they were no longer needed. He looked up at the sky, where the sun's light still reflected off the surface of Venus. As he watched, the first fuzzy edge of the sun's corona crested the trees on the far side of the street and Norman stared into its wavering hot edge until his eyes watered and he had to turn away.

He closed his eyes and tried to imagine what it all meant for the world, but it was impossible. The planet was too vast, its systems too complex, and his mind couldn't hold it all. Everything, *everything* was about to become local. All that would matter in his life was what would happen on this block, what would become of these people and the ones they loved, what choices they would make, and the unpredictable skein of consequences that would be spun from them.

Norman closed his eyes and tried to prepare for the coming storm.

2.

Aubrey Wheeler looked down at the chipped paint on her fingernails and wondered when the last time was that she considered a man attractive. It certainly wasn't now, and it definitely wasn't either of these two guys.

The conference had been in Kansas City, but not even the good Kansas City, whichever one that was supposed to be. Whichever-the-hell Kansas City she'd had to go to was five hundred inconvenient miles from Aurora, a distance that translated into either an eight-hour drive for a six-hour conference or an overcrowded flight on a shit airline. She'd chosen the flight, on a no-frills carrier that didn't assign seats, and after a free-for-all at boarding, she'd ended up in a middle spot between two ex-high-school-football types whose concept of personal space was that her space was for their person. Having no intention of staying stressed and angry for the whole ninety-minute flight, Aubrey had popped a Xanax far too early in the day and was now driving home from O'Hare foggy, crabby, and vaguely depressed.

Actually, her depression wasn't as vague as all that; it was quite focused and specific, because she was headed back into the lion's den. She remembered, barely, the days when business travel used to leave her somewhat invigorated and refreshed—days when it had been a chance to get away from Scott and Rusty for a decent stretch, to sleep better and longer and read and eat whatever she wanted, without worrying about whether anybody else would want to eat it too. But those days were long gone. Gone in the dust of COVID, gone along with her peace of mind, the better part of her thirties, and her marriage.

Before the pandemic, the conference business she'd started and run had done fairly well. But overnight, the number of people who were willing to sit in a windowless air-conditioned room with five hundred strangers dropped to nothing, and Aubrey was forced to contemplate bankruptcy within months. She'd furloughed the entire staff. But three nights later she awoke in the night with a Genius Idea, a revelation that was not-so-slowly dawning on the rest of the business community at the same time. Namely, why do I ever have to leave my house again? She'd pivoted the company to an all-Zoom platform in seventy-two hours and hired back half the staff within a week. By the end of the first year in their new configuration, they had nearly as many employees as in their heady pre-plague days. And more clients than ever, who were willing to pay as much or more for the convenience of attending a conference from the comfort of home. Sure, some morons had eventually insisted on holding in-person conferences again, hence her deeply resented trip to Missouri-or-Kansas, but ninety percent of their work was now online, and profitable. She'd even managed to resume pulling a decent salary, which was an enormous relief to Rusty, as he was a shit and a vampire.

Were those words cheap slurs? You bet! But they were also accurate descriptors that summed up the two dominant aspects of her ex-husband's personality. Rusty was a "shit," used in the classical sense of "waste matter expelled from the body," because he had been an enormous misuse of her time, resources, and love. And as of two years ago, she had most definitely expelled him from her body. He could also be accurately described as a "vampire," if one took the word to mean "a person who preys ruthlessly on others." You could even go so far as to call its primary definition—"a monstrous bloodsucker"—appropriate, because Rusty had drained the spirit and energy out of Aubrey 'til she felt hollow, like an empty suit coat splayed open on the floor.

She knew it wasn't all his fault. She remembered vividly what he'd been like when they'd first met. He was strong and he knew it, in all the ways that confidence is attractive and none of the ones in which it's ugly. He radiated strength and authority, not with gross bravado but in a quiet I-am-possessed-of-a-power-that-I-need-not-use kind of way. Rusty was a general contractor, a good and honest and successful one. Aubrey had always used her mind for work, and she liked the idea of somebody who used their hands for theirs. Best of all, her husband had been the polar opposite of her older brother—Rusty was unserious, physical, and grounded. She'd loved him until he became unlovable.

The last few years Rusty's drinking reached blackout level—which had apparently been the issue in his first marriage, and thanks so much for telling me, Cheryl Anne—and in the end that made it easy for Aubrey. Or easier, anyway. The guy she'd loved wasn't there anymore, and this new guy wasn't welcome. Slowly at first, and then seemingly all at once, the guy she thought she knew was into booze, drugs, rages, long hours lost playing poker, and she was fairly certain he was getting involved in some sort of minor crime; odd sorties at all hours to do God-knows-what with some sketchy buddy of his. No, Rusty had to go, so out he went, out of the house they'd bought together and out of the life they'd planned in such careful detail.

But the twist in the story, the kicker, the sting in the tail, as they say, was that Rusty didn't take all his stuff with him when he went. He left Scott behind.

He didn't actually *leave* Scott; it was more that Scott stayed. Rusty's son from his first marriage was fourteen at the time, old enough to get into trouble, which he did, old enough to know that his mother lived too far away and didn't care enough to take care of him, which she didn't, and young enough to think that if he could just make a few smart choices about his life, he could free himself from the shit cycle of neglect and substance abuse that had consumed both his parents. Outcome pending on that third one.

Because they were both men, and Midwestern ones at that, Scott and Rusty didn't sit down and actually *discuss* a new living arrangement. It was more that they came to realize it in each other's presence at about the same time one morning. Specifically, that moment was fifteen minutes after Rusty had told Scott, "Get your shit and be downstairs. We're leaving." Scott did not get his shit or go downstairs.

Rusty looked up the ancient, rickety staircase that had been first on his punch list for four years—he was for *sure* gonna get to that one—and shouted. "You coming or what?"

Scott shouted back, through his closed bedroom door. "Fuck off."

Rusty turned and looked at Aubrey, who was slouched sideways in the kitchen door, half in and half out, as if there were no room she wanted to be in right now.

"You put him up to this?"

Aubrey just glared at him. *Give me a break.*

Rusty turned back to the stairs and yelled up to Scott again. "You stay now, you're staying for good."

At this point, some teenagers would have shouted something incoherent and slammed the door. Others might have cranked up the volume on something by Death Grips, a rap group rivaled in their abrasiveness only by the sound of someone chewing aluminum foil in your ear. But Scott Wheeler just opened his door, walked to the top of the stairs, looked down at his father, and touched his forehead with two fingers of his right hand in an insouciant goodbye salute.

"Adios, asshole."

Rusty picked up his bag and left.

At 10:47 that morning, Aubrey had been thirty-six, childless, newly single, and ready to accept whatever exciting adventure life held in store for her.

At 10:48, she had a fourteen-year-old to raise. Somebody *else's* fourteen-year-old.

Hey, life, that wasn't what I fucking meant.

It was home to Scott that Aubrey now raced. It was just after one in the afternoon, which meant if she hurried and traffic didn't conspire against her, she'd be at the house by two, plenty of time to toss Scott's room before he got home from school. She'd arranged for him to stay at a friend's for the two nights she was gone, but she'd had no illusions about his true intentions, which had almost certainly been to spend the night with Caprice in the Aubrey-less house on Cayuga Lane. Scott had turned fifteen six months ago, too young to give up one's virginity, in Aubrey's opinion, but that was between him and his consenting partners. It was the substances she was concerned about.

Both of Scott's parents were drunks. Genetics were squarely lined up against the young man, and Aubrey had no intention of letting him fall down that dark hole on her watch. A week before the trip, she'd set up three Zmodo surveillance cameras throughout the house, connected by Wi-Fi to an app on her phone she could access with any decent signal. One camera had gone in the kitchen, hidden in a stack of cookbooks, one in the living room, stashed among a tower of neglected board games, and the third hidden among the dozens of unread books on Scott's bedroom shelves.

Aubrey had quickly shut that one down, after a test run a few days before leaving nearly seared her eyeballs with the image of a perfectly normal adolescent function that she had somehow failed to consider. Look, it hadn't occurred to her, OK? She'd never been a teenage boy. In the end, the video system had proved worthless, unless she was actually in the house and on Wi-Fi. As soon as she was in the car and on her way to the airport, the images had blanked out, one after another, and so the house had been unsupervised, in a digital sense, the whole time she was gone. She'd spoken to Scott, who'd affirmed that he was at his friend Julian's house as they'd agreed, and she'd reminded herself to put a tracking app on his phone the next time she got a chance. So he was fine. But she just wanted to take a quick look through his room to make sure.

Her Uber passed through Stolp Island, the red-hot beating center of things in Aurora, Illinois, if you can call a couple blocks of closed-down shops, a decrepit movie house, and a second-rate casino red-hot. Aubrey had grown up in West Aurora, a mile or two away, in a comfortable two-story house with her parents and older brother. She and her brother had always loved their trips to Stolp when she was little. It was *downtown*, and not the scary kind of downtown full of lost people, like in Chicago, but an old-world downtown that belonged to the 1950s, the type of place where you could buy an Archie comic on the wire rack at the Ben Franklin. Aubrey had never personally encountered an Archie comic, a wire rack, or a Ben Franklin as either a child or an adult, but she'd heard of them in certain books and movies and held a perfect, romantic image of them in her mind. That, she'd hoped, was what she'd give her kids, a place like that where they could grow up and be safe. Her brother had since moved off to seek his fortune, but Aubrey remained, determined to find something that hadn't really existed for fifty years.

Cayuga Lane fit the model of what Aubrey had been trying to build since she was little. Ten minutes from downtown, it was a short cul-de-sac with six houses, most of them old builds from the 1920s or '30s. The house near the end of it was an 1850s Victorian, one of those two-story flat-roofed numbers that were once so popular but had failed to survive much past the quick-build era of World War II. Somehow, this one had staggered on into modern times and had been completely gutted, insulated, and remodeled. In 1958.

Since then, it had fallen into a state of benign neglect, followed by a period of malignant neglect, followed by a "perfect lot with tear-down opportunity!" phase, which was when she and Rusty had first seen it. The decrepit state of the house was the only reason it was on the market at a price they could even consider when they'd picked it up five years ago. They'd known there was a massive amount of work to be done, but Rusty was a contractor and they were young and in love and they looked forward to doing it, and all things, together.

Until they didn't.

Now the house was five years older, and so was Aubrey, though some days it felt like fifteen, and she was in the familiar position of trying, alone, to fix something that was probably beyond repair. On the rare occasions that she and her brother still saw each other, he would mock her mercilessly for her insistence on repair and recycling, as he'd done since they were teenagers. He, who would take one sip of juice from a plastic bottle and throw it away. . . . He, who as an adult decried the use of cheap foreign labor at the same time he profited from it. . . . He, who'd send a computer and a phone jammed with rare-earth minerals off to the landfill every eighteen months, whether they still worked or not, would make fun of *her* for trying to fix a hole in her favorite blouse.

Aubrey's car dropped her off at the house and she hurried up the uneven front walk, her rolly-bag's cheap plastic wheels complaining in the cracked stone. She knew before she got to the step that Scott was inside the house, in direct violation of their agreement that he stay at Julian's 'til she called him. Perhaps the criminal mastermind might have considered closing the front door if he'd really wanted to go undetected. She could hear the TV blaring in the living room.

She came inside and saw the back of Scott's head, silhouetted against the seventy-seven-inch Sony he'd talked her into shortly after his dad moved out. That was early days. She'd told herself the TV was a lure, that it was better to have him interested in being in a central part of the house, where they could commune with each other and she could offer wise and kind guidance, rather than locked in his room at all times. But she'd known the real reason she got it. She just needed a little space to hide and pull her shit together, and maybe the TV would keep him busy.

Scott heard the door and turned. He blinked at her. "You're home."

"So are you."

Scott furrowed his brow, thinking. "I did not expect this."

"Clearly." She closed the door behind her and shoved her bag into the corner.

He turned back to the TV. For some reason, he was watching cable news. Her brain dimly noted that this was not his usual fare. His back still turned, Scott pointed to the TV. "I think you should watch this."

"I'm going upstairs to change, and then you and I are going to talk. This is not what we discussed, and I'm very disappointed."

Scott didn't bother to turn around. Three talking heads in a studio were hotly debating something that was probably pointless. His finger extended, Scott shook it at the screen, for emphasis. "I really think you should watch this."

Aubrey ignored him and bounded up the creaky stairs with as much energy as she could muster. She made a lot of noise going up, then lightened her step when she turned at the top, headed for his room instead of hers. She opened his door softly and looked around. The bed was in its usual state of chaos, impossible for it to look any more unmade if deliberate effort had been put into it. Clothes were every-where, so were the remains of food, and there were glasses scattered around every flat surface, various sugary, colored liquids fermenting within.

Aubrey went to the dresser and opened the drawers, one after the other, running her hands through the contents. No bottles hidden there. Likewise, there were no bags of weed under the mattress or in the nightstand, no scent of smoke in the air, and the glasses she sniffed seemed innocent of liquor. Satisfied, she turned to leave, pleased that she had one less thing to fight about with him. But as she turned, she saw it. Sitting right out in the open, on top of his dresser.

An orange prescription bottle. He hadn't even felt the need to hide it.

Downstairs, she walked in front of him, cutting off most of his view of the gigantic TV, and put the bottle on the coffee table between them.

Scott glanced down at it and shrugged.

"I didn't think you were coming home." He leaned around her, try-ing to see the TV.

"What the fuck do you think you're doing?"

"Would it be possible to discuss this later?"

She resisted the urge to explode. "Scott, it's hydrocodone."

"Yah," he said.

"From my root canal."

"Oh, is that where you got it? Right. Makes sense. That ever give you any more trouble?"

"What is the *matter* with you?"

"I didn't think you were coming—"

"Will you *please* shut up about whether or not you thought I was coming home? You went into my medicine cabinet—or no, actually, you searched my bathroom drawers, until you found some fucking *oxy*, and then you took it, and you're *fifteen years old*, and these are *opiates*, goddamn it!"

Scott turned to her, engaged now. "OK, I didn't search your shit *until* I found some oxy, I searched your shit and *then* I found some oxy, which is, like, super different, OK?"

In a sense, one had to admire, if not the substance of his argument, then at least his willingness to try to steer the conversation onto a path more fruitful for his cause. Aubrey did not feel admiring.

"Fuck off, Scott."

"Nice parenting."

"You are in the wrong here."

"I'm not the only one. You planted cameras to watch me."

She paused. She tried to match his calm. "What are you talking about?"

He didn't bother to answer that, just half laughed and nodded over his shoulder, where she could now see the three Zmodos had been stacked on the entry table. She hadn't noticed them when she'd come in, but clearly, they were there for her.

"I'm not an idiot," he said.

Things were making sense to her now. "You turned them off."

"The minute you left."

"I suppose you didn't practice the piano, either," she said, trying to regain the upper hand.

He just ignored that, looking back at the TV.

Aubrey persisted. "Did Caprice stay here?"

"Celeste."

"What?"

"Her name is Celeste. Not Caprice. You always call her Caprice."

"Whatever. Did she stay here?"

"You call her Caprice because you think she has a 'Black' name, so your brain picks Caprice, 'cause you think that sounds *more* Black, which is actually super racist. Seriously, Aubrey, you gotta work on that. Reflect on your privilege and shit."

"Me picking a name that sounds 'more Black' would not be my privilege; it would be my racism. At least get it straight."

"So you admit it."

"You are exhausting, and I don't like you."

"Well, that hurts my feelings, because I like you."

She took a breath and regained equilibrium. "How many pills did you take?"

He thought for a moment. "Four. Two at a time, four hours apart, in strict compliance with the instructions on the label."

"Incredibly responsible."

"Thank you. Are you mad because oxy is bad for me, or are you mad because they were your secret stash?"

"Both. They're terrible for you, and I was saving them."

"For what?"

"Situations of unmanageable pain."

He nodded. "Well, I'm in one. They helped me."

"Helped you with what, may I ask?"

Once again, he pointed a long finger at the TV screen. "We're all gonna die."

This time Aubrey turned and looked. It wasn't cable news Scott was watching; it was network. But it wouldn't have mattered what station he was on. The news was everywhere, and the headlines and chyrons and scrolling tickers were in a size of typeface generally reserved for the Second Coming.

Aubrey watched, stunned. She couldn't immediately comprehend what the people on television were saying. This couldn't be happening. Hadn't we already gone through everything we possibly could?

Scott leaned over, picked up the prescription bottle, and shook it at her.

"Only eight left. Splitsies?"

3.

MOUNTAIN VIEW, CALIFORNIA

Thom Banning was on the move. He'd been briefed on the solar situation shortly after arriving at the Vida headquarters, on the periphery of Silicon Valley, and was pleased with how quickly he had adapted, how he had *willed* his mind into acceptance of this obvious threshold, this signal event in humankind's technological history. Thom wasn't just unsurprised by the impending disaster, he wasn't just prepared for it. The ugly truth, furiously buried by Thom but obvious to anyone who knew him, was that he was *looking forward* to it.

Like many entrepreneurs, the mental exercise of trying to anticipate the future occupied Thom's mind twenty-four hours a day. There was little cognitive difference, he liked to assert, between his waking state and his dream state, in that both were dedicated to productive thought on whatever was the task at hand. As a little boy, his family had stopped in Fort Myers, Florida, one sweltering spring vacation and taken a tour of Thomas Edison's house and laboratory. The pilgrimage was planned largely as a paean to the boy's budding technical genius, which his parents obsessed over from the time he was old enough to put Snap Circuits together. Edison's house was a bore to the kids and the lab had seemed dusty and uninteresting, but what had stayed with Thom was the nap cot.

It was there—on a tiny six-foot-by-two-and-a-half-foot plank with a thin straw mattress tucked in a corner of the lab—that Edison had taken his famous restorative naps throughout the day. What dreams must have come from those naps, young Thom Banning thought. Not for the first time, he saw his given name as destiny. He decided two things, then and there: that his nickname would never be spelled without the H, lest anyone miss the obvious and appropriate connection with Edison, and that, when grown, he would never ignore the vital creative powers of his dream life.

He kept both vows. It was, in fact, in a semi-waking state that the idea for his robotics firm, Vida, was born. It's harder to nap in your twenties, unless you haven't slept at night, so as a post-graduate Thom would force himself to stay up 'til the morning hours for that very purpose. He wanted to enter his workday sleepy, so that he could drop into a REM state, which he had come to view as the most fertile of all states of human consciousness, at a moment's notice. Vida began, one drowsy August afternoon, as a rather workaday bit of code Thom had literally dreamed up that would provide simple AI enhancement for auto-assembly robotics. Hardly the stuff of great fortunes, but the idea had the distinct advantage of being able to make money right out of the gate. Profit was built into concept. In the years that followed, Thom's ideas, and, increasingly, those of the technological wizzes he hired and whose patents he came to dominate, blended unexpectedly with the emerging nanotech industry. Soon Vida penetrated every corner of the medical and surgical fields, and by the end of its first decade, it was almost impossible to have surgery at any major hospital in the developed world without at least one Vida-produced robotic tool poking around in your flesh.

Thom made his first billion just before he turned thirty-three and threw a lavish birthday party in Belize on Christmas Day. That was not the actual day of his birth—he was born on November 4, and the 25th of December already belonged to another famous historical figure—but Thom picked it to celebrate that year because thirty-three happened to be the age at which Christ died. Thom's intention by this point, stated only to himself, was to live longer and have a greater impact than that guy.

Lest anyone, including Thom, think for a moment that his delusions of grandeur were serious, he would often point them out, to himself and others, in mildly self-deprecating jokes. Thom did not seriously consider himself on a par with Edison or Christ. He was kidding.

Sorta.

One of the hallmarks of Thom's public persona was a famous, somewhat exaggerated case of dyslexia. It made for good press, though it wasn't entirely true. Mostly, he just disliked reading and was easily distracted, so he often found himself re-reading paragraphs three or four times in a row or, worse, skipping over them entirely if they began to bore.

He had no such struggle with direct conversation, however, and had learned at an early age that if someone sat down, looked him in the eye, and told him something, he had a far greater chance of retaining it. As soon as he could afford it, he turned to the idea of paid advisers, experts who would give him an hour of their time and patiently explain a concept, pastime, or industry to him. Renaissance art, the sport of cricket, and brain–computer interface were all introduced to him in this way, with an expert in the field patiently walking him through the basics. At first, he was happy to compensate them, but, as happens, once he got rich he suddenly realized he didn't need to pay for anything anymore. People just did it for free, reaping the dubious benefit of being within the inner circle of the Great Man.

So it was that Dr. Divya Singh, of the Defense Science Board, ended up on the TV screen in the back of Thom's bespoke Chevy Suburban at 11 a.m. on the morning of the event.

"Thanks for taking a minute, Divya. I know you're busy," Thom began.

Dr. Singh nodded tightly, in a let's-get-to-the-point manner. Thom could see from her background that she was in her office in Arlington, headquarters of the National Science Advisory committee, of which she was co-chair. Around her were a number of computer monitors and TV screens. Reams of bound paper covered her desk. Singh, in her late sixties, was old-school and still found it easiest to think with a manuscript and a highlighter in her hand.

"How long ago did you hear?" she asked.

Thom glanced at his watch. "Forty-seven minutes."

"You're going to Hayward?" Singh asked, referring to the largest private airfield in the San Francisco area.

Thom shook his head. "Everybody'll go to Hayward or Buchanan. There'll be a lineup and they won't be able to take off for hours. That's why I hangar at Half-Moon Bay. It's farther, but it'll be just us and the air-show guys."

"Smart. OK, what do you need to know?"

"I understand the CME itself. But I need to know everything about the impact and the effects on infrastructure."

Dr. Singh looked up, muted her microphone, and shouted something to someone off-camera. The place was a swarm of activity all around her. Thom could see hands reaching into the frame, giving her things, taking scribbled notes from her, and the images of people moving in and out of her office reflected in the window behind her. She unmuted.

"Sorry. OK." She thought for a second, then did her best to summarize. "At impact, the electromagnetic surge will begin in the polar regions and travel north and south along the lines of the magnetosphere. The flux fields will change rapidly in intensity and induce massive geomagnetic currents to flow into and through any interconnected electric power grids."

"Meaning power stations and sub-stations?"

"Oh, God, much more than that. Any power-generating or power-relaying structure or wire that is not equipped with a sufficient capacitor is going to blow out."

"*Any* power structure or wire?" he asked.

"Yes. Everything from a nuclear power plant to your coffeepot. If it's connected to the grid and turned on, it will blow."

"But there are capacitors in place, aren't there? To trip the system in case of a sudden surge?"

"Of course there are," she said, trying not to let her irritation show. Thom pretended not to see it. He knew she didn't have time for this, not in the slightest, but he also knew that, like many in her job, she felt a certain obligation to the super-rich, who could theoretically change the entire trajectory of her research and career based on a momentary whim or whiff of good feeling.

She continued, trying to keep her tone level. "But the capacitors would have to be able to handle a sudden and prolonged surge of fifty amps per circuit."

"What percentage of capacitors can handle that?"

"For sustained bursts? Zero. They haven't been invented yet."

"What has the government done to prepare for this?"

"The House passed an excellent bill in 2010, the Grid Reliability and Infrastructure Defense Act. It was never brought to the Senate floor."

"Let's talk post-impact. Where will it be worst?"

"In this country, the most intense areas of effect will be the northeast corridor from Boston to D.C. and the upper Midwest—Illinois, Wisconsin, Indiana, Ohio—gradually diminishing through Western Pennsylvania, with breakdowns accelerating again closer to the East Coast."

"So the West Coast is OK?"

"Not at all. It's somewhat better situated in terms of the length of line between transformers, which is a good thing, but seawater is highly conductive, and where the ocean touches land, the ground conductivity will go berserk. Magnetically induced current will work its way inland in a matter of minutes. You should plan for the complete collapse of the West Coast."

Thom stifled a grim smile. *Oh, I'm prepared, all right.*

Singh continued. "Your repair time could be shorter out there, though."

"How much shorter?"

"Depends on availability of equipment and the damage to manufacturing capacity."

"A range, please?"

"Four to six months for the West Coast, as opposed to twelve to eighteen months for the rest of the country."

"You're saying portions of this country will be without power for *a year and a half*?"

"If you believe the 2013 Lloyd's report, yes. Significant portions."

Thom blew out a long breath. He glanced up and caught the eyes of Brady, his driver, who had been listening. Brady's eyes flicked back to the road.

Thom looked back to Dr. Singh. "But most of the damage will be to the East and West coasts and certain areas of the Midwest. Is that right?"

"At first. I was talking about initial stages—impact to plus three or four minutes. But electrical collapse is contagious. The CME that hit Quebec in '89 caused chain collapse as far south as Minnesota, and that was an off-angle contact. This is a direct hit from the largest energized plasma surge the planet has seen in several hundred years. I'd expect the latent effects of system collapse to ripple throughout the country—and the world, except for perhaps a belt around the equator—for up to thirty days afterwards. Eventually everything's going down. Almost complete destruction of communications and other critical infrastructure."

Thom paused for a moment. Since he was eighteen, he'd been a semi-professional disaster scenarist. The possibility of sudden, catastrophic collapse of one's world was something he'd trained his mind to accept and prepare for. He'd lived it once and refused to repeat the experience. His prepping was an obsession, a sickness and compulsion rooted in personal experience and a profound need to never, ever be caught unaware again. He'd spent twenty years thinking of the worst, most unexpected things that could possibly happen to himself and his world, but never, not in his darkest moments or wildest prognostications, had he expected this. "This is all from one CME?"

"No. The data I've seen, and what NOAA is looking at right now, indicates a CME series in rapid succession, which will inject energy over a period of twelve to eighteen hours. Long-duration geomagnetic-induced currents will overwhelm anything we can do to stop them. Listen, I think I've got to—"

Thom knew what a wrap-up sounded like, but he wasn't done yet. "What's the government response so far?"

"Exactly what you see on TV. There is a robust campaign to get every transformer in the United States taken offline in the next six hours to prevent damage. If the transformers are shut down when the geomagnetic currents start coursing through our power lines, they can't be damaged by it. They could be safely restarted over the next two weeks, as ambient energy levels dissipate. The system could emerge almost completely intact."

"That's fantastic. When will they start shutting down?"

Dr. Singh looked at him the way one looks at a slightly dim child. "They won't, Thom. Power plants are state-controlled. The federal government can't issue a directive or coordinate a policy. It's up to each individual state. Even in the states where the governors are embracing the science, they're still calling it only a 'possibility' of a collapse, rather than a certainty."

"But it *is* a certainty?"

"This is happening. We're going dark."

"We know this, and *no one* will take their power system off the grid?"

"You try selling a voluntary fourteen-day blackout to your state's population on just a couple hours' notice. Listen, I have people here that are—"

Thom barreled over her. "OK, so this happens. What does the government do then?"

She ground her teeth, not bothering to hide her irritation now. But still, she stayed on the line, continuing to play the possible-donor game by a set of rules that were about to not matter anymore.

"FEMA will put the National Response Framework into action. In theory it establishes a complete and effective hierarchy for disaster response. Incident Command System reports to Incident Commander, who reports to DoD, who reports to the executive branch. But that won't work this time."

"Why not?"

"They will have no telephones or internet. There will be no centralized leadership. It will be impossible."

Thom had one remaining question, and it was the most frightening of all. In every scenario he'd studied, the red line was always the same, the clear boundary that would separate the haves from the have-nots, the living from the dead.

"What about water?"

"Yeah, that's the problem. First, it'll be gasoline, though. When the grid shuts down, generators everywhere will switch on, including water-pumping systems. But the generators will burn through petroleum supplies fast. There are strategic reserves, of course, but those too will run out, as oil and gas pipelines will be among the most severely damaged structures in the initial EMP."

"Why pipelines?"

"Long, conductive metal tubes carrying fuel? Why do you think?"

"They'll explode?"

"If they're corroded, yes. And anything with cracks in its welding will split, dumping its fuel into the ground. Once the strategic oil reserves are drained, municipal water pumps will cease to function. Freshwater will become like liquid gold."

"How many dead?" he asked.

"Depends how long it lasts and if they try to run the water pumps twenty-four-seven, which would be suicidal. If they do, think millions dead, just in the U.S."

"What about globally?"

"I wouldn't want to speculate."

"Pretend you have to."

"No, Thom. I'm not a ghoul. I have to go."

Without another word, she ended the call.

Thom was left looking at his own face on the screen, a crystal-clear hi-def image that showed the fear in his eyes in crisp 4K detail. He glanced away, his eyes falling on the rearview mirror, where Brady was staring at him again.

Brady had worked for Thom for seven years, and his job description was best described as facilitator. Brady made sure Thom got where he needed to be when he needed to be there, he expedited problems along the path to solution, and he handled the sorts of things that others could or would not. Two decades as a cop with the SFPD gave him access, confidence, and an ability to see through situations in about thirty seconds, to spot liars and dangers that most people took days, weeks, or never to suss out. Brady greased wheels, opened doors, ran interference, and generally made easy the life Thom wanted to live.

What Brady did not do was ask questions. Though he had no intention of breaking his impassive streak today, the things he'd just heard in the back seat of the Suburban pushed him about as close to that line as he'd ever been. The world, it seemed, was about to end, and his boss, his billionaire boss who had access to anyone and everything, was getting the hell out of there.

Brady wondered what Thom thought would become of the loyal employees he was leaving behind. But Brady did not ask. His job was to handle security, and Thom was secure. That was what mattered.

Thom, catching Brady's eyes in the mirror, started to speak but couldn't find his voice at first. He tried again. "Traffic looks good."

Brady looked away. "Yes, sir. Took the spur at Loma Linda and got around a bunch of it."

"ETA?"

Brady glanced down at the GPS on his dashboard-mounted phone. "Twelve minutes, Mr. Banning."

Thom nodded and dialed up another call. Lisa, his assistant, answered on the first ring.

"Where are you?" she asked, skipping hello.

"Ten minutes out." Thom glanced up at the rearview, where Brady's eyes were seemingly glued to him now, and he winked. "Incentive, Brady."

Brady smiled joylessly. "Yes, sir." He gave the gas another five miles per hour.

Thom turned away, looking out the window at the endless housing developments as they raced past them. "Where are *you*?" he asked Lisa.

"In the hangar."

"How'd you get there so fast?"

"I live five minutes away. Remember?"

"Oh, right. Yeah, you mentioned that." If she had, Thom had absolutely no recollection of it. He moved on. "What about Ann-Sophie and the kids?"

"Francis picked up Ann-Sophie from the house at 9:35, and Antonio got both kids from school at 9:38. The cars met ten minutes later and now Ann-Sophie has both of them and is on the 310 Southbound, ETA four minutes ahead of you."

"How soon can we be wheels up?"

"As soon as you're settled in. The plane's fueled, Marques is ready, and you were right, the only other pilots here are weekenders with prop planes. The weather cooperated. I was worried about the lack of a tower when you picked this place, but you're good to go."

"What's the flight time?"

"An hour forty-seven. You'll be on the ground with a two-hour cushion before onset."

Thom sat back in his seat and allowed himself a tiny exhalation. Everything was going so radiantly according to plan that it was impossible not to feel just the tiniest bit proud of himself. He attempted to banish it—pride was Kryptonite—but then he decided to cut himself a bit of slack and allow a microscopic fleck of self-regard to flourish. Just for a moment.

"There is one complication."

Thom closed his eyes. *You see what happens when you let your guard down?* "What do you mean?" he asked.

Lisa hesitated. "Marques needs to speak with you."

"Is there a problem with the plane?"

"Marques will tell you himself."

"What the fuck are you talking about? What complication? Tell me, right this second."

"I'm sorry. I'll see you in eight minutes." And she ended the call.

Thom felt his body course with rage. Lisa had never, ever, *not one time* failed to obey a direct order from him, and then she'd compounded her unthinkable mutiny by actually hanging up on him? Was he the only one who gave a shit about propriety anymore?

No matter, he told himself, taking a deep, steadying breath. No matter what was about to happen, no matter when it came, Thom Banning knew one thing for certain.

He was prepared.

4.

AURORA

What was suddenly clear to Aubrey was that she'd learned exactly nothing from COVID. Well, that wasn't entirely true. She had learned once again that wildly unexpected events do happen in life and that they can last way longer than you'd ever imagine, with much more far-reaching consequences. Therefore, it's only basic common sense to stock up on supplies and hope the dreadful day never comes. She'd become mindful of the fact that she was no longer a solitary person in this world but, rather, the sole caregiver for a moody teenage shithead, and that she had a moral obligation to be prepared to provide for them both. *Things happen. Be ready.*

Her first step, eighteen months ago, had been to find out exactly what a person would need in the next big emergency. She'd googled "basic home disaster kit" and found hundreds of hits to choose from. The first few were sponsored, overpriced duffel bags jammed with too much of the wrong stuff, but a few links down she found an article with a dot-gov suffix, so she'd clicked on that. The handy checklist seemed to cover everything, not just for another deadly virus but for earthquakes, fires, power outages, even a dirty bomb explosion. Dutifully, she'd printed it out and taped it to the rust-proof black steel storage rack she'd bought on Amazon for $200 and put together one rainy Saturday, just around the corner from the basement stairs.

Aubrey stood in front of the rack now, staring at the two-page disaster checklist, which she'd even laminated before taping it to the support on the right side. She'd gotten off to a great start. The lamination, she felt, was a particularly heads-up touch. One item had been crossed off, the very first on the list: DOWNLOAD THE RECOMMENDED SUPPLIES LIST. There was a neat black line drawn through it, a line so straight and true that it fairly shone with confidence and pride in one's farsightedness. Yes, she'd done that.

The rest of the list, however, was clean, white, and unmarked. The storage rack itself held precisely one item, or eleven, depending on how you wanted to count them, a cardboard sleeve that had once held twelve cans of Goya Black Beans. One of the cans was missing, and she remembered clearly the day she'd made them as a side dish and discovered that both she and Scott despised Goya Black Beans. She'd only bought them because she'd read they could be stored for long periods of time, but, damn, you could hang on to those eleven cans of beans for a decade and still not eat them.

The rest of the storage rack was unburdened by survival supplies. There was no stored water, no battery-powered or hand-crank radio, no NOAA Weather Radio with tone alert, no flashlight, first aid kit, extra batteries, whistle, dust mask, plastic sheeting, duct tape, moist towelettes, garbage bags, wrench or pliers, local maps, extra cell phone with charger and backup battery, extra prescription medications, sleeping bag, or matches in a waterproof container. There was no *anything* else from the list at all.

Aubrey stood staring at the empty storage rack in despair.

"That's pathetic."

The voice had come from behind her. She turned and saw Scott at the base of the stairs. She turned back, in no mood to be harassed. "I'm aware of that."

"You didn't stock up on *anything*?"

"No. Did you?"

"I'm fifteen. It's not my job." She didn't answer. Scott sensed a soft spot, so he pressed on it. "Did you really need to come down here and look at the rack in order to figure out there was nothing on it?"

"No, Scott, I was well aware there's nothing on the rack. I came down to get this." She tore the laminated list off the upright and headed for the stairs, brushing past him. He stayed where he was, staring at the empty shelves.

"I hate those fucking beans."

"So do I. Are you coming?"

"Where?"

"To the store."

He turned and looked at her. She was now at the top of the stairs, and he at the bottom. He furrowed his brow. "The thing hits in, what, four hours or something? Do you have any idea how many people are going to be at the store? Do you honestly think there will even be anything *left* at the store?"

She took a breath, trying to quell the anger that was rising in her, competing with panic as her dominant emotion. "It's not going to get any better if we wait. Meet me at the car."

She went upstairs, got her purse, and pulled out her wallet. A hundred and eleven dollars was, frankly, more than she usually carried, and she was pleased she at least had that much. They'd stop at the bank on the way, take the daily limit off her debit card, and put everything they could get at the Piggly Wiggly on her Visa while the machines were still working. Even if they bought every single thing on the list, in double quantities, it wouldn't last them more than a couple weeks, but there was no point thinking that far ahead.

She scooped up her keys and headed for the front door, pulling her bag over her shoulder. Scott came up out of the basement and drifted toward the TV, which was tuned to increasingly frantic cable news. Scott's eyes were big, his spiking anxiety belying the adolescent cool he was attempting to project.

Aubrey turned back, picked up the remote, and shut the TV off in the middle of the anchor's breathless speculation about the duration of the impending worldwide power outage. Scott turned on her. "You don't think we need to know that stuff?"

She took a step forward and looked up at him. He'd passed her in height about a year ago and she wasn't used to it yet. At least it was good for her posture. She stood, ramrod straight, and looked into his icy blue eyes, the same color as his father's.

"No. We don't. What we need is to get to the store, *now*."

He looked at her, his cheek twitching. The kid was practically biting a hole through his face, either in anger or fear. Probably both.

Aubrey softened her tone. "You know, I read once that if you're sad, you're living in the past. If you're anxious, you're living in the future. But if you're at peace, you're living in the present."

"And if you're completely fucked, you're living with Aubrey."

The urge to slap him was overwhelming. She even pictured herself doing it, in the surge of adrenaline that ran through her body. She saw her arm recoiling, right hand back over her left biceps, and then slicing outwards in an arc, her backhand catching him fully on the right side of his face. She saw his head snap to the side and the angry red patch grow on his cheek. She saw him turn back to her, shock in his eyes, his fingertips going to his inflamed skin, and she saw the expression on his face that said, "Wow, I have completely misjudged this lady and I better pull my shit together right this fucking second." Somehow, seeing that scene play out in her mind was enough, and she didn't need to live it.

Instead, she spoke in a level voice. "I'm sorry your parents dumped you, Scott. I'm what you've got. Get in the car."

She turned and walked out.

In the car, she slammed the door, started it up, and waited. She'd made a strong, unkind play for control and now just had to hope she'd commanded enough of his respect to get through the next few hours. Her eye caught movement and she looked up, into the rearview mirror. They weren't the only ones in the neighborhood who'd heard the news, and everybody was headed somewhere, doing what needed to be done while it was still possible to do anything at all.

Norman Levy, the eighty-eight-year-old former college professor who lived at the near end of the block, was standing in his front yard, holding a boxlike contraption in front of his eyes and staring directly into the late-afternoon sun. Aubrey half smiled for the first time that day. Of course Norman was informed and interested. He was never anything but that.

She turned and looked back at her house. Impatient, she pressed the flat of her hand on the center of the wheel and let out a long, fat horn blast. Scott came out a minute later, the screen door slamming behind him, shoving something thick in his front pocket. He left the front door hanging half open behind him. *Jesus Christ, this is one hell of a disaster sidekick I ended up with.*

Scott got in the car, shut his door, and stared straight ahead. Aubrey put it in reverse and pulled out, faster than she meant to, the front end bottoming out on the uneven sidewalk.

The bank had closed an hour early, and the line for the ATM cubicle snaked out the door and halfway down the block. Scott and Aubrey sat in the car for a moment, just staring at it.

"That line's at least a half-hour," Aubrey said. "Puts us behind at the supermarket. Do it or not?"

Scott had his phone out and was tapping away. She rolled her eyes. "Can whoever you're texting please wait until we—"

He cut her off, reading from the phone. "It says the average ATM can hold as much as two hundred thousand dollars, but almost none of them do. In off-hours, it's more like ten thousand."

Aubrey's eyes skimmed the line in front of the bank, counting fast. "That's gotta be thirty people. Closer to forty."

"What's the most you can take out at once?" he asked.

"Six hundred dollars."

He shook his head, firmly. "Even if we waited, that thing's gonna be empty by the time we get there."

"I have a hundred and twelve dollars on me," she said. "That's it."

Scott looked straight ahead. "I have twenty-two hundred in cash."

"What?"

He kept staring through the windshield, refusing to meet her eye. "In my pocket."

She looked at him, incredulous. "Where did you get it?"

"Would you please just drive the fucking car?"

She stared a moment longer, dropped the car in gear, started to ease her foot off the brake, then abruptly changed her mind and put it back in park. She turned her body, facing him fully with an I-can-wait-all-day expression on her face.

"What the fuck is the *matter* with you?!" he said. "There will be *nothing left* at the store, just drive the car, you fucking—" He stopped himself before he went too far and turned, looking out the windshield again.

He waited. So did she. He had no intention of speaking.

Aubrey backed down. Wordlessly, she put the car in gear and drove.

The line outside the supermarket was even longer. There were two men in bright yellow vests with long guns in front, one a shotgun and the other looking like an AR-15. The crowd waiting to go inside was peaceful aside from some quiet jockeying and the odd muttered complaint about the permissibility of space-saving. But for the most part people were orderly, if only because of the presence of the armed guards. What caught Aubrey's attention, though, was the quiet. No one was speaking any more than was absolutely necessary, and with all the movement, both of pedestrians and cars, it created a strange, unnatural mood. They were all on the move, but there was an eerie absence of sound, apart from the crunch of tires on asphalt and tired, frightened feet scuffling forward in line, a few steps at a time.

They'd all been here before. This was disaster prep as wordless, depressing reflex.

Aubrey reached in the back, grabbed the two big empty Fresh Direct bags she'd brought from under the kitchen sink, and turned to Scott. "You coming?"

He looked at her, and she could see he was on the verge of tears. His voice was barely a whisper. "I can't go through it again."

For the first time today, he looked like a kid. She put a hand on his shoulder and returned his gaze. "It's not gonna be the same."

"No. It's gonna be worse. A lot worse."

"We don't know that."

"I'm fifteen fucking years old. I lived in lockdown for two of those years. I'm gonna be stuck in the Little House on the Fucking Prairie for the next two."

"Wait. You actually read it?"

He shook his head. "Just the first few pages. It was awful. What made you think I would like that?"

"I loved it when I was a kid."

"I sell weed." She looked at him, trying to place the non sequitur. "It's where I got the money."

She nodded. That made sense. "OK."

He frowned. "That's it?"

She looked up at the still-growing line outside the Piggly Wiggly. "Doesn't seem like we have time to get into it any more than that, does it?"

"I have twenty-two hundred dollars in cash from selling weed, and you don't have the time to get into it?"

"OK. Sure. I'll get into it. Don't sell weed anymore, Scott."

"Nice parenting."

"Will you stop that? I'm sorry I said the shit I said. About your mom and dad."

He shrugged. "It's true."

"Doesn't mean anybody has a right to hit you in the face with it. I know they love you. They're just deeply fucked-up human beings."

He tried to laugh, but it came out ugly. He wiped snot from his nose.

Aubrey looked up at the line outside the store again. It was no shorter. It would never be shorter, and she thought about the empty rack in the basement. She thought about the darkness that would descend on them in less than three hours' time, or five hours or one hour or never, depending on which news channel you favored, and she dug around inside herself, searching for the strength and patience to finish this conversation with not-her-kid with anything other than "Dry your fucking nose and get out of the car, you little shit."

She tried something else. "There was this cartoon I saw once. There was a five-year-old boy in it. And somebody tells him to go to school, and he says, 'But I'm only five years old.' And then somebody tells him he's got to go fight in a war, and they shove a helmet on his head, and they push him toward a battlefield, and he says, 'But I'm only five years old.' And then he goes home from the war, and they tell him he has to get married, and he's standing at an altar with some woman twice as tall as he is and he says, 'But I'm only five years old.' And then they show him in a hospital bed, and there's a big chart over him that has the word CANCER written on it in big letters and he says, 'But I'm only five years old.' You get where this is going?"

Scott looked at Aubrey, this flinty woman he'd never asked to have in his life, this thirty-eight-year-old who was just twenty-two when he was born, who wasn't even thirty when she married his father. He regarded this innocent victim of circumstance whom God, in his infinite cruelty, had thrown into his path, and he wished she was anyone else.

He had no fucking clue what the point of her story was.

"I'm making it all up as I go, Scott. I'm only five years old."

Aubrey's phone buzzed and they both looked down at it. The screen lit up with a picture of Scott's father. It was an old picture, Rusty was smiling in bright sunlight in the backyard of the house she and Scott still lived in, shirtless. Aubrey wished to Christ she'd changed it, but Rusty called so infrequently and upset her so thoroughly that she'd usually forgotten about it by the time they hung up. The result was his picture bugged the shit out of her every single time he called but remained unchanged.

She was about to answer, but Scott beat her to it. He pressed the button on the side of the phone, declining the call. He looked at Aubrey.

"I don't want to go through this with you."

"I don't want to go through it with you either."

Their feelings clear, Scott took the empty shopping bags and got out of the car. Aubrey followed.

5.

Rusty seriously doubted the world was coming to an end. But there was chaos in the making, no question about it, and if things were going to shut down he knew he needed to be ready. His first and most immediate problem was, as ever, money. He'd called Aubrey to try to get a sense of her general cash-on-hand situation, but of course the bitch didn't pick up.

So now he'd had to move to plan B. He had exactly five hundred dollars to his name, money he'd just earned for fixing storm damage to Mrs. Krauthafer's garage roof. He knew five hundred wouldn't last him long. It was almost like having nothing at all, so there was really very little risk involved in treating it as seed money and trying to turn it into a larger, more comfortable amount. If that plan collapsed, he could always move back to option A, badgering his ex-wife for cash. She usually came through in the end.

Rusty got in his truck and headed over to the Lucky Star as soon as his head had cleared from last night's indulgences. He had no intention of risking the entire five hundred—he wasn't *that* kind of compulsive gambler—plus he had very specific plans for the party he was going to have with some of the cash. No, *four hundred* was a sane and sober amount to risk. He'd pick a color, put four hundred on three spins of the roulette wheel, and let it ride three times. If all went well, he'd come out of this with $3,200, a respectable amount of cash with which to ride out this supposed blackout that was coming. It felt good to be proactive, to take matters into his own hands swiftly and decisively, but he kept getting hung up on the ageless binary question "Red or black?"

Black, to Rusty, had always seemed to be asking for trouble. It was the color of night, of death, of darkness and defeat. Then again, Black is Beautiful, Black Don't Crack, and *Black Panther* was an awesome movie. But he knew that was superstitious thinking, which is what usually steered him over to red, until he started thinking of Blood Red, the Red Menace, and Red Tide, which was either a kind of ocean pollution or a Southern football team.

But today was going to be different. No waffling.

Rusty pulled into an alley around the corner from the front entrance, parking in a spot where, he knew from experience, he was less likely to get a ticket for the expired smog inspection sticker on his dashboard. The casino was even more crowded than usual, the general assumption among the gaming set being that they wouldn't bolt their doors 'til the power was actually out. Rusty wasn't so sure even that would stop business. Rusty figured the Lucky Star for the generators-and-armed-guard type of concern if things went dark. There was too much money to be made.

It was busy today, for sure, a lot of last hands being played, and the big-screen TVs all around the place were tuned to sporting events. Unless you knew already, you'd have no idea that ten thousand billion metric tons of highly charged coronal mass were headed toward the earth at just over six million miles per hour.

As Rusty came into the place, Espinoza, all six foot three inches of him, was coming right toward him down the center aisle. Rusty saw him first, turned away, and ducked into a row of slot machines. Espinoza worked for Zielinski, Rusty owed Zielinski well over ten grand, and the nasty little Polack expected his five hundred a week, every week. It had been almost a month since Rusty had made so much as a good-faith payment. Zielinski wasn't Chicago Outfit, and he never would be—he wasn't Italian—and he overcompensated for this lack of criminal standing by being a vindictive dick. On his bad side you did not wish to be.

Espinoza had some other unlucky bastard by the elbow, a Hispanic man who looked pretty bummed out, and the big guy was escorting him from the premises. But Rusty's luck was bad, as usual, and Espinoza spotted him in between two Slots O' Fun machines.

"Don't be rude, Rusty."

Rusty turned, feigning surprise and delight. "Hey E, what's up? Didn't see you there."

Espinoza didn't bother addressing the obvious fiction. "You park in the alley where you always do?"

Rusty narrowed his eyes, trying to think fast. Did they want his truck? 'Cause that would be fucked up and seriously impair his ability to earn. He sorted through a few options for how to express that, but Espinoza cut him off.

"Just give me the keys. I gotta borrow it."

"Where you going?" Rusty's eyes darted to the Hispanic guy, whose afternoon had turned sharply for the worse.

"Nowhere. Z has to explain things to my man here. Let him use your truck, just to sit in. Ten minutes."

Rusty looked at the Hispanic man again, but the guy wouldn't meet his eyes. He fished his keys out of his pocket, thought about promising Espinoza he'd give $1,000 of his theoretical winnings to Zielinski on his way out to buy time but bit back on that impulse. If nobody asks, for the love of God don't offer.

He held the keys out to Espinoza. "Seriously, ten minutes. I'm just here for a quick hitter."

"Sure, that'll go great." Espinoza took the keys from Rusty and headed for the exit, his charge in tow. Rusty watched them go, finally catching eyes with the Hispanic guy. *It's your day, fucker, not mine.*

Rusty cruised past the poker tables, no time for his usual game, five-ten Texas Hold 'Em. Today was going to be a surgical strike, three spins of the roulette wheel. He picked a nearly empty table, always his preference. He firmly believed that good luck couldn't rub off on you from others but *bad* luck was a deadly plague that spread through the air. He chose a table with a slightly hot lady croupier, also a prerequisite of his, not for reasons of luck but just because he preferred good-looking women to cranky-looking men. He waited 'til she spun the wheel and sent the ball on its way, then he pulled four clammy hundred-dollar bills from his pocket, folded them the long way with a snap, and set them confidently on the black square.

"Four hundred plays," the croupier announced, and, hey, her voice was even prettier than her brown eyes. She looked up at him and smiled. "Good luck, sir." And she liked him! Maybe, who knows, if he hits this, he goes home with a new blackout buddy, he thought. You never know. Women didn't treat him like they used to a few years ago—Rusty sometimes thought it would have been easier to never be good-looking at all than to have been good-looking once—but they still liked winners, and he was about to be a winner.

The wheel slowed, the ball dipped, bounced around the steel-edged slots, landed briefly in red 19, and then leapt, as if discontent, the hell out of that loser space and settled contentedly into black 26, where it stayed.

"Black wins."

You bet your cute ass it does, Rusty thought. He was surprised at his relative calm at this good fortune. His heart didn't skip a beat, he didn't pump a fist in the air, he didn't even raise an eyebrow. He'd known he was going to win, and watching it happen was an almost clinical experience. Interesting. Maybe the start of something.

The croupier set four black chips on top of his four hundred-dollar bills with a satisfying click, then scooped the losing bets off the table. Rusty stared down at the green felt, where his now eight hundred dollars lay still. The croupier spun the wheel, picked up the ball, and looked up at him. Rusty just nodded. Let it go.

"Black lets it ride," she said to no one in particular and tidied his stack. Rusty tried something different this time. Rather than attempt to psychically will the ball into a black slot, he turned his back on the table, looking out into the casino. He'd been turning away at crucial moments since he was a kid watching football, and more often than not, he'd found it worked. Need that field goal to go through the uprights? Don't watch. That worked, didn't it? And that time you were in the kitchen on a third and eight and they ended up getting a first down? Better get the hell back into the kitchen every time it's third and eight. They say a watched pot doesn't boil, but if you look away from a roulette wheel, does that make it come up your color? It was worth a try. He took a breath and stood a little straighter while that honey of a croupier set the ball in motion around the spinning wheel and called for last bets.

Suddenly, Rusty furrowed his brow, struck by a thought. It was a new one for him.

Maybe he should stop early.

Maybe, if this spin comes up black, which he was nearly certain it would, he'd take his $1,600 and leave. Maybe he'd settle for two good spins instead of hoping for three, maybe he'd shove the cash in his pocket and walk the fuck out of there for once. Yes. Yes, that was what he would do, that was exactly what he'd do.

Except the money should be on red.

The thought came, unbidden, into his mind, landing like an ember spit out of a fire. His whole body twitched, desperate to turn around and move the bet from black to red. It wasn't too late. The ball hadn't started to drop yet; he could still hear it circling the top ledge. There was time. It was going to be red, he knew that now, of *course* it was going to be red, Red Letter Day, Paint the Town Red, Roll out the Red Carpet, *shit*, and he started to turn.

But he stopped himself. No. That was the old Rusty. That was stupid, superstitious, and self-defeating Rusty, and he would not surrender to him. He'd come in with a plan, and he was now going to execute that plan. The money would stay on black, and he would remain calm. He took a deep, cleansing breath, closed his eyes, and listened to the sounds of the casino as it hummed and clinked around him. He loved the sound of chips, of slot machines paying off, of ice clinking in drinks, and, most of all, of the erratic bounce-click of a roulette ball starting its descent from the rim of the slowing wheel, doing its jumping-bean act around the wheel, and finally dropping neatly into—

"Double zero. Green pays."

Rusty turned around, uncomprehending.

Green?

The answer to "red or black" was fucking *green*? He looked at the wheel, incredulous, and saw the ball riding around in the loathsome double-zero slot, that odious American invention, a second green space.

The ugly, hateful bitch of a croupier scooped up his chips, dropped them on her stack, and staked his four hundred-dollar bills through the slot in the table without remorse. She didn't look at him, she didn't say she was sorry, and she sure as fuck wasn't going to be his blackout buddy.

Rusty winced at the light and skulked down the block, headed for his truck. The universe, as usual, had turned on him in the cruelest and most sadistic way possible, teasing him with the good fortune of some unexpected cash and a win at the table, only to come swooping back like a bird of prey, scoop him off the ground, and rip him apart in mid-air to remind him of the pathetic, endless losing streak that he was still on.

As he came into the alley, he saw Espinoza leaning against his back bumper and could make out two people in the cab through the tinted window. It was Zielinski on the passenger side. He could see the outline of the straw fedora the stupid Polack wore, one of his several affectations. Rusty figured the other guy for the Hispanic dude, and Zielinski was leaned over close to him, something glinting in his hand. The Hispanic man's muffled shrieks of pain were audible through the thick glass.

Rusty stopped short, looking at Espinoza for an explanation he didn't want. Espinoza, who now had a leather glove on his right hand, shrugged. An awkward moment passed between them as they both considered the alley walls, the ground, the sky, anything but whatever was going on in the front seat of Rusty's truck.

"Why don't you take a hike?" Espinoza offered, his voice almost kindly. "I hate this shit. You know that. Bad enough I gotta be here."

"How long's he gonna be?"

Espinoza shrugged. "I'll leave the keys on the tire."

But Rusty didn't want to walk away. He needed to get the fuck in his truck and scrounge cash and food and water in whatever way he could, and he certainly did *not* want to do so on foot. "I can give it a minute," he said, the soul of reason.

Espinoza looked up, squinting into the lowering sun. "You think, what they're saying? With the power and all?"

Rusty shook his head, skeptical. "C'mon."

"I don't know, man. Everybody's saying."

"They say a lot of stuff. Gotta get ratings."

"I don't know, Rusty, feels like shit's about to get very real in the world." He jerked a thumb back over the truck, toward the window. "Z wants everybody paid up if the power's gonna go."

From the front of the truck, there was a muffled wet gawping sound, someone choking or crying or both. Espinoza looked back at Rusty, agitated this time.

"Seriously, take a hike. You don't want to see Z right now."

"Maybe I should talk to him. If shit gets weird, could be some good opportunities coming up, you know what I mean? I could help him."

"It ain't your help he wants, Rusty. I'm not coming for you, fam. We go back. But you know what you gotta do. Can you please just take care of it?"

"It is at the top of my list, I promise you."

"Yeah, well, take care of it faster. Keep him off your back. Feel me?"

The passenger door of the pickup truck opened abruptly, and a man in a pressed white dress shirt and straw hat stepped out. The word that came to mind most readily to describe Zielinski was "dense." Not dumb, far from it, but thick, stout, compactly built. He gave the impression you could punch him in the gut and do more damage to your hand than to him. He resembled no one so much as Nikita Khrushchev. Maybe he'd seen old news clips, and that was why he favored the crisp white dress shirts and hat. He didn't notice Rusty at first, as he was wiping his hands on some kind of kerchief, just out of Rusty's line of sight, behind the cab of the truck.

Espinoza moved right away, meeting his boss before he came around the corner of the truck and taking a small, red-smeared pliers from him. He muttered as he approached, but Zielinski had already noticed Rusty. His face darkened into a frown.

"Hey, Z, what's up?"

"I left something in there for you," Zielinski said.

No idea what that meant, Rusty managed only an "Oh, OK. Thanks, man."

Zielinski muttered again to Espinoza, who went around the front of the truck, opened the driver's door, and pulled the Hispanic guy out. There was gentleness in the big man's gesture, the way an undertaker is cautious with a body that no longer needs caution.

Rusty looked at the guy as Espinoza helped him past. He was moaning in pain, his left cheek swollen, a long, ropy string of bloody tissue running out in a perfect line down his neck and across the front of his shirt. The Hispanic guy looked up at Rusty, his left eye nearly swollen shut and his right asking for help. But he kept his mouth shut.

Rusty watched as Espinoza led the guy out of the alley. A jingling sound drew his attention back to Zielinski, who was holding his car keys out to him.

"See you soon, Rusty."

Rusty took the keys, grateful to be nearly out of there. "You got it. Be safe, Z. Crazy times."

Rusty turned, hurried around to the driver's side, and got in the truck, slamming the door behind him. He looked up into the rearview mirror, but Zielinski was gone, around the corner of the alley already.

Rusty turned, shoved the key in the ignition, and stopped, his eyes focusing on an object perched on the dashboard, directly in his line of sight.

The tooth was a molar, maybe the one from all the way in the back, judging by the tripod of thick roots on which it stood. The gooey strand of red tissue from the Hispanic guy's shirt made more sense now, as it had once been connected to the biggest of the three roots. Two clusters of periodontal ligaments were splayed out on the dashboard on either side of the tooth, visible in the space just over the steering wheel. Rusty let out a long breath and took a moment to compose himself.

How had it all come to this? He'd had everything, once. A decent job, a strong body and handsome face that women went nuts for, a house, a kid. It seemed booze and coke expected a lot from a person in return. Now everything he'd had was gone, all of it. Now he was a scared, beaten dog.

Worse, he was a dog that owed money.

He started the truck, opened the window, and found an old Starbucks napkin on the floor. He used it to pick up the tooth and chucked it into the alley, hearing it click across the pavement in two or three skips. So, Z did teeth now. God knew what the fuck would be next, and ten grand was a lot of money.

He leaned forward and looked up at the sky as he pulled out of the alley, wondering when or if you'd ever be able to see the thing everybody said was coming.

6.

HALF-MOON BAY AIRFIELD

Brady muttered into his cell phone when they were half a mile from the airfield's driveway, and the chain-link gate was swinging open before they pulled up to it. From the back seat, Thom could see the Gulfstream 650 parked just ahead, beyond the doors to the aviation center. The other custom Suburban was parked in front of it, and Ann-Sophie, a tall, anxious woman whose overwhelming blondness made Eva Braun look swarthy, stood beside the open rear door, fidgeting with an Hermes overnight bag. Thom admired her, even now. Oh, hell, *especially* now, but his admiration was really a way of appreciating himself: here he was, whisking his Swedish-model wife away to safety moments ahead of an impending apocalypse. What, exactly, was there not to like about him and his situation at this moment? Who on planet earth occupied a place higher on the food chain than he did, even in comparison with his exalted peers who had just as much money, had done just as much planning, and were possessed of a plane with the same number of seats, covered in the same creamy Italian leather upholstery? They may have made plans, but they hadn't made *Plans*. Not the way Thom had.

These thoughts, Thom knew, were perfectly normal. To be pleased with one's station, if it is advantageous, to feel possessive and desirous of one's wife, to take honest stock of one's fortune, if it happens to be outrageous, and think that all this is a positive thing, and to take a private moment, every now and then, to consider oneself truly hot shit—this is common fucking gratitude.

You just gotta be careful not to say it out loud.

Thom's Suburban swung around and pulled to a stop ten feet from where Ann-Sophie stood waiting. Thom opened his door himself, moving faster than the airport worker who was lunging toward it, and he opened it with such conviction that the guy rapped his knuckles on the handle.

"Sorry," Thom threw at him, and he meant it, but, *hey, c'mon, how many times have I asked Lisa to tell you guys I open my own goddamn doors?* He covered the ten feet between himself and Ann-Sophie in a rush. He pulled her into an embrace.

"You're all right," he murmured in her ear. "The kids are fine. We are going somewhere safe." He was holding her tightly, and she returned the embrace for a moment, but when she moved to pull away, he held on a moment longer, not releasing her. "Just take a second. Stay calm."

"I'm fine. Let go of me."

He did, and she pulled back. He was surprised by the animosity in her eyes. *Really? Now?* Sure, they'd had that Thing they'd been trying to work through, but every married couple had their thing, and aren't times of crisis supposed to bring people together? But he realized, as he looked into Ann-Sophie's bottle-green eyes, that nothing had been forgiven, nothing was going to be put behind them, and he was about to trade a nineteen-thousand-square-foot house overlooking the Pacific Ocean for a thirty-two-hundred-square-foot apartment in a reconditioned nuclear-missile silo a hundred miles outside of Provo, Utah, that he would share with a vindictive Nordic witch.

For the first time that day, the end of the world was sounding like a teensy bit of a drag.

Over Ann-Sophie's shoulder, Thom saw his second distressing sight.

Lisa, his assistant, was hurrying toward him, her heels click-clicking in that self-important way he hated. She had her hands out in front of her, palms down, making a "please be calm" gesture before anybody had even begun to freak out.

Thom pulled away from Ann-Sophie and spoke to Lisa before she could speak to him. "Where are the kids?"

"On board."

It occurred to Thom later—much later—that if your wife, the mother of your children, is angry with you for a thousand offenses and holds myriad grievances and you're about to go into isolation together and you'd rather not enrage her further, it is better to direct questions about her children's welfare to *her* and not to your assistant.

Lisa, no dummy, caught herself after her instinctive two-word reply and gestured to Ann-Sophie, as if to cede the matter to her. Ann-Sophie just shook her head, the question already answered. "Yep."

"Bags?"

Lisa hesitated. She was a likable person, brisk, competent, and not looking to her job for social advancement. She was extremely well paid, which was all she asked, aside from a modicum of respect, which she got from everyone she dealt with except Thom. Her boss could be snappish, demanding, and never, ever remembered a single personal detail she shared with him. In that regard, Thom's spouse and his assistant had an unspoken sense of allegiance, and an uneasy peace.

Ann-Sophie answered Thom's question about the luggage on Lisa's behalf, completing the role reversal between spouse and personal assistant. "The bags are on the plane, Thom. The clothes were last washed a week ago, the phones are charged, and the batteries were all refreshed in February." She looked at Lisa. "Would you like me to tell him?"

Thom looked back and forth between them. "Tell me what? What's going on? Why are we—"

He stopped mid-sentence as the first Suburban, the one from

which Ann-Sophie had alighted, was pulling away, giving him a clear view of the air stair that had been folded down from the Gulfstream. There, standing at the base of it, was a tall, athletic-looking man in his mid-forties in a crisp pilot's uniform and aviator shades. Marques fully looked the part of the former Air Force pilot turned sky chauffeur and he was, in many ways, Thom's favorite accoutrement of his success. His own *pilot*, a decorated veteran, no less, who was ready to go anywhere in the world at a moment's notice. And there he stood now, tall, fit, shoulders squared, chest thrust out, ready to lift them all the hell out of there and tear into the sky, headed for safety while the world lit on fire beneath them.

But Marques was not alone.

For a moment, Thom didn't understand the image. His brain couldn't decode the light waves that were reaching his retinas, couldn't turn them into a rational perception that matched his understanding of reality. Marques, his pilot, his transportation guru, his getaway driver, for God's sake, was not alone. There was a Black woman next to him, six or seven years younger than Marques, with the fingers of her right hand interlaced with the fingers of his left. OK, so Marques had a woman with him.

But it got even weirder. Because the woman, the one who was acting like Marques's, uh, *companion* or something, had another human beside her. This person was small—maybe three feet high, so what's that, four years old or so?—and this undersized human was clinging to the left leg of the woman for support and safety.

Marques has a fucking wife and kid? And he *brought* them?

"Marques needs to speak with you," Lisa offered, pointlessly.

"No," Thom said.

She hadn't asked a question and wasn't looking for a decision, so Thom's answer made no real sense, except to him. To him, the single word meant "No, Marques cannot bring his fucking-news-to-me wife and kid to my fucking Sanctuary," but he was too stunned to get the words out.

Marques, seeing his boss's face, turned to his apparent spouse, said something quiet and reassuring, stroked the little girl's hair with a smile and a wink, and walked toward Thom.

Thom met him halfway. "What the fuck, Marques?"

"Got an issue, boss."

"You're married?"

"Her name's Beth. Been together two years now. You sent us a housewarming present last July."

Thom nodded, thinking. Important not to come off like an asshole here. He needed this guy. "OK. Well, good. Uh, congratulations. But you're not, you know, married?"

Marques took off his sunglasses. "Like I said. We've been together two years." It was a strong delivery, particularly with the removal of the sunglasses and the steady eye contact.

Thom straightened. He couldn't match Marques's height, the deepness of his voice, or the moral authority of the uniform, even if it bore no relation to the military or any official air service or airline. Still, it had epaulets, and they tend to square one's shoulders rather impressively.

"The thing is," Thom started, and Marques lifted his chin, as if to say, "Yeah, motherfucker? What is the thing? Tell me the thing."

Thom cleared his throat and started again, from a different angle. His eyes fell on the little girl, and he pulled his lips back from his teeth in an approximation of a smile. "Who's that cutie?" He waved, and the girl buried her head in her mother's thigh.

"Her name's Kearie. She's four."

"I see. And you and—" Shit. Lost it already.

"Beth."

"Yes, I was about to say, you and Beth, you guys have been together for—"

"Two years. Kearie's father passed away not long after she was born. I'm her daddy now. Boss, I know this is not what you had in mind, and it is not something we ever discussed, but it is the reality of the situation. I'm not leaving without them. You are welcome to get another pilot if you can, because if they don't go, I don't fly."

"You know I can't get another fucking pilot at two minutes to fucking midnight in a goddamn *societal meltdown*, Marques."

Whoops. That one got away from him. But it was a valid point, and, well, it was out there now.

Marques took off his hat and wiped his brow. He looked back at Beth and Kearie and forced a smile, made a tiny gesture to say hang on, I still got this. He looked back at Thom. "Right. You can't get a pilot. So that's it? They're coming?"

Thom played for time, thinking as fast as he could. "Hang on, hang on, can we please just—you know, it's a twist. You've thrown me a curve here."

"I know that. And I apologize."

"We had an agreement. Anywhere, anytime, if the shit hits the fan, that's what we said. And in exchange, you're with me, taken care of, all the way, right down the line. You're safe. That was the deal."

"I know. And I have always appreciated that."

"As long as you get me there. That's what we said."

"And I intend to."

"But I thought there was just one of you. That you're single, Marques. You see? *I hired you because you're single.*"

Marques just looked at him. "I thought you hired me because I embodied excellence as a professional pilot."

"That too. But—I don't know, I just thought you were single, that's all."

"I was. And then I wasn't. And you knew that."

"I didn't fucking know that!" Again, Thom caught himself. Now it was his turn to look back, over his shoulder. Ann-Sophie was staring at him, her arms crossed over her chest. Lisa had her head down, hands clasped in front of her, waiting this out. Thom gestured to both of them—don't worry, I got this—and turned back to Marques.

"It was a set of patio furniture," Marques said.

"What?"

"Your housewarming present, when Beth and I moved in together, a year ago. Teakwood patio furniture. It's beautiful. Thank you again.

That was very thoughtful." He steadied his gaze, his point proven. *You knew about us. Or you don't remember that you knew and just had your assistant send an expensive present, which then makes it your own damn fault for being a jerk.*

Thom tried one last tack. "How about this? They can wait here, in my car. You fly us to Provo, then you fly back here, and Brady drives all three of you wherever you want. Anywhere."

Marques furrowed his brow, trying to figure that one out. "Like where?"

"Anywhere."

"You're offering—what are you offering, exactly?"

"I'm offering to release you from your commitment to stay with me and my family for the duration of whatever is about to happen. I'm offering to leave my plane wildly out of position, should I need to move again. I'm offering to strand myself at—actually, no. Never mind. I'm not offering that at all. That offer is no longer operative. It is not on the table."

Marques tried hard not to roll his eyes. He looked at his watch. "Boss. Clock's ticking."

"There isn't room."

"Of course there is," said a voice from behind him. Thom turned. Ann-Sophie looked at Marques and nodded. "There's plenty of room. We'll figure it out."

Marques smiled tightly and nodded his thanks to her, then shifted his gaze to Thom, waiting for final approval.

Thom shrugged. "Looks like you have me."

"I was hoping for something a little more understanding."

"Oh, fuck off, Marques, you've got me over a barrel and my wife just offered you and your common-law family shelter from the fucking storm, but that's not enough, you want me to offer it myself, and I have to *mean* it?"

Marques took his sunglasses from his pocket, unfolded them, and slipped them back on. "We can be wheels up in four minutes."

Ann-Sophie turned and walked to the base of the air stairs, bent down to give the little girl a caress on the cheek, then straightened and slipped an arm around Beth's waist. She leaned over and whispered something to her, giving Thom the distinct impression that they'd spoken before he got there and his wife had assured her everything would be fine. Ann-Sophie then turned them toward the stairs, meaningfully, and with a gentle hand on Beth's back, invited them to precede her on board the plane.

Thom looked back at Marques. There was nothing left to say.

Marques shrugged, in the generous manner of a winner. "Thanks, boss." He turned and hurried up the stairs, following his family through the door and turning left, toward the cockpit.

Thom turned back to Lisa, fury in his eyes. She handed him a bound leather folder. "This is everything we discussed, in terms of paperwork. The rest is being downloaded onto the server at Sanctuary as we speak. I'll head to the office and be reachable in the usual ways until we lose power here, and then on satellite thereafter. All the numbers are in the folder. Vital documents are in the vault and will stay there."

"You could have warned me," Thom said.

"It wouldn't have changed anything."

"You could have *handled* it."

"Yes, Thom, I'll be fine," she said, showing irritation for the first time he could ever remember. "Don't worry about me. Thank you for asking. Good luck to you." She turned and hurried away across the airfield, toward the row of parked cars just to the side of the tiny terminal.

Thom looked around. He was the only one left on the runway except for Brady, who waited in the Suburban, the engine still running. Brady was staring at him.

Thom muttered to himself, under the rising whine of the plane's turbines. "What, I'm the bad guy?"

But there wasn't anyone there to reply, and he wouldn't have been interested in the answer anyway. He turned, hurried up the stairs, and got on his plane. He settled into his usual seat, left aisle, forward-facing, in front of the dining table. He looked around. His kids, Anya and Lukas, were on the couches in the back, throwing cracker packets at each other and shouting "Daddy!," thrilled to be out of school and apparently going someplace fabulous. Beth (was that her name, Beth?—better make a note of that) and her daughter were behind them in the way-back area, by the bathroom, the little girl curled up in her mother's lap.

Thom looked at them for a long moment and attempted to reframe his thoughts. Reframing was always possible; it just took a moment sometimes. OK, yes, this situation was eminently reframable. He had not been strong-armed by his own pilot. No, no, not at all. He had, in fact, been given an incredible gift, the benefit of perspective. How remarkable it was that he, just a middle-class midwestern kid, really, was now able to provide for this whole other family in the midst of a global disaster, and in rather spectacular fashion. He'd go chat up Marques's whatever and her daughter later, invite the kid to come up into the cockpit, and let them know he was glad they were here, despite his initial surprise. He'd explain about the shock of the new and how changes in carefully thought-out plans always took a moment for him to come around to. But, yes, he would assure them, they were welcome here, very welcome. Everything was going to be OK. Thom was proud of himself. He'd done the right thing.

Ann-Sophie, who had stopped in the cockpit to have a quick word with Marques, headed back. To Thom's simultaneous relief and disappointment, she settled into the seat directly opposite him, her usual seat.

She leaned forward and, in a gesture of peacemaking, put a hand on his knee and gave him a squeeze. "It's the decent thing to do."

Thom smiled. "My very thoughts."

"How's your sister handling this?" Ann-Sophie asked as she buckled her seat belt and the plane's door slammed shut.

Thom looked at her blankly.

Shit.

He hadn't thought of Aubrey all day.

7.

CAYUGA LANE

Aubrey took the corner onto Cayuga a little faster than necessary and almost hit a kid on a bike. Scott shouted and braced himself against the dashboard as she locked up the brakes, bringing the car to an abrupt, squealing halt. The kid didn't even look back, just bore down and pedaled harder, banging up onto the sidewalk and heading west, into the setting sun.

Scott and Aubrey caught their breath.

"The hell is that kid doing out?" Aubrey asked.

"It's a blackout, not a tornado," Scott said, but his tone was unconvincing, and his voice quavered.

Aubrey pressed the gas, gingerly, in case there were any more ten-year-old lunatics racing home, and continued down the block. The neighborhood was still busy. Most of the cars that had headed out earlier had returned and were now backed into their driveways with trunks and doors open, in various stages of unloading. Whatever could be bought, borrowed, or otherwise rounded up had been crammed into them and was now being lugged into kitchens and basements. Stocking up was instinctive at this point; most people had gotten pretty good at it.

As they drove past Norman Levy's house, thoughts of the professor flickered through Aubrey's mind again. "Remind me I need to check on Norman right away if this happens. See if he needs anything."

Scott grunted. "If this happens, I wouldn't bet the over on Norman. He's like a hundred."

Aubrey turned. Again, the urge to slap him was strong. Instead, she leveled her voice. "That's a shitty thing to say."

"My bad."

"I hate that expression."

"My bad."

She looked at him. Was he trying to enrage her?

Scott half smiled. He was. Sometimes the kid could be funny. "I won't let you forget Norman. But you know he's got this shit more under control than anybody."

Scott had once been unabashed in his admiration of Norman. They'd been great together, a grandfather figure and his unlikely protégé. Norman's place was an intellectual funhouse. There was always something interesting going on there, and for a couple years Scott had been an almost daily presence, coming home with stories of telescopes assembled, radio rigs he'd been allowed to fiddle with for hours, and endless conversations he'd had with the string of smart and entertaining characters Norman kept in his life. But then Scott hit fourteen, his father was thrown out of the house, and the boy clammed up, to everyone.

"Talk to me," Norman had told him then, "like you used to," and instead Scott stopped going over to Norman's house altogether.

"Maybe you should be the one to check on him," Aubrey suggested.

But Scott was staring past her, his face flushing. "He's here."

"Who?"

"Dad. He's here."

Aubrey turned and saw the black pickup, parked in their driveway in a proprietary fashion. She took a breath, kept cool, and swung a wide U-turn in front of the house, parking at the foot of the walk as Rusty pushed open the screen door and came outside. Waltzed right out of *her* house, the one she'd bought him out of, and overpaid dearly for the privilege.

"Left your front door wide open," Rusty said, in lieu of a greeting. Scott got out, slammed his door, shoved his hands in his pockets, and started up the walk, intending to blow past Rusty in an adolescent stalk, but Aubrey called him back.

"Can you help carry, please?"

Scott and Rusty answered at the same time—"Sure"—and started walking toward her.

"I meant Scott."

Rusty stopped, rolling his eyes. "Sorry."

Aubrey opened the trunk and she and Scott started picking up bags stuffed with toilet paper, pasta, cleaning products, canned goods, and the like. Rusty, rebuffed, drifted a few feet closer and looked at the bags, frowning.

"That's a lotta perishables. Hope you like milk."

Scott and Aubrey ignored him and kept working. "I can take more," Scott offered to Aubrey.

"You sure?"

"Yeah, put it under here." He lifted his elbow, creating a space on his left hip, and she tucked a box of Tide under there. He lifted the other arm, asking for more. She obliged. In Rusty's presence, they were suddenly working together better than they had in months.

Rusty nodded toward a plastic bag jammed full of frozen items. "That's all gonna melt."

Aubrey didn't respond.

Scott headed inside, studiously avoiding eye contact with his father as he passed.

Rusty stepped down off the curb and came to the trunk, reaching for a bag.

Aubrey waved him off. "I can get it."

"Oh, come on. You're worse than him."

"What do you want, Rusty?"

"What do you think I want? I'm checking on you guys."

"We're OK. You should get home and get ready."

"For what? They're yanking our chain again. The sun's gonna blow up? We're going back to caveman times? C'mon, Aubrey. Three-day blackout, tops."

She closed her eyes, thinking how little she missed Rusty's opinions about the world, his distrust of every single institution, corporation, and loose affiliation of like-minded individuals in existence, whether formally organized or happenstance. She bit her tongue. "I hope you're right."

"I know I am."

"Please take your arm off of there." She'd picked up the last of the bags and was waiting to close the trunk, but he was in the way. Rusty closed it for her, and she started up the walk. He followed. She glanced back, over her shoulder. "If you don't think it's happening, why did you feel the need to check on us?"

"Just wanted to make sure you guys weren't panicking."

"We're not. We're taking precautions. There's a difference."

She moved up onto the front step and Rusty lunged in front of her, opening the screen door. Aubrey paused, because the next logical step would be for him to follow her into the house, help unpack the groceries, and generally become part of things, which was a development she urgently wanted to prevent.

"Would you close the door, please?" She backed up and set the bags of groceries down at her feet. Rusty complied, closing the screen door. From inside, they could hear the sound of the TV as Scott turned it back on, checking for an update. Aubrey turned to Rusty. "Thank you for checking. We're fine."

Rusty just looked at her, saddened. His icy eyes, courtesy of his Irish mother, sloped down at the sides, and when he'd hit his forties, he'd acquired a permanent heavy-lidded look. The resulting effect was that he struck most people as a man who carried a burden of great sorrow. It wasn't so terribly far from the truth; it just missed the mark. He had inflicted far more suffering than he'd endured.

"It's not natural," he said.

"What?"

"You. My kid. Living together. You're not even related anymore."

"That was his choice, not mine. I thought it was brave."

"I want him to come live with me."

"Then you probably shouldn't have hit him."

She regretted it immediately. Not because it was unkind or uncalled for, but because it meant this conversation was going to go on a lot longer than she'd hoped.

"I told you, I don't remember doing that."

"Well, Scott and I do."

"Did I ever hit you?" She didn't answer. *"Did I ever hit you?"*

Aubrey turned, looking inside. Scott was looking back at them over his shoulder, his senses hyper-attuned to the slightest change in the calibration of a conversation's hostility level. Aubrey called to him. "Can you get all the cold stuff into the freezer in the basement? And move it in there all at once, don't leave the freezer door open for long, OK?"

Scott nodded and headed into the kitchen. She knew the coffin-size freezer Thom had gifted her during COVID was empty, save for a single five-pound bag of ice, and she hoped to get it as full as possible while they still could. It was a plan that was doomed to failure after a few days if the power did go out, but it was all she had at the moment.

Rusty was still looking at her. "I stopped. Drinking. So that you know."

"I'm glad. Rusty, I have a lot of work to do."

"It was the times I blacked out. That was it, right? Because every other time, I was myself, and I was in control. You know that. But I can't remember what I can't remember, and I couldn't control it either. It wasn't me."

Aubrey turned and looked across the street, westward, where the sun had fully set behind the row of maple trees that bordered the school behind the houses. It was cool mid-April, so it would be dark soon. Maybe *really* dark. She was desperate to wrap this up.

Rusty wasn't finished. "If I got pissed off, I could tell, and I could always control it, no matter how much I'd had. I could feel it coming and I could walk it down, I could make it go back in, and I never, ever hit anybody or anything when it was like that."

"But you did, Rusty."

"*In the blackouts*, that's what I'm saying. But I don't remember those, because I was switched off. I couldn't stop it because I wasn't there. It sounds stupid, but it's true, and that's why this is all so unfair."

He'd leaned in on that last sentence, and when he hit the *f* in unfair, she could smell his breath. Southern Comfort, maybe? A spicy, earthy thing, the kind of booze nobody sits down with a glass of, the sort of thing you only drink if it's the very last thing in the cabinet and you gotta get a buzz on right this fucking minute. She saw the little red streaks in his eyes then, and she marveled at her defensive ability to miss things she didn't want to see. The last two years of *not* seeing Rusty drunk had dulled some of her formerly razor-sharp observational skills. Of course he was fucked up, and of course he was scared and full of regrets, and she wanted nothing to do with it.

She attempted a neutral tone. "Thank you for checking on us. I hope you're right about all this."

"Oh, come on. Like you never wanted to smack the kid?"

"No. Never." She picked up her groceries, glancing at the screen door. "Would you mind?"

With exaggerated gallantry, he reached out and opened the door for her. She stepped through, but instead of closing it, Rusty leaned in the doorframe, lingering.

"Look, it's a weird time."

"It is."

She turned, bags still in her arms, hooking her foot under the front door to close it.

"And it catches me at just the worst possible moment," he continued.

She paused, realizing what he was actually there for. She sighed. "How much?"

"I've got a twenty and a ten in my wallet and the ATMs are shut down. How much can you spare?"

"Wait here."

She turned and walked into the house. He watched as she went into the kitchen, put the bags on the counter, and turned to the half-open door that led to the basement stairs. Leaning slightly to his right, he could just see her back as she spoke to Scott, who was still downstairs, probably loading up the freezer. Rusty frowned, wondering why on earth she was asking Scott before dipping into her own finances, but that was a puzzle he knew he was never going to figure out. Those two had been tight since the day he'd first brought her home, when Scott was seven or eight, and they'd been conspiring against him ever since.

The more he watched, the less Rusty liked the conversation. Aubrey was at the top of the stairs, gesturing, trying to make some kind of point to Scott, who must have been resisting it. He could hear the boy's surprisingly deep tones countering her emphatically. Wait a minute, was this the actual situation here? Was Rusty a man standing on the threshold of what had once been his own home, watching while his ex-wife attempted to convince his fifteen-year-old son that it was OK to give him *a couple of twenties*?

Shit. That's low, man.

After another heated back-and-forth, Rusty saw Aubrey dip into the doorway, heard her feet bang down a few stairs, then stop, turn around, and come back up. She marched across the living room and came back toward him, carrying something in her right hand. She extended her arm as she drew close.

"That from Scott?"

"None of your business. Do you want it?"

"Yeah, you got everything under control here."

"Do you want it or not?"

He looked down. She was holding three bills in her hand. But they weren't twenties. They were hundreds.

Rusty controlled his reaction as best he could, but his right hand shot up pretty quickly, wanting to secure the money before she changed her mind. He closed his hand around the bills and shoved them in his pocket. Far down, as if he was afraid she might come after them.

"Tell him his old man says—"

But the front door was already closing. "Please don't ever come in this house when I'm not here again."

"You left the goddamn door open. I was worried."

She stopped, the door still opened a foot or two. "And to answer your question, no. You never hit me. I got you out before you had a chance." In her pocket, Aubrey's cell phone rang. She closed the door without another word.

Rusty turned, trying not to smile. The kid, for God knows what reason, had just forked over three hundred dollars in cash, at a time when those two chuckleheads were obviously convinced the world was about to come to a crashing end. That meant the little shit had, at a minimum, at least three times that much cash that he had *not* given over. Why on earth his moronic ex-wife had put a teenager in charge of their finances was beyond him, and unimportant.

This was a fascinating development that needed a good, long think.

8.

Inside the house, Aubrey let out a breath of air and tried to lower her shoulders, which had been cranked up around her ears. She rolled them back once, pulled her phone from her pocket, and answered.

"Hey, Thom."

"Heeey."

It was funny how a single word out of her brother's mouth could drive Aubrey right up the fucking wall and down the other side. Just the way he'd say "Heeey" in that low, sympathetic register one uses when speaking to someone they pity. It was a hey that said, "Sister, I get it, you're broke, divorced, loveless, pushing forty, and presiding over a failing business, but I do not judge you at *all*."

She played past it. "I was just thinking about you," she said.

"Don't worry about *me*. What about *you*?"

"I'm fine," she said. "Just laid in a bunch of groceries." She felt her initial irritation with him easing. They'd been through hell together, and his personal faults, annoying ways, and galactic ego aside, she knew he only wanted to help. It was just the way he did it that was maddening.

"Did you fill the freezer?"

She headed into the kitchen, glancing at the still-opened door to the basement and pictured the enormous freezer now maybe ten percent filled.

"Yep. I can hardly get the lid closed."

"Good. Don't open it unless you have to. But don't overreact and throw everything out too soon either. Aside from meat, almost everything frozen can be eaten unfrozen."

Aubrey wondered how to prevent a discussion of her failure to plan for disaster, as Thom had repeatedly implored her to do. He'd gone so far as to send a team of three handsome and muscular men to her house one day, offering to assess her wants and needs and return in three days to Take Care of Everything. They were from some sort of Chicago-based concierge apocalypse-supply firm, but she'd sent them away. No, she hadn't filled the freezer, no, she hadn't let the survival warriors stock her house, and, no, she hadn't filled the fucking rack in the fucking basement, OK?

"Where are you?" she asked, trying to change the subject.

"On the plane."

"On your way to the *Fuhrerbunker*?"

"May I ask once again that you please not compare me to Hitler?"

"I don't compare you to Hitler, I compare your bunker to his. But I take it back. I'm sure yours is much nicer."

"This is *serious*," he said. "This is *happening*. I was on the phone with the National Science Board not twenty minutes ago."

"What did they say?"

"Ninety percent outage worldwide. Four-to-eighteen-month repair time."

"Do you believe that's true?"

"It doesn't matter what I think. I believe they believe it."

On that she knew he was right, and it was one of the things she'd always admired about him. Her brother's ego was the iceberg into which his ship would one day crash and sink, but, intellectually, he was able to put it aside when he was in the presence of people who knew more about their own field than he did. The ability to admit ignorance, to shut up and actually listen, was something Thom had acquired early in life, and it was, to Aubrey's mind, the single greatest reason for his enormous success. But he was the last person she'd admit that to.

"Please let me send for you."

"No, thank you."

"There's a place here I've set aside for you. You need to at least see it."

"I've seen pictures. I know what it is. I don't want to live there."

"Two weeks."

"I don't want to live there at all."

"No, no. I mean I can't fly for two weeks. That's not just me, that's all planes, everything will be grounded until they're sure the energy's dissipated in the magnetosphere. Just too dangerous. But I can have you picked up in two weeks."

"Thank you, but I'm fine right here."

"This could be turned into a positive. It could be the perfect opportunity for you to get out of Aurora for good."

"It's my home. It was yours too."

"Yeah, but I left. I assumed you would too. That's what rational people do."

"I'm not rational. I'm a woman."

He groaned. "*Once*. I said that *one time*."

"And I wrote it down."

"No one else in my life is as hostile to me as you are."

"Sure, they are, just not to your face."

There was a pause.

"Please let me help you," he said, softly. "I owe you."

"Ancient history, Tommy. We're OK now."

Scott came up from the basement and nodded at her. "Who is that?"

"My brother."

"Who is that?" asked Thom.

"Scott." Jesus, all she did was answer demanding questions from the men in her life, of whom she had actually chosen exactly one, the one who turned out to be the abusive drunk.

"Why don't you ask Scott if he thinks you guys should come here?"

She was losing patience. "Because, Thom, Scott is not making the decisions for me, and neither are you. *I* am making the choices, and I choose to ride this out here, for however long it takes."

She'd actually made no such choice yet, but she'd been saying no to things Thom offered for so many years it was a reflex. It had started out as plain old childhood resentment, and she had perfectly good reasons for it, but only herself to blame for her choices. Ten minutes in adolescence had shaped the rest of both their lives, the way it fucking does. Maybe, she figured, if she refused to share in his obscene wealth she wouldn't feel quite as bothered about the way she'd helped create it.

"OK, reality check, all right?" Thom said. "You will be without power for an extended period of time. *Months.* In the short term, you will run out of battery for your phone, which wouldn't work anyway, because cell towers will go down. Longer term, the supply chain of food will strain and break, the water will stop flowing from your tap, and your neighborhood will descend into lawlessness. I don't have to ask if you ever bought a generator, because I'm sure I'm correct in guessing you did not. I doubt that you actually filled the freezer in the basement, you have no weapons of any kind because you are philosophically opposed, and you are living within one hour of the third-densest urban population in the country, all of which will soon be starving, panicked, and on the run. You will be living WROL: without rule of law. I know you don't like reality, Aubrey, but there it is. So the next time we talk, and I again make the offer to have someone come and fly you to safety, I hope you will give it better consideration than this."

"Do you think it's possible you overprepare?"

"There is no such thing. Just because something hasn't happened before doesn't mean it never will. Your thinking is stuck; it's called initial occurrence syndrome. But I have seen how easily things can get out of control, and so have you. I won't ever let that happen again."

"I'm fine, Thom. We stood the drought, now we'll stand the flood."

"What drought? What flood?"

"It's a song."

"Well, you're not going to be able to hear it for the next year and a half."

Scott had wandered back into the living room and was flipping through channels. They were alight with news broadcasts, each with a different terrifying spin on the events to come. As the hour grew later and night began to fall on the East Coast, the tone, even among the most denial-based political viewpoints, had grown pessimistic. An anxious spokesman, Perry somebody from NASA, or NOAA, or the NSA, was making a public plea to power utilities nationwide to shut down before it was too late.

"I gotta go, Thom."

"Did you get the money?"

"Did you send me money? I haven't looked today."

Thom paused. He was exasperated but spoke in a measured tone. "I sent you twenty thousand dollars last fall in case a situation like this arose. You were to go to the bank, withdraw it in twenties, and leave it in four different places in your house. In a case of social collapse, cash is going to be the most valuable commodity. That and pre-1965 silver American coins, but we won't get into that. Did you do it?"

Aubrey turned and looked at the beautiful Ian Dunn oak cabinets that she'd ordered for her kitchen the day Thom's money showed up in her account. They had the heavy, solid feel of excellent carpentry and made her happy every time she got a water glass. OK, so she didn't refuse *everything* Thom sent.

"Yes, I have cash."

"You're lying."

"I am. You bought me kitchen cabinets."

"This isn't a joke, Aubs. It's real, and it's happening."

"I know. I'm scared. But we're OK. Thank you for calling."

"Do you still have the satellite phone I sent? It had three extra bat-teries, all charged. Check them. I will call you on it in the morning. We'll discuss this again. It's you and me, remember?"

"Because everyone else is dead," she answered, automatically. It was their routine, and it had been funny once. It wasn't right now.

"Let's get you through this one day at a time," he said.

"I plan to."

"I love you."

"You too."

He hung up first. She walked into the living room, joining Scott at the TV. They fell into disaster posture, sitting upright at the edge of the couch flipping between channels, no news good enough or bad enough to satisfy.

9.

Monarch Air had an executive terminal at the Provo Municipal Airport, which was eighty-six miles from the site outside Jericho. It was a longer drive than Thom had hoped for, but he'd looked at numerous closer airports and none had air-traffic control towers. He didn't want to risk being airborne with nowhere good to put the plane down once the event had started. The likelihood of bumper-to-bumper traffic on the outskirts of Provo seemed low, so that was where they landed. So far, aside from the wrinkle Marques had put in the plan, everything was going pretty much exactly as expected.

Ann-Sophie and the kids were the first ones off the plane, and they headed toward two waiting Suburbans, customized with exactly the same details as the models they rode around in back home, down to the apps on the iPads waiting in the seat backs and the brand of hand sanitizers in the door pockets. Thom had called ahead to order another car so that he wouldn't have to ride with Marques, Beth, and her kid. There was a limit to his beneficence, and the phone call with Aubrey had irritated him. What was the point of caring about people, planning ahead for them, allowing them to borrow the use of your well-developed consequence-foreseeing frontal lobe, if they ignored all your advice? Kitchen cabinets? Great. I hope you enjoy them when you're burning them for heat this winter.

Putting his sister out of his mind, he stood at the cargo hold in the back of the plane, supervising the unpacking of the bags, counting them off one by one as the handlers loaded them onto luggage carts. The plane would be hangared and serviced here for a few days, until Marques returned to fly it to the private airstrip near Sanctuary, where it would reside on a more long-term basis. A qualified mechanic was the one detail Thom had let slide so far, but that wouldn't be hard to find, once the trouble hit. Who *wouldn't* want a cushy, high-paying job in a safe environment once things got dicey? And this time Thom would be double- and triple-checking that guy's marital status, you could bet your ass on that.

The baggage handler slammed the door at the rear of the plane and walked toward the SUV. Thom frowned.

"We're missing one."

The handler turned around. "Sorry?"

"You unloaded four bags. We have five."

The handler turned back, opened the hold, and looked inside. "Nothing else in there."

"Where's the blue one?" Thom asked. The handler looked at him blankly. There really was nothing else in the hold. Thom turned to Ann-Sophie. "Honey!"

She turned from where she was helping the kids into the back of the car.

"Where's the blue one?"

"What blue one?"

Thom maintained an even tone. "We have five go bags. Two red—those are the kids'. Two black—those are you and me. One blue. That one's missing."

"I'm sorry, I didn't see it."

"You had them take all the bags out of the locked cabinet in the garage, didn't you?"

"Yes."

"*All* of them?"

"Well, I thought so. I don't know, Thom, I was upset. Your phone call was upsetting. I was trying to get to school to get the kids."

"You didn't *have* to go to the school," he snapped, then reined in his tone. "You didn't have to go to the school because Antonio was going to the school. That was the whole plan."

Ann-Sophie straightened, turning icy. "I wanted to see my children."

"That just—that wasn't what we agreed. Remember? In the disaster-planning meetings?"

"I'm sorry, I guess I wasn't really listening. Was the bag important?"

"No. I bought the stuff, packed it, systematically unpacked and re-packed it for three years, and cleaned and tested everything in it on a rotating schedule because it was *un*important."

"Knock it off," she snapped, drawing herself up to her full height, which was an inch and a half taller than him. The baggage handler turned away and busied himself with unnecessarily repacking the four bags in the back of the SUV.

Ann-Sophie softened her tone. "You got us here, Thom. You did a great job. I'm sure whatever was in the bag, there are a dozen identical items like it at the place."

She was right. The missing bag hadn't been long-term provisions at all, it was a short-term PERK, or personal emergency relocation kit, to be used only if they'd been unable to fly and were forced to drive. And not just drive but maneuver through a hostile landscape with limited fuel reserves. There were extended-life body warmers, boxes of water-purification tablets, freeze-dried stroganoff and macaroni and cheese, tampons (for blood from wounds as well as their usual purpose), chain-saw blades for harvesting wood, and condoms.

Because, you know, you never know.

Obviously, they would be fine without all of that here. It was more the principle of the thing. Here it was again, the best advance planning in the world rendered useless by poor follow-through. Thom knew he was going to be fine. He had taught himself to be a master of radical self-reliance; he could literally eat a pine tree if he had to. But he was worried about everyone around him. Clearly, he was going to have to lift them all on his back and physically carry them through this ordeal. Fine. So he would.

"Sorry I snapped at you." They headed for the car.

Eighty-six miles took just over eighty minutes. The stretch of road was long and flat, cutting a line more or less straight southwest from Provo through Spanish Fork, Eureka, Jericho, and eventually to the five-hundred-acre parcel that had once been the property of the United States government. The Little Sierra Missile Range had gained notoriety in the early '80s when it was proposed that it be converted into one of the nation's first Dense Pack ranges. Dense Pack was a configuration pattern developed under Reagan in which ten to twelve hardened silos for LGM-118 Peacekeeper ICBMs would be evenly spaced along a north–south line, all within a few miles of each other. The thinking was that since incoming Soviet missiles would likely come south from over the North Pole, a long string of identical missile placements stood a greater chance of survival in a first-strike scenario, rather than scattering them in easier-to-target one-offs spread around the country. The idea met with intense opposition when it was pointed out that, perhaps, grouping twelve silos in the same place made it far more likely for enemy firepower to be concentrated on that one area. Local and not-so-local residents were unamused, and the idea was dropped. The Little Sierra Range was therefore poorly named, as it had only ever served as home to a single nuclear missile silo.

But what a silo it was. It was built in the early 1960s to house a Titan II missile, the largest and heaviest ICBM ever built by the United States. The missile was a hundred and three feet tall, weighed a staggering 330,000 pounds, and was the first U.S. missile that could be launched from an entirely subterranean complex. The silo was a hundred and forty-six feet deep and fifty-five feet in diameter, super-hardened with twelve-foot concrete-and-steel walls all around. It was a gargantuan structure whose only aboveground portion was a large, circular lip that sat a modest three feet above the ground, like a very thick and wide manhole cover.

The Little Sierra silo was decommissioned in 1991 as the U.S. government made the move to smaller, more lightweight missiles that required less in the way of infrastructure. The silo and land surrounding it, all five hundred acres, sat empty and unpopulated, except for a revolving series of twenty-four-hour marine guards, who may have had the most boring job in the entire United States military, which is really saying something. It wasn't until the late nineties that the government realized there were actually people crazy enough to buy these things.

Little Sierra was first picked up by a real estate speculator whose gamble that the surrounding badlands could be made into usable housing developments proved resoundingly wrong. After his bankruptcy, the next buyer up to the plate was the Chickasaw Tribe, of nearby Oklahoma, which was looking to invest some of its casino profits in large chunks of real estate in nearby states. After one visit to Little Sierra, they decided to look somewhere else. Finally, in the early aughts, the government found a willing buyer in Thom Banning, who had, post-9/11, correctly predicted that the market for survival bunkers was something worth keeping an eye on. He'd picked up the land for $1,000 an acre, a steal no matter how barren, and after $30 million in renovations, he now owned one of the world's premier post-apocalyptic survivalist enclaves.

The twin Suburbans pulled up to the main entrance. The manhole-like cover that had once sat just over the nose of the Titan II had been removed, replaced by a discreet concrete guardhouse, which was set into a rolling hillside that had been graded, landscaped, and irrigated with care. It was an imposing entrance but not a terrifying one. The only other aboveground structure was a six-thousand-square-foot modernist château nestled into the artificial hillside beside the gatehouse. It was designed to shelter a single family, Thom's family, for as long as things stayed somewhat docile out in the world at large.

But the real masterpiece, for when the shit *really* hit the fan, was all underground, inside the converted silo, which was now fourteen floors of scrupulously conceived subterranean living space.

Thom's car was in the lead and pulled up to the gatehouse, where they were met by ex-Major Jimmy Rutland, casually dressed in fatigues, Kevlar vest, and wraparound sunglasses, with a semiautomatic weapon slung across his chest. Ex-Major Jimmy made no move for Thom's door. He knew to let the man open it himself and get out. Thom bounced out of the car and came forward to address Jimmy with a grim we're-all-men-of-the-world expression.

"Jimmy."

"Mr. Banning. Good to see you, sir. Sorry for the circumstances." Jimmy wasn't sorry at all. Jimmy had been born for this day; he'd enlisted on his eighteenth birthday, trained his way up through anti-terrorism security forces in the marines, and was making serious money in the private sector when Thom had recruited him.

"How's it looking?" Thom asked.

"Clear and fine, sir. Glad you all made it OK."

Thom turned and gestured to the others, in the cars behind him, that it was OK to get out. They did, the kids spilling out of both cars and taking off across the dirt road, which wasn't actually dirt at all but DryCrete, a weatherproof material made to look and feel like an unused country highway. The kids didn't care. They raced up the hill and rolled down its lush grass.

Jimmy frowned, noticing Beth and her daughter, and looked down at a clipboard on the stand in front of him, scanning the list of names there. "Do we have a change in the guest list?"

"We do. I chose to include some friends. Let's treat them well."

"You got it, boss."

"Who else is here?"

"All active guards reported within an hour of your call. Dr. Bordwell lives in Provo, so he was one of the first resident staff to arrive." He gestured to the nearby grassy slope, where a middle-aged man in khakis and an untucked blue shirt sat staring out at the desolate landscape. Jimmy leaned in and lowered his voice, for Thom's ears only. "Dr. B. could use a little bit of a charm offensive. I think we're dealing with some shell shock."

Thom frowned and glanced over at the figure sitting on the grass, who did indeed look bereft.

"What's the matter?" Thom asked. "Our dentist didn't like his room?"

"Oh, I wouldn't worry about it. Situation's got everybody on tilt. He'll settle in." He continued. "We've had contact from nearly all the other contract hires, in one form or another. Dr. Rahman is ten minutes behind you, and the Friedmans and Ms. Hyland should be touching down at Provo as we speak. The others are in various phases of transit. All in all, everybody seems to have mobilized on the double."

Thom nodded. Marques, he noticed, had gotten out of the car and joined them, overhearing that last part. Thom glanced at him, annoyed all over again, and looked back to Jimmy. "Please get our bags into the main house and show our guests to, let's see, I'm thinking number nine. That sound good?"

"Sounds like a good plan today, sir, and that is the best kind of plan." Jimmy turned to Marques. "I'll be back in five"—for some reason he felt the need to hold up a gloved hand, fingers spread to denote the exact number of minutes he was talking about—"and will show you to your quarters."

With that, he spun on his bootheel and headed for the gatehouse. Marques turned back to Thom, confused. "Exactly how many people are going to be living here?"

"Exactly as many as are necessary for the successful long-term functioning of a community. We have a dentist, an internist, two chefs, a trainer, two schoolteachers, a physical therapist, a yoga instructor, an agriculturalist, a spiritualist, and you, an airline pilot. They should all be here by dark. What can Beth do?"

"Sorry?"

"For a living, what does she do? Everybody has to contribute."

"Oh, right. She's a real estate broker."

Thom stared at him for a long moment. "I'll keep that in mind if we sell." He turned and started walking toward the big house, gesturing to the entrance to the silo itself. "Jimmy will show you to your place. Ask him to see the gym, the movie theatre, the hydroponics, the works. He likes to give the tour. I think you'll see you bet on the right pony."

He walked away, up the hill, and Marques looked around. The scale of the place, the degree of planning and building, the armed militia guards, the imposing landscape—he'd known Thom was rich, and he thought he knew what that meant, but build-your-own-society rich? That had never occurred to him.

He walked up the short hill to where Beth and Kearie were playing. He smiled and circled his arm around Beth's waist, pulling her in close.

She looked up, into his eyes, and spoke quietly. "How is it going?"

"It's going how it's going. It'll be fine."

"I'm sorry I got you into this," she said.

"Don't be. It was my idea."

He kissed her. It was awkward, and she hadn't been expecting it.

He pulled back, tucking her hair behind one ear. "I'm sorry. I won't do that again. He was watching us, though."

Beth looked over his shoulder and saw Thom, who was indeed eyeballing them. She turned back to Marques and smiled. "It's OK." She leaned up and pressed her lips into his, the feeling more familiar this time, and she minded less when she was the one initiating it. She made it good, counting to five in her mind, then pulled back and rested her forehead on his chest. "I have to admit, I was wondering about that. Like if you were going to—you know, expect anything."

"It's not like that. I'll sleep on the floor."

"Thank you."

He smiled. "Tell Kearie she's gotta try to be more affectionate with me."

"She's kind of freaked out."

"Who isn't?"

Thom walked into the big aboveground house and looked around. The living room was stunning, with enormous, angled plate-glass windows that looked out on the stark badlands and snowcapped mountains in the distance. The place had been built all on one level, bedrooms radiating off the great room and kitchen like spokes on a wheel. Everything else was underground, starting with the playroom, family area, library, and gym, and eventually leading to the emergency exit tunnel. The tunnel opened onto the private elevator down into the main complex, where all other residents were housed in a series of stacked apartments ranging from eighteen hundred square feet for singles all the way up to the bunker penthouse, which was about twice as large. It was to there the family would retreat if and when things got rough. Until then, they'd live above ground, the lords of the manor, the only ones not confined to the lower depths.

Thom went first to the kitchen, to check on food and other supplies, which had been laid in exactly as discussed and signed off on. All was in readiness there. He could hear Ann-Sophie in the master bedroom, putting things away, and he took a deep breath and wandered over to take her emotional temperature once more.

He stopped in the doorway, watching as she unpacked. The closets were already reasonably full, doubles of all her favorite things that were appropriate to the desert climate had been bought, laundered, and hung up, the spaces opened and aired regularly. There really wasn't much, if anything, for her to do.

Or for Thom, for that matter, and for the first time all day he wasn't sure what to do with himself. Prepping was more than a hobby. It had been his avocation, and a competitive game for he and his fellow billionaire friends. Who had anticipated the most? Who had actually implemented their plans, and how sturdy were they? But now the prep was over, the game strategies had been put into motion, and there wasn't anything left to do except watch things play out and see who had the most chips when it was over.

Ann-Sophie stood between the bed and the closet, holding a plum-colored cashmere cardigan in one hand and a bottle of coconut water in the other. She had her back to the door, and Thom could see her head moving from the sweater to the water bottle, wondering to herself how on earth she'd ended up with them, why *those* two items, above all others, and what was she supposed to do with them now? She backed up, felt the edge of the bed with the back of her knee, and sagged down onto it.

"I wonder—"

She turned, startled. She hadn't heard him in the doorway. Two-foot-thick walls, twelve-inch soundproof glass, and carpet-over-wood-over-concrete floors made the place as quiet as a recording studio. You could snap your fingers and practically feel it evaporate in the air around you.

Thom gestured, sorry, and tried to continue. "I wonder if maybe this isn't a good chance."

"For what?"

"For us. To start over."

He took a step into the room and closed the door behind him. Immediately, she got up from the bed, sensing an implication.

He sighed. "That isn't what I meant."

"What did you mean?"

"Come on. It's been shitty, right?"

"Yes. It has."

"Well, I've apologized. Several times. Now the world is going to fall apart. We're all we've got."

She looked at him. She wondered when she might ever be able to watch him undress again. She wondered, if that day ever came, if the sight of his overworked abdominal muscles would arouse the same revulsion in her that she felt right now. She wondered if she could ever see him naked and aroused again, and she wondered how long, exactly, would persist the image of his stupid fucking abs, tensed and sweaty, while he stood in the middle of their home gym, his head down, one hand caressing the dark hair atop his trainer's head as she took him in her—

Never. That's when she'd watch him undress. Never ever. It was the sheer corniness of his behavior that enraged her the most, the wild, over-the-top clichéness of it all. Your *trainer*? Are you *joking*? The rest was just going to be the sorting-out. The kids would love Stockholm. She was sure of that, as sure as she was that he wouldn't even try to fight her.

"What do you want?" he asked. She didn't answer. "Darling. What do you *want*?"

Still no answer. He turned and walked out of the room.

Ann-Sophie, who loathed conflict and had spent most of her adult life managing to avoid it, walked in the opposite direction. She stopped at the window and looked out, not at the spectacular view but at Marques, Beth, and Kearie, who were now playing with Anya and Lukas. The little ones were racing up the grassy hill, then flopping onto the ground to roll right back down it, giggling delightedly, leaping to their feet and drunk-walking back to the top, bragging about who was dizzier.

Marques and Beth tried a roll too, ended up going mostly sideways, and crashed into each other halfway down, laughing.

Ann-Sophie watched them. Now *that's* what a family looks like, she thought.

Beyond, the sun slipped beneath the mountains.

10.

The power still hadn't gone out. Scott kept watching the TV reports, but Aubrey grew tired of the expanding deadline, the horizon that never seemed to be met, the confusing explanations about solar weather, and why this death blow's travel time was impossible to estimate. Four hours became seven hours because nine hours became maybe-we-were-wrong-about-this-whole-thing, which led to more shouting, blaming, and finger-pointing on the TV. Sometime after midnight, Aubrey went upstairs, took a long hot shower, got in bed, and turned out the light.

Every three or four minutes until she finally fell asleep, at 2 a.m., she'd open her sleepless eyes, feel for the switch on the bedside light, and flick it on, just to see. Every time, the bulb would blaze to light. She wondered if everybody was just . . . wrong.

They were not.

When the CME erupted from the sun's surface and entered interplanetary space, it created an enormous magnetic cloud containing counter-streaming beams of electrons, flowing in opposite directions.

The massive, billowing cloud made first contact with the earth's magnetopause, the outer limit of the magnetosphere, at thirty-seven minutes past 3 a.m., Central Daylight Time.

Normally, plasma in the solar wind is deflected around the earth into the long magnetotail, which then caroms harmlessly into space or is disbursed, without significant impact, into the atmosphere. In this case, the sheer volume of the coronal mass was overwhelming. Ten thousand billion metric tons of charged electronic particles surged into the earth's magnetic field like a Mongol horde and cascaded toward the polar regions. Once there, they ricocheted back and forth between the polar mirror points, creating a current flow of unprecedented ferocity that roared above the earth at an altitude of 100,000 meters. Once inside our atmosphere, the resulting voltage potential on the surface of the earth shot off the charts, and the overpowering pulse of direct current invaded power lines through their ground connections.

The Aurora Generating Station—an 878-milliwatt, simple-cycle, natural-gas-fired facility on the outskirts of town and part of the Upper Midwest power grid—picked up the charge within ninety seconds of first polar contact. From the Aurora station, the super-intense power surge spread through the lines, both above and below ground, in DuPage, Kane, and Kendall counties, tripping breakers, blowing transformers, and melting power lines everywhere within a sixty-mile radius.

In the living room of Aubrey's house, the seventy-seven-inch Sony TV winked, unceremoniously, and went dark. Scott, who had fallen asleep on the couch, failed to notice.

The light woke Aubrey. Not its intensity but its weirdness. Even asleep, her brain knew something wasn't right. She blinked, looking at a sideways, blurry image of her bedroom curtains. She'd never liked blinds, preferring to have natural light wake her in the morning, and it was doing that now, but the reddish hue coming through her bedroom window was anything but natural.

She sat up on one elbow, waiting for her eyes to focus. Outside, the sky was alight, which meant time to get up, but when she picked up her phone and looked at it, the time was 4:11 a.m. Even in April, that was way too early. She sat up, swinging her legs over the side of the bed. She stared dully at the sky outside her window, awash in a blood-red glow, and looked back down at her phone to double-check the time. She noticed there was no signal.

Her breath quickened. She reached for the bedside lamp and clicked the switch. The bulb failed to light. She clicked it two, three, four more times with the same result. She glanced over at the TV mounted on the far wall, which always had that maddening little red light in its lower left corner, even when it was off.

Except for now. Now, there was nothing.

"Wake up. Scott, wake up."

He rolled over on the couch and squinted up at her, but she was already leaving the room, headed outside. She'd pulled on a pair of pants, her shirt half-tucked in. The room was bathed in a reddish glow, and when Aubrey threw open the front door, more colors streaked across the floor. It was nighttime, and it wasn't.

Scott got up and followed her. She walked down the front path, her head back, taking in the huge, weird sky above her. It was majestically streaked with a half dozen vivid colors: reds, blues, and the most otherworldly swirls of electric green he'd ever seen. The aurorae were spread in great, soft arcs across the sky, with patches that had billowing surfaces like clouds. But they were completely different from moonlit clouds, in that the stars beyond were clearly visible through them. There were rays of lighter- and darker-colored stripes that undulated through the sky, radiating upward, increasing rather than fading in intensity the farther they rose from the ground. The sky seethed and billowed.

Scott drew up next to Aubrey and they stood there, at the edge of the sidewalk, staring upward in disbelief. Aubrey heard voices and looked down, seeing Cayuga Lane turned into something not quite daytime and certainly not nighttime. Some of her neighbors had walked into the street to get out from under their trees for a clearer view. Mrs. Chen and her boys lingered in their doorway, afraid to come out any farther, and a few were inside, their slack-jawed faces visible in their windows, lit up by the rainbow-colored reflections on the glass around them.

All of them were staring up at the sky, then at each other for confirmation, and then back up at the heavens. Scott drifted over toward Phil, the amiable pothead in his mid-forties who lived across the street, and they muttered together. There was something Aubrey didn't like about their rapport, but she had no time to think about it at the moment.

Norman Levy stood in the middle of the street in a pair of torn khaki pants, a flannel shirt, and enormous, unlaced hiking boots, staring up at the sky, hands on his hips, his face lit up with the widest, most childlike grin Aubrey had ever seen.

"You OK, Norman?"

The old man looked at her, opening his mouth and trying to find words, but he couldn't. He gestured back up at the sky, as if to say, "Have you *seen* it?" Then he turned away from her again, his eyes back on the heavens.

"Norman? Are you all right?"

He answered softly, without looking at her. "Oh, I don't know about that," he said. "But goddamn it's glorious, isn't it?"

Up and down the block, and as far as Aubrey could see in any other direction, not a single window, door, or streetlamp was lighted.

Aurora, Illinois, had gone dark.

Seven hundred and twenty-nine miles away, Perry St. John stood in the parking lot of NOAA headquarters, shoulder to shoulder with his co-workers from the solar monitoring station and stared up at the same sky. It was just after 5 a.m. on the East Coast, and Perry was approaching his twenty-fourth hour on the job, in what was the longest, most terrifying and exhilarating day of his professional career.

He stood there silently, Murtagh and Fitz on either side of him, and the other dozen researchers, some of whom had been there in the morning when it started, and others who had poured in as the day had worn on. None of them spoke, because none of them could think of a single word that could capture the beauty in the sky above them.

Nor could they find words to express the completeness of their failure over the course of the day. They had rung society's alarm bells as they had never been rung before; they had called every government official all the way up and down the line, from the lowliest O&M manager at a tiny power plant in Christine, Texas, all the way up to the Chief of Staff to the President of the United States, and their increasingly desperate entreaties had been largely greeted with skepticism, hostility, and a strong desire to get off the phone. As the day wore on and the anticipated impact was delayed and delayed, they were met with outright anger, and their successes, such as they were, became fewer and further between. A tiny relay station in Wichita agreed to go offline. They cheered wildly. Ethos Energy said they'd get back to them, actually did, and said they were "seriously looking into" taking all transformers in Central California off the grid. They cheered, less wildly. And a plant manager in Tallahassee saw immediately the peril of the situation and swore he'd call back in five minutes but had been sent home for the day by the time they reached the facility again, three hours later.

By the time the CME breached the earth's magnetosphere, the crew inside the NOAA station had given up and braced themselves for the worst. Their power was among the first to go out, within sixty seconds of contact, connected as they were to the massive Eastern Seaboard supply grid. Reports of fires and explosions at towers all up and down the coast popped up on their cell phones, which beeped with strange alerts and evacuation orders they'd never heard before, until they

stopped working completely, the cell networks collapsing minutes after the electrical towers failed. At one point, an "Incoming Nuclear
Missile" alert popped up on the phones of all Verizon customers but
was just as quickly replaced by a "Recall Alert" message, just before
that network went dead.

With their computer screens blank, their cell phones dead, and the
land lines fried, there was nothing left for the staff to do but go outside
and watch the show. The black-sky event had begun.

In that moment, Perry felt only wonderment. Suddenly, it was magnetic midnight everywhere on earth. His eyes scanned the heavens;
his brain digested the details. At the higher altitudes, the charged
particles moved rapidly in the thin atmosphere and excited the oxygen atoms, giving the sky a deep crimson aura; moving down, he
saw that more frequent collisions were suppressing the red and allowing nitrogen to dominate, hence the powerful green; still lower
down, the nitrogen was ionizing rapidly, radiating at a large number of wavelengths, splashing red, blue, and purple across the skies.
Perry closed his eyes—which took a force of will—and listened. High
above, he could hear the auroral noise, a hissing and cracking sound,
two hundred feet above him as the charged particles of the inversion
layer dissipated in the night sky.

Everything about the contact was so utterly, so precisely as it
should have been.

Perry took a deep breath and forced himself to look away.

He looked down at his watch, an analog model that had been his
grandfather's. It was still ticking, and said it was 5:26 a.m. He thought
for a moment. There was nothing more he could do here, he realized.
There was nothing anyone could do. Prediction, preparation, and
warning—those times were all past. Now there was only survival and
recovery. The Northeast Corridor, that stretch of the East Coast running from Boston, through New York City, and down to Washington,
DC, was home to fifty million people. Perry knew if he wasn't out of
that urbanized megalopolis within the next three hours, there was a
very good chance he would die there.

Without a word of goodbye, he walked quickly across the parking lot, digging in his pocket for his car keys.

Thom Banning stood in the living room of his house and looked out at the mind-bending light show that lit up the desert floor for hundreds of miles in every direction. In Utah, it was just after 3 a.m., and he was the only one awake. Ann-Sophie and the kids, asleep behind motorized blackout shades, had been undisturbed by the coronal event, their white-noise machines pleasantly whirring, generating the soothing sound of an air conditioner, a spring rainfall, and ocean waves, sound-mixed to Thom's personal specifications. The other residents of Sanctuary, all of whom had arrived over the course of the evening, were presumably asleep in their subterranean beds, unaffected, the LED "windows" in their apartments still projecting whatever soothing view they had personalized for their sleeping areas.

Thom himself had been awakened by a dull thrumming sound six floors beneath him. He was a light sleeper anyway, but he had spent enough trial-run nights in the silo to recognize the sound of the liquid-cooled Generac Protector diesel generators kicking to life. That could mean only one thing—the expected thing, that the underground power lines that fed the silo from the main generating complex in Jericho had gone dead and Sanctuary's auxiliary power supply had engaged, according to plan.

Nothing was changed, nothing was interrupted. Not so much as one digital clock would need to be reset. The facility had shifted seamlessly to backup power.

Looking out the windows, Thom noticed a tiny smudge on his glasses. He took them off, cleaned them on his T-shirt, and realized the smudge was a scratch. He knew his need for eyeglasses was a weakness and a dependency. He'd explored Lasik surgery but had been told his eyeball was of a shape that was inconsistent with surgical success. Irritating, but he'd adapted accordingly. He had twelve pairs of spare prescription glasses, neatly lined up in the second drawer of his bedside table here at Sanctuary, an idea he'd had while watching an old *Twilight Zone* episode. He'd swap the scratched ones out for a fresh pair in the morning.

He took a deep, contented breath. All was in order.

Except for one thing. One detail that still wasn't crossed off his list, a wrinkle that refused to be ironed down. His sister.

He picked up his satellite phone from the table and dialed her number. It didn't even ring on the other end. She hadn't bothered to turn it on.

Fighting back his initial flash of anger at her stubborn foolishness, he tapped the phone on his lips, thinking. Aubrey was not ready. Aubrey had *refused* to be ready, despite everything he'd done and said. Aubrey, in some way, was doing this to spite him.

But Aubrey must be protected. Aubrey must be repaid. That had always been the case, and it was no different now. The situation just called for stronger measures. A freezer, a phone, an armed guard, a lifetime supply of power—none of that was going to make any difference, and none of it was going to even be possible to arrange within the next few days or weeks. There was only one thing that would matter for any of them in the new world, and of *that* thing, Thom had control. A lot of control.

Thom raised the phone again and picked another number. Brady answered on the first ring.

"You OK, Mr. Banning?"

"All fine here. Is your power down?"

"Yup. 'Bout ten minutes ago. Do you need something, sir?"

Thom smiled tightly. Brady. Thank God for Brady. Decent, reliable, *unmarried* Brady. "Yes. I need you here. As soon as possible. I want you to pick up a certain amount of cash from me here and drive it across the country, to my sister."

Brady paused. "Now?"

"Yes. Leave tonight, if you can. I'm worried about her."

"How much cash are we talking about, sir?"

"Two hundred and fifty thousand ought to do it."

Brady said nothing.

"Are you still there?" Thom asked.

"I'm here."

"What's the matter?"

"A quarter million is a lot of cash to be driving around with right now."

"I know, and I'll be grateful. When I get word that she's received it, twice that amount will be transferred into your bank account."

"How are you going to do that, sir," Brady asked, not unreasonably, "with the power out?"

"There are backup systems. It'll be fine. Are we going to keep books, now? You know I'm good for it."

As a joke it was unfunny, and it fell flat, Brady thought. A self-described problem-solver, he did not appreciate when problems were merely perceived, or created, or urgent situations were catastrophized into existence. Doubtless, a quarter of a million dollars did not need to be ferried across the country *right this minute*, in the early stages of what was probably a worldwide blackout. Contrary to his boss's opinion, he did have a life of his own. He weighed that life and those concerns against the value he placed on his job and the pride he took in it, and he stifled his urge to tell his boss to shut up and go to bed.

When Brady spoke again, his tone was soft but firm. "I can't make it by tomorrow. But I'll be there as soon as I can." He hung up.

Thom tossed his phone on the couch and looked out the windows again, pleased. OK, so Brady was a little grumpy about it, but he'd do it. Brady always got it done, no matter how unpleasant the task. Brady was his Man, and his Man would handle this thing, and for once Aubrey wouldn't be in a position to refuse help.

He looked out at the majestic western skies, lit up like daytime.

He looked down at the stained-glass Tiffany lamp on the end table nearest him. The room was brightly lit by nature's glorious light show outside, but Thom reached down and turned the switch on the lamp anyway.

The frosted bulb glowed, lighting the irregular, hand-blown glass panels.

Thom smiled.

He still had power.

Rusty Wheeler sat in the folding lawn chair on his front walk and looked around his darkened neighborhood. People were out, hooting and hollering and generally making assholes of themselves.

Rusty took a long pull from the can of Pabst Blue Ribbon in his hand, probably the last good cold one he'd have for quite a while, and he thought about things. He looked up, at the row of darkened streetlights all up and down the road, through the entire neighborhood, across the whole city, the state, the entire country, and maybe the world. Or so they said.

OK, so he'd been wrong about the solar deal. But there was one thing Rusty knew for sure. Opportunities were about to present themselves.

When nothing works, anything goes.

PART II
DECAY

11.

The drive from San Francisco to Provo was eleven hours with no traffic, but Brady didn't leave right away after Thom summoned him. There were a few things he needed to tend to at home before going. He had no wife or kids of his own, and his only significant relationship was with his longtime girlfriend, Paula. The fires of romance were turned down to a barely perceptible level between them, though; they hadn't been sexual in years and only saw each other once every few weeks. Brady wasn't even sure what kind of relationship it was anymore, other than one of habit. He stopped by her place outside of Mill Valley to check on her in the immediate aftermath of the power going out, and she professed to be fine. Paula was even more of a loner than Brady was, and he believed her when she told him that she didn't anticipate any real discernible change in her lifestyle without electricity, except perhaps that she'd get out less. Some of Thom's prepper obsession had rubbed off on Brady, and then onto Paula. She had a basement full of canned goods, a generator with plenty of gas that she kept in a shed out back, and there were, of course, her cats to take care of.

Paula had no intention of going anywhere, and Brady wouldn't have wanted to take her if she did, so as he left her place that afternoon he wondered if it was the last time he'd ever see her. He supposed it might be and tried to feel something, but it just wasn't there.

Brady's mother, however, was another matter. Madeline was in the middle stages of dementia, and Brady and his brother had put her in assisted living two years earlier. It was a decent place, largely paid for by Dennis, who ran the treasury department of a large mortgage lender, but Brady had chipped in financially, and he did most of the calling and visiting. There was no question of leaving Madeline in the care home; in an extended crisis it would be one of the first places to suffer loss of life. Brady decided, on his own, to go pick her up right away, rather than wait 'til events deteriorated to the point that they must.

Madeline had surprisingly few questions for someone who hadn't been out of the building, other than for a walk around the block, for two solid years. She stared pleasantly as Brady packed her things, then sat in the lobby, holding her handbag in her lap and watching the families rushing in and out while Brady signed the discharge papers. Madeline looked up and down the chaotic street with bright curiosity as they inched their way across it to his waiting car, hanging heavily on his arm. Something was in the air, but damned if she knew what.

"Will we see Terrence?" she asked, as Brady put her seat belt on.

"No, Ma. We don't care about him no more, remember?"

"Oh, that's right," she said, having no idea what he was talking about. "Not anymore. Don't care." She made a flippant gesture with her hand and smiled, as if batting away cares.

Terrence, the youngest of the three brothers, had been lost to drug addiction a decade ago, and after several years of frantic interventions, cell-phone tracking, and private investigators, his trail had gone cold, and the brothers gave up trying to find him. Perhaps Terrence got what he'd always seemed to want, which was to annul himself. Brady had mourned and moved on. Brady was good at moving on.

The drive from Madeline's facility to Dennis's house, on Marin Drive, was only about twenty minutes in no traffic, but it took almost two hours the day after the lights went out. Everybody was headed somewhere, some in a bigger hurry than others, and Brady drove cautiously. He was conscious of having his mother in the car but also mindful of the risk of an accident, with the whole world addled, anxious, and aggressive.

Despite Brady's inability to call ahead, Dennis and his wife Holly weren't surprised to see him, or to find that he had Madeline and her two small suitcases with him. They had a sprawling house at the foot of Mount Tamalpais, with a freshwater stream running through their backyard, and they'd often joked that they were uniquely situated to ride out the next COVID. Even though it had arrived in the form of solar chaos rather than microbial infestation, Dennis and Holly were fine with taking the old lady in. It had, in fact, been the original plan for Madeline's sunset years, until dementia made her more of a medical challenge than they thought they could handle at home. Now they would just have to make it work. As Holly settled her mother-in-law into the first-floor guest room that had already been remodeled for her, Dennis and Brady stood in the living room, staring down the hallway, conversing without looking at each other, as was their custom.

"You sticking around?" Dennis asked.

"Gotta get to Utah ASAP."

"Guy can't wipe his nose without you."

Brady just shrugged.

"What, he forgot his Tic Tacs?"

"Got an errand he wants me to run."

Dennis turned, trying to make eye contact with his brother. It wasn't easy. Brady was six foot four, a good five inches taller than his brother, and would have to deign to look down. "What kind of errand?"

Brady turned, met his brother's eyes, and scowled.

Dennis held up his hands in surrender. "You will do what you will do."

"I have a job."

Thom paid Brady $260,000 a year, which at first had sounded like a lot to Brady, who was former San Francisco PD, the son of an ex-cop himself, and wasn't used to a six-figure salary. But after taxes and the exorbitant rents in the area—Thom had insisted Brady live within a ten-minute drive of him—Brady found he was no further ahead financially than he had been when he was walking a beat in the Tenderloin. Sure, there were perks, like the car, the kickass health insurance, and an enticing retirement package, but he still had less than $30,000 in savings, at the age of forty-seven. It was a less-than-terrific feeling, especially when he looked around the garage at Thom's house and counted seventeen vehicles of various models and types, the vast majority of which were never driven.

"What do you really get out of that job?" Dennis asked.

"What do you get out of foreclosing on people?" Brady responded, and so the matter dropped.

Had Brady answered his brother's question honestly, "proximity to unspeakable wealth and power" might have been the most accurate reply, but that was a kind of clarity that was only sporadically available to him. Even if it had been on the tip of his tongue, his millionaire brother was the last person he'd have shared that insight with, because he knew the absurdity of it. What good was being *close* to unspeakable wealth and power, what possible gain was there in it, for anyone? It was rubbernecking, that's all, peering over the rich neighbor's fence. Brady's was a job that was the employment equivalent of slumping on your couch watching the Kardashians.

Sure, you could look. You could pick up stories that your friends wouldn't believe, if you hadn't signed an NDA and could actually tell them. Or you could, as Brady and innumerable others in his position often did, lie awake at night occasionally, dreaming that the wise and kind billionaire, *their* wise and kind billionaire, would die unexpectedly, leaving you lavishly remembered in their will. Brady knew of no specific examples of sudden billionaire death and excessive employee inheritance, but that didn't stop a person from hoping.

Mostly, though, Brady just did his job, as his father had taught him to. He performed the tasks that were required, he did them all the way, and he left no mess for anyone else to clean up afterwards. To Brady's mind, driving a quarter million dollars in cash across the country to deliver to Thom's sister was no different from cleaning out the garage when he was a kid. Make sure everything ends up at the curb, tightly bundled in black trash bags. Leave it broom-clean.

Same thing here. Deliver the money safely, wish the lady well, and return.

And let no one stop you from doing your job.

Once or twice over the years, Thom had made unseemly requests; he'd asked Brady to do jobs that were not the sort of thing that could be talked about in polite company. Or anywhere, for that matter, except perhaps in the confessional. There were payoffs, of course, and in the past couple years there had been mild intimidations that he was asked to perform. His size made it easy, and most of the time they had it coming. On those occasions Brady had made certain to tidy up his eternal soul afterwards.

After he'd said his goodbyes to his mother and brother, an emotionless experience Brady was used to by now, he went directly to Thom's house. He was waved through the gate by security—how long would *those* guys stick around if this thing lasted as long as he'd heard it would, Brady wondered—and went to the massive garage. He had no intention of making a cross-country drive in a gas guzzling Chevy Suburban, no matter how comfortably tricked out it was. Gasoline itself was going to be a major problem, as would finding an open recharging station for an electric car. He needed to have both capacities and knew the exact car he wanted from Thom's fleet.

The black BMW X5 hybrid had a twenty-four-kilowatt-hour battery that could return up to fifty-four miles on a single charge, as well as a three-liter turbocharged gasoline engine that added another three to four hundred miles to its range. There was a spare battery in the trunk, kept fully charged and rotated three times a year, and a lead-lined spare fuel tank that had been custom-built into the wheel wells, with its line running beneath a false floor of the trunk. The modifications didn't leave much in the way of trunk space, but as an emergency vehicle built for crisis evacuations, it was ideal. The combined reach of the car, without any refueling or recharging, was nearly seven hundred miles, if you knew how to change a battery. Which Brady most certainly did. He would need to gas up exactly once, which he would do halfway through the 781-mile drive to Utah, at the refueling station they'd established near Battle Mountain, Nevada. Stopping was a risk he was prepared to take. Go get the cash first, then figure out how to get to Illinois with it and not get robbed or killed in the process.

Brady reached into the Suburban and removed the Saint Christopher medal he kept hanging from the rearview mirror. He'd wound it tightly so as to attract no attention from the boss, and it took him a minute to get it free now. But he wasn't leaving without it. Christopher was the patron saint of travelers in general and motorists in particular, and he had some serious motoring to do.

Medallion in hand, he turned to the BMW, opened the driver's door, tossed his lightweight gym bag in the back seat, and slid behind the wheel. The leather crunched in a pleasing manner. Brady had tried hard to get Thom's attention regarding this car, which was, after all, the ultimate go-car, and he hoped some of it had gotten through.

Because this fucking BMW was where it was *at*.

Brady lifted the lid on the storage compartment between the two front seats, revealing a lock with a three-digit tumbler. He spun the digits to 0-4-4—Mr. Banning's personal choice for the code—and opened the MicroVault gun safe he'd had installed. He pulled the Glock G23 from its sleeve inside the vault. The Glock was a tight little forty-caliber, solid and reliable, with a modified mag capacity of sixteen shots. More than enough for anything that might come up along the way.

But Brady believed in the inviolable principle of redundancy and hadn't stopped there. He squeezed the left armrest in the driver's door with one hand, popping the lever just under its lip with the other and flipping it open. He'd sent the armrest back for two redesigns, unsatisfied with the trickiness of its release the first couple of times. Like a mystery box he'd once bought in a souk in Marrakesh (awful, sweaty trip with bad food, it had been Paula's idea early in their relationship), the armrest needed to be easy to open *only once you knew how.*

He knew how. He pulled out the J-Frame M&P Scandium he kept there, the one he'd special-ordered with the external hammer. Sometimes you wanted a weapon that operated on simple mechanical basics: pull this back, squeeze the trigger, bang. It was the type of gun with which nothing could possibly go wrong.

The M&P was there, it was loaded, and it had been cleaned and oiled recently.

Brady put both guns back in their sleeves and shut the lids. He gave the driver's door a tug and it closed with a soft whoosh. He hung Saint Christopher around the rearview, letting it dangle at whatever height he pleased, adjusted the seat and mirrors, and started the engine.

He'd be at Sanctuary in eleven hours.

Battle Mountain, Nevada, was just off the I-80, more or less midway between Silicon Valley and Thom's silo complex in Utah. The unincorporated town was, at its roaring peak, home to about three thousand citizens, most of them spread out on the flat, arid badlands surrounding it. Its high-desert location meant hot days, cold nights, and a scarcity of population that suited some people well. There were three reasons to settle in or around Battle Mountain: you were born there, you planned to die there, or you couldn't stand the sight of people but still liked the idea of running water.

The old Arco station two miles outside of town had once done a decent business, until the local highway, 51, was killed off by the construction of the interstate and the slow death of the area's mining facilities. With no more copper or ore to mine and truck away, there was little demand for gas this far off the beaten path. When Thom was looking for a wholly-owned refueling station, the Arco's location, rock-bottom land value, and pristine underground tanks made it a perfect choice.

The late-afternoon light was fading into a cold blue as Brady pulled the BMW to a stop, got out, and stretched his back. He'd made the drive out of San Francisco easily enough, after steering his way through surface streets to escape the clutch of refugees on the 580. He'd gone due north from Mill Valley instead of east, getting on and off the 37 as traffic dictated, then north on the 29 and east on the 12, until finally hooking up with the I-80 at Cordelia. It was refreshing to be forced to use his memory to find the route instead of his phone; it had been years since those old synapses had been asked to connect, and to him they felt grateful for the use. It was like putting his fingers on a manual typewriter again, after all these years—you forgot how physically satisfying the act of typing used to be and how pleasantly drained you could be afterwards.

He'd stopped to pee only once, so now he hurried across the gravel parking area to get inside the old Arco building, noting with some satisfaction that his breath was curling up in little clouds in front of him. He'd always loved getting out of the city and didn't understand why he didn't do so more often, especially when there was so much natural beauty within a short drive of San Francisco. It was funny, he thought, turning the key in the lock of the old service station's front door, how it always seemed to take a crisis to remind a person of the extremely simple things that were important to them. It was then, mid-thought, that he first noticed the shadow moving on the tile floor in front of him, growing bigger at his feet, and right around the moment that he realized the shadow was not his, the crowbar whooshed through the air beside him, coming down toward the crown of his head.

The last few microseconds were the ones that saved Brady's skull and life. The red alerts in his brain went off, all at once, silenced his pointless reverie about getting out into nature more often, and reminded him that he had just committed the cardinal sin of walking into a darkened room without so much as pausing in the entrance to make sure it was safe.

His police training kicked in, angry at his neglect, and he managed to twitch his torso just a few degrees clockwise, tilting his head and rotating his upper body away from the blow. The crowbar came down not on his skull or clavicle but on the thick, ropy muscles of his rotator cuff. The impact was still enough to make his vision flash hot white, and he collapsed in pain and surprise, his knees hitting the hard floor first. He managed to put out a hand to stop himself from going all the way down, and the shock of pain now spread into his wrist as well. Two seconds into the assault and he'd suffered injuries in four critical areas: shoulder, both kneecaps, and left wrist.

But none was debilitating. He turned his head sharply and saw a pair of decrepit black high-tops, a pair that might have been top-of-the-line once but were now ratty and torn, victims of years of abuse and stink, only the rotted traces of laces left in them, and the bare, dirty skin of filthy shins peeking over their tops.

Brady rolled once, to his left this time, and the crowbar came down in the middle of the tile floor, sending chips of white ceramic flying. Ordinarily his right hand would have ducked into the shoulder holster he wore around his left side, just inside his canvas jacket, but he didn't bother this time, because he knew there was nothing in it. Still only a few seconds into the attack, he decided to give himself a break and leave aside the utter idiocy he had shown by strolling, unarmed, into an unguarded, abandoned fuel station during a worldwide emergency without carrying a weapon or even pausing for so much as a "Hello, anybody home?" first. He was due for a fearless and searching self-evaluation, once he got out of this predicament, should he be lucky enough to do so.

Brady knew that taking a look back at his attacker was likely to prove fatal—he'd be low, looking up, in a helpless posture, as the crowbar came down for a third time—so he scrabbled across the hard tile floor without so much as a glance, scuttling like a crab toward the still-open front door. He passed over the threshold on throbbing wrist and aching knees, dragged himself up onto his feet, and ran to the car, fleeing like a seventeen-year-old camper in a horror movie.

He got to the car, yanked open the driver's door, and didn't dare to look back at his pursuer until he had both hands on the armrest, squeezing the outer ledge of the plastic lid and simultaneously tugging upward on the front lip. The compartment clicked open and Brady's right hand dove inside, closing around the cold, pebbled handle of the M&P Scandium, the one with the hammer.

Looking up as he raised the gun into the space between the open door and car frame, he finally laid eyes on his assailant. The meth head couldn't have been more than twenty years old, but they must have been twenty hard years, because he was as leathery as a saddlebag, dirt-encrusted, and unshaven. His appearance was striking enough, but the stench of him was worse; it was swept up on a breeze blowing off the mountains behind him and washed over Brady in a wave.

"Motherfucker."

Brady was never much for cursing, but when he did that was his go-to word, and he went there now, in a commanding voice that left no room for discussion. The meth head paused, feeling the sudden shift in Brady's attitude and, even in his addled state, not failing to notice the guy he'd once had dead to rights now had a gun trained on him.

Brady was about to shout his next instruction—put the crowbar down and get on the ground, or words to that effect—when the meth head's two friends came stumbling out of the gas station as well. They were a couple, a few years younger than the first guy, teenagers still, and they were just as angry and unreasonable as he'd been. With the door to the place fully open now, Brady could see inside, and he made out just enough of the bedrolls, empty tuna cans, and piles of garbage to figure out what had happened here. The refueling station had been neglected for a few months—it wasn't Brady's job to check on the place, but he sure as hell wished it had been—and had been discovered, broken into, and homesteaded by this trio of addicts.

Again, Brady's momentary distraction nearly killed him. While his eyes were diverted to the two new arrivals and the open door to the building, the first guy had moved toward him again, crowbar raised. He was within six feet of the car before Brady detected the movement, shifted his aim, and squeezed off a shot meant to go over the fucker's head.

But the trigger of the M&P was set light, much lighter than he'd remembered since the last time he'd taken target practice with it. Instead of whistling over the addict's head and hitting the roof of the gas station with a satisfying warning thud, it sliced through the cartilage of the guy's left ear.

The meth head howled in pain, dropping the crowbar and cupping a hand to his ear, which released a healthy spray of blood. The couple in the doorway screamed, the meth head whimpered, and Brady resorted to his go-to curse yet again, only this time low, under his breath, meant only for himself.

"Mother*fucker*."

The next twenty minutes were among the most awkward he could remember. The three homeless kids, because that's what they were—drug habits and horrible decision-making aside, they were practically still children—dissolved quickly into apology, remorse, and fear. Brady helped bandage up the older guy's ear as best he could, cautioned them about the situation that was rapidly unfolding around the world, invited them to remain at the refueling station as long as they needed, and stressed the importance of never, *ever* raising a crowbar to him again. He vowed to check on them on his way back home, and he meant it.

"What the fuck is going on out there?" one of them asked. "Like, rioting and looting and shit?"

"Not yet, but I'd imagine there will be. Anybody who says they know anything for sure is lying. Get used to not knowing. For a long while."

Half an hour later, he was back in the BMW, now fully gassed up, and was mentally tearing himself a new one. He had lurched, weaponless, into an unfamiliar and potentially hostile environment, he had shot and wounded someone he'd only intended to frighten, and he'd suffered several needless injuries.

They were less than twenty-four hours into the start of the crisis. He'd better sharpen up his fucking game right now or he wouldn't live to see how it ended.

12.

AURORA

On Cayuga Lane, things were quiet at first. The night of the event, as they stood under the strange and wonderful sky, Aubrey and her neighbors had greeted each other in a way they hadn't in several years. They learned or were reminded of first names, shared shaky smiles at the compelling oddness of it all, and, nearly to a person, clung to the belief that it would be over in two, three, maybe five days at the most.

The second day, things got more real. Aubrey heard sirens in the distance almost constantly. She tried to tell herself they were utility trucks racing to the scene of the damage, super-competent men and women who'd have things fixed up in no time, but in her heart, she knew what the wailing horns really meant. Panic. Chaos.

On night two, the northern lights were visible again, the streaks and billowing shapes every bit as vibrant and oddly colored as at first oc-currence. Whatever weird electrical shroud had taken up residence in the earth's atmosphere had dissipated not even a little bit on night two, nor would it on the third night. That first night, every man, woman, and child on the block had come out to look at them, but by night three it was down to just Norman, the astronomer, and Phil, the pothead. Phil was out every night, lying on his front lawn, arms folded into a pillow beneath his head and staring up at the sky, occasionally exhaling a puff of smoke.

Thom had been right about another thing—the contents of Aubrey's freezer did not spoil as quickly as she'd feared. She'd gone to cook the meat the next day, but her stove was electric, so that was out of the question. She'd tossed all the meat out before it could rot and ruin everything else. It had not yet occurred to her that garbage pickup might soon be a thing of the past, so at the moment it was stinking up the big plastic trash can in her driveway. The rest of the stuff in the freezer was intact, but it wouldn't last more than seven or eight days comfortably, and three weeks uncomfortably. If they ate those goddamn black beans. After that, she had no plans.

The morning of day three, Aubrey had noticed Phil boarding up what looked to be a broken window on the half-sunken basement level of his house. She hadn't gone over to ask, but she'd wandered into the street, close enough to hear him talking with Derek and Janelle, who lived next door. Apparently, there had been a break-in on the second night, and why they'd picked Phil's unassuming house was as big a mystery to him as it was to them. Nothing much was missing, he said, they'd mostly just ransacked the basement, but he'd startled them in the act and had a black eye to show for it. He was actually grateful for the lack of power, as he'd been able to scurry away in the darkness of his house and hide until the burglars were gone.

That was as close as violence had gotten to Cayuga Lane. So far, anyway.

Now, on the morning of day four, Aubrey sat on her front steps, smoking one of the last of her secret cigarettes before Scott got out of bed. She'd dug out the Iridium Extreme satellite phone Thom had sent her two Christmases ago and checked its battery—still at forty percent. She wished she'd returned even one of Thom's calls, which had come at a rate of about five per day so far, as surely he'd have better intel than the scuttlebutt on her block. But she hadn't felt like talking to him. Everything he'd ever told her had turned out to be right, but that wasn't going to be enough for him, he'd want her to know and admit it. She shoved the bulky phone back in her pocket. Maybe in a little while.

Honestly, though, what did it matter if she knew what was going on in the rest of the world? What would it change?

She felt clearheaded this morning. Thinking and planning seemed to be getting easier. Abruptly losing coffee from her diet was certainly a part of that. She hadn't realized how much she'd been drinking, but when you cut it off abruptly, your addiction has a way of standing up and introducing itself. The massive headaches subsided after forty-eight hours, and turned into more of an emotional pang, a longing for something that had been underappreciated and was now impossible.

She'd slept better the last couple of nights too, in spite of the dire circumstances and her overwhelming anxiety. She woke when the sun was up, she got sleepy when it went down, and during the times in between there were no electronic distractions. She'd never been a big consumer of TV, but the internet and its discontents were a major part of her life.

No more. That whole world was suddenly gone and wasn't coming back for a long time. Aubrey was surprised by how quickly she'd begun to mentally disconnect from the infinite online distractions she'd used to seek. She had kicked the internet to the curb with a speed and conviction that surprised her, awakening as if from hypnosis and realizing what a prisoner of algorithm her thoughts had been. No coffee, no internet? Thank Christ.

Scott's adjustment was more gradual. He'd always slept a lot, and he was still sleeping 'til noon, but now he was also in bed most nights by 10 p.m., which meant he was officially asleep more than he was awake. Aubrey knew incipient depression when she saw it, and his general listlessness and monosyllabic conversations were danger signs. Then again, he was looking down the barrel of a year or more of living in Little House on the Fucking Prairie with his ex-stepmother. So, you know, he had a right.

Aubrey heard the roar of a car engine. A beat-up black Dodge Ram had just come around the corner, noisy and rude in the heavy quiet of the morning. She frowned. It was Rusty's truck, and he and it were the last things she wanted to see. He drove past her house, fast, and cut the wheel. He made a showy U-turn, curving around in a big arc 'til the back end of the truck was directly opposite her driveway. There he stopped with a jerk, threw it in reverse, and backed up, bouncing over the crack in her sidewalk and parking in her driveway.

Aubrey sighed and stood up from her front steps. Now what?

"Relax, everybody, the cavalry has arrived," Rusty said, without charm, as he got out of the truck. He dropped the rear gate and leaned in, getting a gloved hand on one of the metal bars that stuck out on either side of the large yellow machine in the bed of the truck.

Aubrey walked over and looked at it. "What is that and why is it here?"

"You're welcome very much." Rusty slid it back toward him, bent his knees, and hoisted it out of the truck. He was strong, but this thing had to go eighty pounds. He duck-walked it, with some effort, over to the side of the house before dropping it down on the cement apron under the kitchen window.

"Seriously, Rusty, what is it?"

"What does it look like? A generator."

He went back to the truck, jumped up into the bed, and walked to the front of it, flipping open the equipment cabinet that ran beneath the rear window. He pulled a two-gallon can of gas out, hopped off the back of the truck, and returned to the generator.

"I had an extra one at the site I'm working on. Won't be doing anything there for a while, and I thought maybe you guys could use it."

Aubrey, unaccustomed to an even remotely kind gesture from him, didn't know what to say. "Thanks" seemed obvious but inadequate, but then again, so was Rusty, so she went with just that.

She watched while he unscrewed the generator's cap, upended the gas can, and filled the tank. "It's kind of a pig, and a gallon of gas won't last you more than an hour or so," he said. "The tank's two gallons, so I'm gonna fill it up, and I can come back every few days if you want. I'd say run it no more than one hour at a time, maybe every other day."

"Wow," she said. "OK. Um, I appreciate it."

"Don't fall all over yourself."

Once the tank was full and he'd put the can back in his truck, he took out a set of cables, opened the electrical junction box in the boxwoods at the base of her kitchen window, and set about connecting the generator. A stuck panel gave him some trouble and he pulled out the Buck hunting knife he kept in a sleeve on his belt, using the butt end to jam it back into place. He was good with his hands and knew what he was doing.

Aubrey watched, appreciating his ingenuity at first, but she was conflicted. Something about this seemed very not right. Maybe it was the fact that Rusty had never, in the eight years she'd known him, ever once done anything without expecting something in return.

Yeah, that was it.

"The shithead up yet?" Rusty asked, stepping back from the electrical setup and glancing toward Scott's window, which was just over the driveway.

"Not for a few hours," Aubrey said.

"Figures. You're gonna need him to get that thing in the basement. That's where it's gotta go, whenever you're not using it. Do *not* forget, and don't let him weasel out of it. You know what people would do to get their hands on a genny right now?"

"I can imagine."

He looked at her and smiled. She noticed he'd let his teeth go. "You want to fire it up?"

Aubrey shrugged. "Guess so."

He gestured to the house. "Go turn off anything that's on."

She hated the way he tried to order her around. He always had, mostly without success, but failure had never stopped him from attempted bossiness. But she did what he said, because she wanted power, mostly to see if it was possible, but also because, well, *she wanted power*. For the past couple days, she'd been getting herself used to the idea that there wasn't going to be any, not now, not tomorrow, and not for a very long time, and all of a sudden somebody shows up and says here you go? She was exhilarated and disappointed at the same time.

The screen door banged behind her as she went inside, flicking switches here and there, unsure if she was turning them on or off, until she decided to unplug a few things instead. She got to the kitchen and opened the window next to the table. She could see the top of Rusty's head outside.

"All set."

He bent down in front of the generator, shouting up through the window as he worked. "There's a fuel valve on the front, it's black and round. Turn it to OPEN. Move the choke rod from right to left, then you just flick the switch." He did and, after a moment, the generator chugged to life, spitting a small black cloud before settling into a low-level hum and rattle. He continued, raising his voice over the engine. "Once it's on, move the choke rod back to the right."

In the kitchen, the lights over the sink flickered and turned on. Aubrey tried not to gasp, but she was delighted.

"There you go," Rusty said, stepping back and wiping his hands, grinning.

Aubrey went to the counter, picked up her dead iPhone, and shoved it into the cradle on the kitchen counter, next to the sink. She held her breath and then, after a moment, the phone's screen blinked and the Apple logo appeared, signaling that it was charging.

Her hands went to her mouth, involuntarily. Oh, shit, was she *tearing up*? She was, and, goddamn it, that made her mad, it was a fucking *phone* for Christ's sake, and hadn't she been happier without it?

"Again—you are welcome." Rusty's voice was lower because he was in the house now, standing in the doorway between the kitchen and living room. She hadn't heard him come in, and she definitely hadn't invited him. But he had given them power back.

"Maybe just run a half hour now," Rusty said. "Let it warm up. Then another half hour if you want to, before it gets dark. And definitely get the goddamn thing in the basement before night falls."

Again not asking permission, he turned and went to the base of the steps, shouting up the stairs. "Scott! Hey, shithead!"

"Don't do that."

"*Scott!* Get your ass out of bed. I gotta show you something."

"*Rusty.*" She raised her voice, calling from the kitchen doorway. "Do not shout up the stairs."

But Scott opened his door and came to the top of the stairs in his pajama bottoms, squinting down at Rusty, then turning to Aubrey. "The fuck is he doing here?" he asked.

Aubrey noticed their positions—Scott at the top of the stairs, Rusty at the bottom, and she around the corner, in the doorway to the kitchen. She felt an acute sense of déjà vu. This was exactly where they stood the day Scott had cast his lot in life with his thoroughly unprepared stepmother.

"He was just leaving," she said to Scott, trying to keep her voice even.

Scott blinked and looked around, noticing the lamp at the top of the stairs was turned on. "The power's back?" he asked, incredulous.

"It is so long as I'm here," Rusty said.

Scott looked down at Aubrey. "What is he talking about?"

Aubrey came forward and looked up at him. "He hooked up a generator. So we could charge a few things and have some power for a bit."

"I thought we had rules about him coming here. Like, call first."

"The phones don't work, numbnuts," Rusty said. "How am I supposed to call?"

"OK, so there *are* no rules anymore," Scott said, his tone flat and declarative. He turned, disgusted, and went back to his room, closing the door behind him.

Rusty turned back to Aubrey. "I'll leave it to run for about an hour. Should give you time to charge your stuff, cook something if you want. Then I'll pack it up and take it. I can bring it back day after tomorrow."

"I thought you said you were leaving it."

"I changed my mind. I don't trust shithead to get it in the basement every night, and you're not strong enough."

Aubrey shook her head. That was enough. "Could you wait outside while things charge, please?"

"Suit yourself." He headed for the door but stopped, thinking. "So, with the gas and my time and everything, two hundred seems fair."

Oh, for Christ's sake, how could she not have seen this coming? How could she possibly have thought this trip to supposedly check on his son and ex-wife could have been rooted in anything other than a scheme to squeeze more cash out of them? With a liar, it didn't matter how many times you made the vow never to fall for their act again; they kept coming up with new ways.

"Two hundred dollars?" she asked. "For a couple gallons of gas?"

"For a couple gallons of gas when there's about to not *be* any gas, yeah. And for the trip over, and the wear and tear on the generator, and my expertise in hooking it up. Fuck, Aubrey, are you actually *negotiating* with me, the guy who brought you power? When you didn't even have to *ask*? What is wrong with you? Seriously, you've changed."

Aubrey refused to engage. "Wait here," she said and went upstairs. Rusty waited, listening, and heard her go into her room, or what had been *his* room, he thought. If she hadn't closed the door, he might have even been able to tell which dresser drawer she opened to get the cash out. But the location was good enough. It was a start.

A few moments later she came back down the stairs and held out a hand with two hundreds in it. He took them from her without making eye contact.

"I'll be in the truck." He left the house and stalked across the front walk, the victim of a great offense. She watched as he ripped open the door of his truck, got inside, and slammed the door.

Exactly fifty-four minutes later, he shut off the generator without warning, packed it up, and roared away with it.

As soon as his truck turned the corner on the block, Aubrey went into the kitchen, yanked her useless cell phone out of the charger, powered it down, and threw it in a drawer, pissed at herself. The goddamn thing wouldn't even have worked with the towers down.

She went upstairs and found a new hiding place for their thinning stack of cash.

A few minutes later, Scott thundered down the stairs, cleaned up and dressed.

"Can I take the car?" he asked, without looking at her.

"Where are you going?"

"I have to check on someone."

It was only mid-morning, and she was already tired of fighting. "We only have half a tank. Is it less than a couple miles?"

"Yep," Scott said, with the patient air of one summoning every bit of noblesse oblige they had inside in order to deal with the idiot in front of them.

She handed him the car keys, graciously declining to mention that he only had a learner's permit, and he left without saying thanks. Aubrey was still in day-to-day mode, she told herself, and the idea of Scott feeling a sliver of freedom and possibly containing his geyser of resentment for a little bit seemed like a price worth paying in gasoline.

She went back out front and sat down on the steps again. She kicked herself for allowing Rusty's distraction. She needed to get serious. She needed to plan for a future, a *long* future that did not include electric power.

Counting everything she and Scott had bought, they had maybe seven days' worth of food. If they ate sparingly. And if they didn't? Well, if they didn't, they'd go hungry, and if they went hungry long enough, they'd die.

She had Rusty to thank for one thing. He'd pissed her off. Shown her the danger of slipping back into old ways of thinking in a world that had fundamentally changed.

Her eyes focused across the street, where Phil was out in front of his house as usual, sitting in a webbed lawn chair, trying to conceal the one-hitter he was taking occasional hits from while he read an old paperback in the morning sun. He seemed to be taking a break from some yard work, a newly furrowed dirt row to his left and a long-handled, flat-bladed tool of some kind leaning against his lawn chair.

Aubrey squinted her eyes, staring at Phil, thinking. She looked up and down the block, at all the yards, filled with rock gardens and perennials and the odd trampoline or two. An idea was trying to form in her head when her eyes fell on Norman's house, two down and across the street from hers.

His front porch lights were on. She blinked, trying to register that. Why were Norman's lights on?

OK, maybe he had a generator too. But it was 9 a.m.

Why were Norman's lights on?

13.

Earlier that morning, Perry St. John had been headed west on the I-80, about a hundred and fifty miles outside of Bethesda, when he too had thought of Norman Levy.

After his initial flight instinct in the parking lot at NOAA, Perry had tried to develop some counterintuitive strategizing. Fleeing the cities was what everyone was thinking, he realized, and the gossip around the courtyard of his apartment building in Bethesda was that all roads out of the major eastern cities were already packed, traffic crawling if it was moving at all. People were running out of gas and water on the roadsides, and Perry was determined not to be one of them.

He wondered if maybe just keeping cool and staying put would give him a leg up on the knee-jerk responders. If everyone got the hell out of there in a hurry, there was no way they'd have the chance to clean out all the stores and storage depots, which meant maybe he could create Fortress Perry right here in Bethesda. Maybe he'd turn into a sort of latter-day Robert Neville, the hero of Perry's favorite book of all time, *I Am Legend*, the famous last man on earth, fighting his lonely daily battle with a world full of vampires. It worked out OK for Neville, foraging and killing in the daytime, building a house full of booby traps. The book had made it sound kind of fun, actually. Well, until the ending.

But after a few days Perry had realized that, as with most things, his initial instinct had been correct. The city, no matter how empty, was still too full of people; it was undergoing a rapid and complete infrastructure collapse without electrical power, and no doubt it was only days away from an epidemic of crime and violence far worse than anything that could happen in the countryside.

The only place Perry could think to go was his parents' house outside Iowa City. It was nine hundred miles away, at least three tanks of gas, and there was no guarantee his folks would be home when he got there. He'd lost track of their comings and goings between the house and their condo in Florida, and there was no way for him to contact them. Still, it was the best plan he had, so day three of the black-sky event for Perry meant stealing gas cans from a locked hardware store with a smashed front window, siphoning fuel from the tanks of parked cars all up and down his block, and shoving two boxes of peanut butter protein bars that had mercifully just arrived from Amazon three days earlier into a large suitcase with the rest of his clothes.

Thus equipped, he set off, pleasantly surprised by the lack of traffic on I-80 West. Right around the time he started feeling like this plan was going to work and he'd actually started looking forward to the idea of spending a year or so back home in Iowa, he remembered Norman.

Professor Levy lived alone in Aurora, Illinois. Perry flushed, feeling a burst of shame that he had completely forgotten about his mentor in this situation. An old man on his own, without power and water?

Perry glanced down at his gas gauge, saw it was still on three-quarters, and fumbled for the map on the seat beside him. Finding any physical map at all had been more of a challenge than almost anything he'd rounded up before setting out on the road, and, looking at it now while he drove, he saw that Aurora was only twenty or thirty miles off his route to Iowa. He could easily stop in and check on Norman. But, his concern now pricked, he decided he couldn't wait that long.

He took the next off ramp, pulled over on the first hilltop he could find, and dug out the portable radio he'd shoved into one of his suitcases. Norman was the one who'd introduced him to the joys of shortwave in the first place, and he felt certain the old man would be all over the airwaves in a situation like this.

Norman had been chasing signals for sixty years, and of all his myriad hobbies and interests, it was one of the old man's favorites. He'd talk about it with anyone who seemed remotely interested, and even those who didn't. But a few friends and former students would show momentary interest, mostly for the nostalgia quotient, and at some dinners they'd allow themselves to be dragged into a session on the shortwaves.

"They're not goddamn shortwaves," Norman would chastise them. "I'm not some trucker with a CB talking about Smokey in a blanket or what have you. It's HAM. Short *and* long waves. I can talk to Canberra on this thing."

Perry unspooled the reel of long-line antenna, looping it around the luggage rack on top of the car, then gave the radio's hand crank a couple dozen turns for power and switched it on. He keyed the microphone and called out, using the frequency on which Norman could most often be found.

"CQ, CQ, this is, uh"—he looked down at the map to see where the hell he was—"Somerset County, PA, looking for you, Aurora, Illinois, on two hundred thirteen megahertz. Come in."

He waited but heard only static.

He tried again, and this time, halfway through his call, the radio squawked angrily, three times in a row, as with someone keying it in irritation. Norman's voice came through, loud and mostly clear.

"You've got to say 'over,' dummy."

Norman was there, up at dawn as usual, and sounded undiminished. Perry keyed the mic again. "Hey, Norman, it's Perry. How you holding up?"

"Best as can be expected. How's things out east? Over."

"Like the early part of a zombie movie, before the brains start to fly," Perry said. "I'm headed to the folks' place in Iowa. Want me to stop in on you?"

No answer. Only static. Finally:

"For the love of Christ, will you please say—"

"Over! Sorry, over. Want me to stop in? Over?"

"What would you do here? Over."

Perry thought for a good long while. "Not much, I guess. Over."

"Thanks for thinking of me, kiddo. I'm fine. Worry about your folks. You're a good man. Over."

Perry thought for a long moment, then keyed the mic again. Something about Norman had always brought out his tender side, and he could feel the emotion welling in him just hearing his old professor's tones.

"What are we gonna do, Norman?"

There was a long pause, Perry added "over," and Norman finally answered.

"The only thing humanity has ever done. Wait and hope."

Perry smiled. Norman had been saying that for as long as he'd known him. It still helped.

"The house is freezing," Norman said. "I gotta go hit the generator for an hour. Stay safe, kiddo. Over and out."

"Over and out."

14.

After she'd seen the porch lights on at Norman's house, Aubrey had sat quietly for a moment, listening. There was a low humming sound coming from Norman's driveway.

She got up and headed toward it, walking at first, then picking it up to a jog as her concern mounted. She knew the house; she'd been there several times over the years. The professor was a gregarious and capable host, inviting former students, old colleagues, and an occasional neighbor for long, boozy dinners that had left Aubrey feeling awkward. She honestly didn't know why he included her. She tried to decline the invitations, preferring to see Norman one on one in a more neighborly way, but he'd kept at her, insisting she belonged, as long as she didn't bring that shit-for-brains husband of hers. He'd actually said that, while she and Rusty were still married, which had simultaneously enraged and delighted her. Who had *that* kind of nerve?

Norman was always there for her. When she was debating starting her conference business, it was Norman who told her to do it. When she agonized over kicking Rusty out of the house, Norman was the one who told her she must.

"I can't believe I ever got involved with him," she'd said.

"Low self-esteem," Norman had replied, then shrugged. "You see these things. You gotta get over it, though."

The moment she reached his driveway, she could tell there was something wrong. It wasn't just the porch light that was on; the kitchen and living room were lit up too, even though sunlight was streaming through the windows. Aubrey called out.

"Norman?"

No answer. She walked up the driveway, and the faint humming sound grew louder. It was coming from around the side of the house. She called Norman's name again, got no answer, and reached the garage.

The door was wide open, and Aubrey laid eyes on the trouble right away. It was a small, red Honda generator, the kind you could wheel around from place to place, that had been set up just a few feet back from the open garage door. It was running, and when Aubrey put a hand on the side, she could tell it was hot enough to have been on for quite a while. Her eyes widened, she realized at that same moment that her lungs were constricting, and she looked up, to the air vent that was at the top of the nearby wall, almost directly over the top of the generator.

"Norman!" she shouted, and in three quick movements she snapped the generator off, shoved it out of the garage so it could vent in the driveway, and threw open the door that led into the house.

She came inside, coughing from the accumulated CO_2 that had shot through the place, and ran down the short back hallway that led to the kitchen.

"Norman!" she yelled, and tore around the corner from the kitchen and into the living room. The old man was sprawled on the couch in flannel pajama bottoms and a T-shirt. His head was back, his mouth open in a gasp, arms and legs splayed. Aubrey could tell in a second what had happened. Norman had gotten out of bed before sunup, felt a chill in the house, and turned on the generator for what he thought would be a quick burst of heat. Having parked it in the wide-open garage door, he probably figured the CO_2 would just blow outside, but then the wind must have shifted, trapping the gas in the garage, and therefore letting it seep into the house, following a swirling draft inside through the vent. And there the invisible poison set upon the professor, settling into his lungs, clouding his mind, and putting him to sleep.

The only question was how long ago he'd succumbed. Aubrey raced across the floor, grabbed him under the armpits, and dragged his body off the couch. He was still warm. She pulled him down the kitchen hallway, inadvertently banging his head off a door frame. He moaned. He was alive.

Aubrey dragged him down the garage steps, across the cement floor, and laid him out over the wood bark, fifty feet from the house. There, she moved the old man's arms and legs up and down, like she'd seen in an old movie where somebody had almost drowned, until Norman finally gasped, choked, and gulped fresh air.

A few hours later, after the house had been aired out and Norman had good-naturedly listened to a ten-minute lecture from Aubrey that could have gone by the title "Carbon Monoxide: The Silent Killer," he smiled at her.

"Aubrey. Of *course* it's Aubrey who saves me."

"Why of course?"

"Because Aubrey takes care of everybody. But who takes care of Aubrey?"

"Aubrey takes care of Aubrey."

"Well, she does a lousy job."

She waved off that tedious line of conversation and looked around the place. "You rearranged the furniture."

"Every six months. Keeps things fresh. You'd know that if you still came to dinner."

"I don't belong at those dinners, Norman."

"Horseshit. You're smarter than ninety percent of the people I ever taught. Why didn't you go to college?"

"No school would have taken me."

"Oh, right. Your so-called tragedy."

She looked at him, pissed off. "That is the most insensitive thing I've ever heard you say, and I've heard a *lot* of offensive shit from you."

"Honestly, who gives a goddamn about what happened a hundred years ago? You are wasted potential."

"I forgot. I don't actually like you that much."

"There is no time, Aubrey. For any of us. Look around. Could the hour possibly be any fucking later?"

"I should be getting back. I was in no way prepared for this."

He shrugged. "Some people prepare. Some people don't. Both get in the grave just the same."

"Yeah, but some get in the grave a lot sooner. I really gotta go."

"I want to show you something first."

He led her into his den, with its desk that held his home radio setup.

He turned to his nineteen-fifties-era Zenith Trans-Oceanic radio setup, a truly gorgeous museum piece that dominated most of the space, its silver microphone sitting alertly on a stand in front of it.

"Your radio's OK?" Aubrey asked.

"Newer setups would be fried, but this thing's a warhorse. I was even on it when the CME hit. Vacuum tubes are very resistant to EMP—arcing, surges, no damage at all."

"Scott'll be glad to hear that. He loves that radio."

"Tell him to come over, we'll talk to some people."

"I try, Norman." She pointed back to the radio. "Have you raised anybody on it?"

"First forty-eight hours, not a thing. Sizzle and pop, that was it. Once the surges eased off in the magnetosphere, though, I started to get some decent signals, mostly down in the lower ranges, three to ten hertz. Just this morning I picked up the long-gig waves and I was really getting somewhere, but then go figure, I started feeling sick, nauseated and dizzy, so I went out to the couch to lie down for a few."

"Which you will never do again."

"No, ma'am," he said.

"Problem is," Noman continued, gesturing to the radio, "all I'm hearing is anecdotal. Everybody's out there telling their horror stories, but good numbers are hard to come by. I've got a general global picture, but it'll be days before I can really sort it out."

"What countries are out so far?"

"It's easier to say which ones still have power." He picked up a yellow legal pad, crammed with notes, and pulled his reading glasses off the top of his head. "Parts of Colombia, Brazil, Uganda, Kenya, the Maldives, Indonesia."

"Anything that's near the equator."

"Highest marks."

"They never lost power?"

"Zero interruption. As the magnetic surge rippled south and north from the poles, it diminished. Lost its disruptive ability. It spared the entire equatorial band. But everything south and north of that, in both hemispheres? Infrastructure is almost completely gone. And the dominoes are still falling."

Aubrey contemplated that. "What do you think is next for—"

Norman shook his head in furious agitation, the way he'd used to do with a student who wasn't fully grasping his point. "Don't blow past this, Aubrey. Take a moment and think about it. The United States, Canada, Scandinavia, England, France, Germany, Russia, most of China, Japan, I don't know, name any other wealthy first-world country—we're back in the Stone Age. Or, hell, give us some credit, the Bronze Age. And that's where we're going to stay for a *year*. Or more. But the Congo? Somalia? São Tomé and Príncipe? Fucking *Kiribati*? They are up and running, like nothing ever happened." An incredulous smile spread across the professor's face. He reached out and grabbed hold of Aubrey's wrist, the fire of intellectual excitement burning in his eyes. "And do you know what else, Aubrey? Do you know what they're up to in all these downtrodden places that have had the shit kicked out of them for a thousand years or so, by all of the assholes that are now in the dark? Do you know what they're *doing* in these poverty-stricken countries that are suddenly the kings of the fucking world?"

Aubrey didn't.

"They're organizing relief efforts." Norman shook his head again, tossed his notepad on the desk, and sat back from the console. "Offering to fly in contractors to increase their food production capabilities, so they can start to feed the rest of us. They're giving free leases on land, tax-exempt status, and unlimited power draws for any nation or corporation that wants to base humanitarian work there. And the stuff produced won't even be for *them*, mind you. It's all for export. They don't want anything in return. They just want to help."

He drew the back of his hand across his eyes. "I think it's the most touching goddamn thing I've ever heard in my life."

Aubrey nodded, her mind racing ahead. "Money and power won't matter."

"Well, I wouldn't say that."

"Everything will be about food."

She stood up, recapturing the line of thought she'd started an hour earlier on her front steps, while she stared at the pothead across the street.

"Food."

Norman smiled. "Look at you go."

"Shut up, I'm thinking."

"About time."

15.

As of 8 a.m. on April 18, four days after onset of the event, the power had been out for eighty-six hours and the United States Army was not riding in on a white horse to save the day.

Thom didn't understand why. "It's a question of jurisdiction?"

"It's a question of priority," Divya Singh responded. Her image was on the big screen in the communication room of the silo complex, a two-hundred-square-foot underground Faraday cage with signal continuity that was exceeded only by certain military-grade bunkers.

Thom sat in his ergonomic desk chair, his hair wet and a bib around his neck while he soaked up valuable time that Dr. Singh did not have to offer. He'd been insisting on a briefing for two days, and Dr. Singh had consented only after Thom had Lisa call and offer a one-time $10 million grant to fund the research project of Dr. Singh's choosing. In exchange, she would continue to advise him "on an ad hoc basis during and in the immediate aftermath of the crisis." Dr. Singh had grudgingly agreed, and now here she was, bought and paid for. She stared resentfully into her laptop's screen from the living room of what looked like a rustic mountain cabin. A lamp burned in the background behind her. Wherever she was, she still had power.

She tried to clear up Thom's confusion. "Power supply isn't a priority for DoD, except as it affects defense readiness. In a time like this they have only one focus: maintaining national sovereignty."

"What, they're afraid we're going to be invaded? Isn't this happening all over the world?"

"Ninety percent of it, yes. But the Defense Department's first responsibility is maintaining critical infrastructure. *Their* critical infrastructure. Army installations have to tie into the grid too, so their primary mission will be to protect and restore their own assets."

"What about food?" he asked. "Water? Social order?"

Dr. Singh started to answer, but then squinted into the camera. "Is that—I'm sorry, there's a pair of hands that keeps coming in and out of—Are you getting a haircut, Thom?"

Irritated, Thom waved away the hands. Chloe, the yoga instructor, had been personally selected by Thom to be the beneficiary of a twelve-week course in hair styling, in order to fill a double role at the bunker. She'd never taken to hair and, if Thom's current cut was any measure, she hadn't practiced in the two years since she'd finished the course.

"Sorry. Little shaggy. I'm done." He pulled the bib off and glared up at Chloe, instantly regretting it. Chloe was young, just in her midtwenties, and she was sensitive to criticism, as well as racial injustice, income inequality, misgendering, and apparently, frowning. "Sorry, Chloe. Thank you very much. We can pick this up later." Noticing her expression, he added "It's looking great. Really fantastic. You have a natural gift."

Chloe let her straw-colored hair flip down in front of her face and hid behind it as she packed up her things without a word.

Chloe was a problem in the making. It had not gone unnoticed by Ann-Sophie that Chloe bore a resemblance to her, both in coloring and body type, with the notable and irritating exception of being at least a decade younger. Chloe, alert to vibes of all kinds, had picked up that the boss's wife disliked her, almost as much as the boss seemed to take an interest in her. She was navigating the hostile waters as best she could.

Thom turned back to the screen. "Sorry. You were saying?"

"I was saying," Dr. Singh continued, "that the army will hunker down, island their assets, and try to maintain combat readiness in case of attack."

"What about continuity of government? All those plans—the President, Congress, that enormous bunker under the Denver airport. Where are they all? Do they have power?"

"Probably, but you have to understand, the federal government doesn't *matter* anymore. It is incapable of helping, except in its capacity to direct resources to local governments so that *they* can handle it. FEMA stopped supply-chain-resilience oversight a decade ago. Do you know the distribution organization the government has planned to use, in the event of a widespread food crisis?"

"I do not."

"Walmart."

"You're joking."

"It makes sense. Who has better infrastructure for the mass dissemination of cheap goods? Who's got a wider spread throughout local communities? The federal government will simply pay Walmart to give away food and supplies. That's all it *can* do."

Thom thought. "You're saying there is now, or soon will be, *no* hierarchy of command in the United States?"

Dr. Singh nodded vehemently. "Things are already beginning to break down much the way they were detailed in the New Madrid mega-scenario FEMA developed a few years ago."

"I missed that one. What did it say?"

"Basically? Be nice to your mayor. You're going to need her. Communities will become localized and insular. Then again, that's not entirely a bad thing. With the internet down for the indefinite future, rumor and disinformation will transmit much more slowly. It's a lot harder to spread lies face to face than it is online. Local truth will become the only real truth, which I guess is how things ought to be anyway."

Thom declined to argue her simplistic, Luddite view of information technology. She took advantage of the pause and glanced at her watch. "I should probably get going. Does that give you enough of a picture for now?"

"Not yet." Since she'd accepted the $10 million, Thom felt free to dispense with conversational niceties. "What are the cities like?"

"Not post-apocalyptic, or not yet anyway. Exit flow from New York and New Jersey was better than expected. But we're still at the threshold. Most people don't have a problem maintaining a 72-hour personal sustainment mindset, but longer than that—well, after the first week we're headed into the great unknown."

"Have you heard anything about the Chicago area?"

"No. Why?"

He wasn't interested in a two-way flow of information. "Where did you say you are now?"

"My family's cabin in the Alleghenies. Western Pennsylvania. I knew power would last the longest here, but I imagine it'll go in the next few days."

"What is the status of recovery efforts?" he asked.

"Way too soon to tell. We're still in reaction mode, then we move to resiliency, and *then* we can start to think about recovery. But it will be a spectrum of recovery. First resources will always be directed to"—she ticked them off on her fingers as she spoke—"electrical water pumping, sewage treatment, and hospitals. In that order. Given a choice between pumping fresh drinking water to a city and running power to a hospital or care home, a local government will choose the water every single time."

"As they should," Thom added.

"Opinions vary," she shrugged. "Abundant water flow leads to massive waste. Intelligent, restricted flow, with agreed-upon hours . . ." She could see she was losing him and stopped herself. "We don't have to get into that."

Behind Thom, ex-Major Jimmy had come into the room and was gesturing that Thom was needed. He looked back into the camera. "That's it for now. I'd like to speak again in twenty-four hours."

"I'll do my best. But when it goes dark here, I switch to survival mode too, Thom."

"I guess ten million doesn't go as far as it used to."

Dr. Singh just looked into the camera with a level gaze. "I guess it doesn't."

Thom hit the LEAVE button on the conference, dissatisfied. He picked up one of the two phones that were on the table in front of him, this one a clunky satellite phone. He checked the screen, didn't see what he wanted, and tossed it back down on the table, where it landed with a clatter.

"Is my sister the worst person in the world or *what*?"

Jimmy just looked at him, unsure how to respond.

"Rhetorical question. What do you need?"

"Brady's set to go, sir."

"About time." Thom got up and left, muttering under his breath, and Jimmy only made out a few words. Something about never having to work so hard to save somebody in his life.

And then there was Brady. The indispensable Brady had arrived from San Francisco more than forty-eight hours earlier but had dragged his feet about leaving for Aurora ever since, citing the need for "thorough preparations."

"Finally decided you're ready?" Thom asked as soon as he came outside. Brady was leaning against the side of the black BMW, eyes closed, soaking up the sunlight. The day was crisp and bright, the sky cloudless, and the air so clear you could pick out the pine trees on Black Crook Peak in the distance. Brady opened his eyes and stood.

"I know you would have liked me to leave sooner."

"I'd have liked you to *be* there by now. I haven't spoken to Aubrey in three days. Her sat phone's off and you can bet she doesn't have any money stashed. I have no idea what's going on, and you're daw-dling."

"It's a long drive to Aurora, sir," Brady said. "Fifteen hundred miles, that's twenty, twenty-two hours if I go straight through. There's a lot to consider."

"What are you so worried about?" Thom asked. He looked back at Jimmy, still in his fatigues, semiautomatic slung across his chest, and made a "What is this guy so afraid of?" face. Ex-Major Jimmy shrugged. *Some people.*

"Personal safety," Brady replied. "The drive here was a little dicey." He hadn't shared the details of his encounter with the meth heads in Battle Mountain, in part because he believed it was wrong to burden one's employer with the details of a difficult job but also out of sheer embarrassment. He had been stupid and careless and nearly gotten his head caved in for it. The encounter had left him shaken, mostly by his low level of awareness, and the realization that the more complex the plan, the more stress points at which things can go wrong. Sheltering in your house is one thing, but trying to maintain a fuel-supply chain across eight hundred miles, all the way to your underground commu-nity in a decommissioned nuclear missile silo—you know, there could be some hitches in that plan.

He'd vowed to learn from the experience. He'd spent the forty-eight hours since he arrived at Sanctuary checking every cable and contact on the car, cleaning and oiling the guns, charging batteries and filling gas tanks, eating and sleeping as best he could, treating his bruised joints with Voltaren and ice, and gathering every bit of intel he could get about weather and societal conditions across the Great Plains. He was going to need to make two fuel stops on this trip, and neither one of them would have the pre-planning of the Bald Mountain gas station—and look how that had turned out. He was highly invested in the idea of nothing going wrong this time.

"Don't worry about your sister. I've got her."

Thom nodded, but he was distracted. Chloe had come out of the complex and was in a huddled conversation with Jimmy, who was half turned away from him, speaking to her in low tones. He put a hand on her shoulder, and she looked up at him, forcing a smile. What the fuck was this? Was he comforting her?

He decided he didn't care and turned back to Brady perfunctorily. "Have a good drive." He turned to go.

"Just need one more thing, Mr. Banning."

Thom turned back, annoyed.

"The money?" Brady asked.

Thom and Jimmy went down to the vault on their own, leaving Brady to wait up top. The strong room was in the lowermost level of the silo, beyond two sets of multiple-key locking doors. Like a safety-deposit box, the main vault needed two authorized keys to be opened, and an additional key for each of the four antechambers beyond that. Thom trusted Jimmy more than anyone else, but he still had given him access to only the first of the cash storage antechambers. The architect's design had been such that the presence of an additional room wasn't revealed until one was fully inside the previous room.

There was no corridor; it was a series of interconnected chambers. Thom's theory had been that, once someone entered the first room and made a ballpark estimate of the amount of cash inside—in the case of the outer room, that number was $1 million, in twenties and hundreds—if they knew the number of additional rooms, simple math would reveal the total amount of the horde. And when big numbers got out, big trouble often followed.

But by limiting knowledge of the additional rooms, Thom figured he could keep a lid on things. The amount of cash in each of the five chambers was a million greater than the one previous, and the grand total, $15 million in U.S. dollars, was known only to Thom. His biggest threat, he figured, was from the security guards who had transported the money in the first place, but since he had never moved more than $2 million at a time and no guard ever made the trip twice, there was no way that total could be arrived at by anyone but him.

It took a few minutes for Thom and Jimmy to load $250,000 in twenties into the small blue duffel bag. In total, the money weighed just over twenty-seven pounds. While they moved the packets methodically from the boxes into the bag, Thom tried his best to speak casually.

"Everything OK with Chloe?"

"Chloe? Sure, why?"

"Saw you talking to her outside is all. She seemed upset."

Jimmy waved a hand. "Oh, she's just being Chloe. You know Chloe."

Thom nodded. "Oh, sure." He kept loading the bag, daring a look up at Jimmy.

What he wanted to say was "Yeah, I know Chloe. How well do *you* know Chloe?" What he actually said was nothing. Feeling jealous of attention paid to any young, attractive woman in his orbit was a habit he had been trying to break. He decided to drop it.

But with uncomfortable subjects apparently now on the table, Jimmy cleared his throat.

"So it seems Dr. Bordwell is leaving us," he said as casually as he could muster.

Thom looked up. "I beg your pardon?"

Jimmy kept working, moving the packets of twenties from the silver box to the blue duffel bag. "A problem with his father. Apparently, he had a heart, uh, episode just before the power went out. Probably stress-related. Dr. Bordwell got worried when he couldn't contact him for a few days, so he, uh, went back to Provo."

"You mean he *left*?"

"Yes, sir. Oh nine hundred this morning."

"So he isn't *leaving*, Jimmy. Our dentist has already *left*."

"Right. That's what I meant. Dr. Bordwell has left."

"And what the fuck am I supposed to do if I get an abscess?" Thom asked. He caught himself and rephrased. "If one of the kids gets an abscess? Or Ann-Sophie? Or you, Jimmy. What are we supposed to do, *die*?"

"Well, sir, he did give his apologies, and he said he'd be more than happy to come back in the event of an emergency," Jimmy offered. The truth was, David Bordwell had hated the place on sight and wondered how the hell he'd ever made this hellish deal with the devil. He'd spent a couple nights in the hole in the earth that had been reserved for him, luxuriously appointed though it was, and decided no fortune was worth living like a mole for a year. He'd left without explanation. Jimmy had made up the sick father to cushion the blow for Thom, to give it an aura of respectability that might contain the boss's reaction. It wasn't working.

"Come *back*?" Thom said, incredulous. "Oh, sure, we'll just drop him a text or send an e-mail or call him up, except, oh, no, we won't because *there's no fucking power*."

Jimmy didn't answer. He went back to counting the cash, moving his hands back and forth, filling the duffel bag. After a moment, he cleared his throat. "Anyway, with him leaving, I started thinking. His apartment is empty now, nobody's using it, shame for it to go to waste—"

Thom winced, bracing himself.

"So I thought this might be a good moment for me to bring up my cousin Mike's situation."

Thom closed his eyes. What was the *matter* with everyone?

"No more new people," he snapped.

16.

AURORA

Pothead Phil was asleep in the webbed aluminum lawn chair on his front lawn. Hearing a sound, he looked up and saw that Aubrey was coming toward him. She seemed determined, so much so that Phil glanced behind him to see if she was headed toward somebody else. But, no, she was coming straight for him, a purposeful look in her eye. She raised a hand and waved.

"Hi there."

Phil stood, uncomfortable. Many things made Phil uncomfortable, but his attractive neighbor across the street was near the top of the list. "Hi."

"You don't have to get up," she said as she reached him.

"OK," he said, sitting back down for a nanosecond before realizing, no, that made him even more uncomfortable, and standing up again. "How's it, um, going?" he asked.

"You know. Shitty. How about you? Doing some work on your yard?" she asked, nodding toward his clothes. Phil was dressed in dirty chinos and a faded I LIKE PI T-shirt that hugged a little too tightly around his slightly thickened middle. He smiled at her beneath the brim of the old straw hat he wore, like the kind you'd find on a scarecrow's head.

Phil looked pretty ridiculous. But Phil also didn't care. Somehow, it was a look he pulled off.

"Some. Fell asleep."

Aubrey turned, looking at the long-handled lawn tool that was leaning against his chair. "What's that thing?"

Phil picked it up and flipped it around, showing the half-moon-shaped blade, which looked sharp along its outer edge. "Sod lifter."

"Why are you lifting your sod?"

"Planting." He gestured to his front yard and the small but decent patch of grass he was in the process of upending. "We're really lucky this happened now."

"We are?" she asked.

"Oh, God, yeah. Mid-April? Kinda couldn't be better, if you think about it. We gotta get started. I have a full garden in back, but I was going for mostly herbs and such. Those won't be much use now."

"What *kind* of herbs?"

Phil's cheeks colored. "Nah, I know what you mean, but I'm not into that."

"Uh-huh," she said.

Phil continued, some rising anxiety in his voice. "Anyway, I was turning some sod, you know, out here, 'cause I wanted to do some planting. But it's a fuckload of work. I got that six-foot section up and had to take a nap."

"Do you know anything about gardening?"

"I know kind of a lot," he said, enthusiastic. "But so far it's mostly been little stuff that I grow, you know, um, inside the house."

Aubrey stared at him for a long moment, the picture becoming clearer in her mind. She turned and looked at his house, a single-story number with a half-exposed basement. The top halves of the basement windows were above ground and looked to be blacked out. One of them was boarded up. She turned and looked at Phil again, assessing the state of his black eye.

"How's the eye?"

He touched it self-consciously. "Oh, you know, fine. I'm fine. I got off lucky, probably."

"Phil, you grow hydroponics in your basement, don't you?"

"Yeah. Little bit. Some. Veggies and such."

"Weed. A lot of it."

"What? No!"

"C'mon."

"I don't know what you even mean," Phil said, anger creeping into his voice. "I thought we were talking about *vegetables*."

"This is where Scott gets the pot he told me he sells. From you. You grow it in your basement, he sells it, you split the profits. And somebody you sell to knew where it was and came and stole it when the power went out. Is that right?"

"This is, this is uncool. I got robbed, I'm the *victim* here, and you're, you're—I don't have to stand here and—" Not finishing his sentence, he turned away from her, picked up his chair, and began to fold it. The webbing, half-torn, got stuck in the aluminum frame, leaving him wrestling with it. Aubrey watched him, waiting.

"It's OK. I know it's legal now. Just maybe not to sell it?"

Phil threw the chair down on the ground, frustrated, and turned around to her. "*He* asked *me*, OK? I was growing strictly for my personal use, and that's it. *Your* kid came over—"

"Step-kid."

"Whatever. He came over, I don't know how he knew—"

"Maybe it's the blacked-out windows and that you smoke pot in the yard every night?"

"And he just started pressuring me. Scott is very, you know, he's very *ambitious*."

That was not a word Aubrey had ever heard used to describe Scott. In a way, she was kind of proud of him. "Anyway, the fuckers stole most of it, and the rest is dying without the grow lights." He looked over at the boarded-up window morosely. "Worst part is they made me help load it in their truck."

She looked at him. She didn't exactly feel sympathy, but she knew loss when she saw it. The guy took pride in his plants.

"What do you do, Phil?"

"I'm a data analyst for CRB?" He said it like a question, as if clearing it with her.

"Well, there's not going to be any data to analyze for a long time," she said, "so you're a farmer now. If we turn all the soil out here, what kind of edible food could we get down in the next week or so?"

Phil squinted at her. "Is that necessary? You really think the power's gonna be out for a year?"

"I think we're fucked," Aubrey said. "Degrees of fuckage, I don't know. Do you really want to wait around to find out?"

Phil turned and looked at the strip of exposed soil, thinking about it. "Well, space is a premium, so you want anything that's got good bulk. Tomatoes, obviously, you can make just about anything with them, or eat 'em cold. I'd grow a bunch of tomatoes and can the shit out of those, if I could find enough salt and vinegar."

"Now you're talking," she said. "What else?"

Phil kept thinking, warming to the challenge. He looked around his front yard and gestured at the locations of imaginary crops. "Zucchini, that's good and chunky, doesn't rot, keeps you for a while. Carrots, obviously, if I could scare up enough chicken wire to keep the critters out. Spinach, eggplant, pumpkins, squash. Don't have room for any more than that."

"What if you did? What if we opened up all the yards?"

"Well, then, *yeah*. Sky's the limit. First off, any kind of bean we can possibly get in the ground, we should do it. It's protein."

"Corn?" Aubrey offered.

Phil laughed out loud, then realized she wasn't joking. "No. Not corn. Takes up too much space and has, like, zero nutritional value. Don't get me started on the corn lobby."

Aubrey made a mental note to never, ever get him started on the corn lobby.

"We're not looking for cash crops here," he said. He looked around the neighborhood, expanding his thinking. "If I had that half-shaded plot down there, by Janelle and Derek? I might just put some orange watermelon in. Wouldn't that be a treat? You ever had orange watermelon?"

She shook her head.

"Oh, you don't know. Come August, I can eat a whole one of those in a day. Man, it's sweet."

She looked at him, coming to life in front of her. Four days ago, they both would have sounded like nutters, some kind of crazy survivalists, tearing up their front yards to plant seeds for the apocalypse, but today, standing here on the strangely quiet block, under a sky empty of airplanes, it sounded to her like the most rational conversation she'd ever had in her life.

She looked down at the sod lifter he held between his dirty hands. "Is that hard to use?" she asked.

"Not at all. Here." He held it out to her, and she wrapped her hands around it. "Hold it straight up and down, like that, at the end of the row I just started." She did, putting the rounded end of the blade upright on the grass. "Now turn your hands, like this."

He came around behind her and reached up, not physically adjusting her grip but gesturing at her with his hands in the air, twisting them just so. Aubrey had an innate creepiness detector that kicked into gear when a man was about to put his body too close to hers, but Phil kept a good two feet between them. That was nice.

"Now hold it tight and just hop up a little bit, enough to get the soles of your feet up onto the flat edge. It'll drop right into the sod."

Aubrey did as he instructed and jumped up onto the flat back of the blade. Sure enough, the curved edge sliced into the soil with a satisfying crunch.

"Good. Now step back, lever the handle over flat to the ground, and shove it under. You're gonna slice all the roots in one go."

Aubrey did, and with minimal resistance, the chunk of sod in front of her separated itself from the dirt below. She lifted it. "Do you have a wheelbarrow or something?"

"We don't throw it out. We *use* it. Fertilizer. Just flip it over."

She did. The chunk of sod plopped neatly back into the dirt upside-down, revealing the rich, dark soil underneath it.

Phil looked pleased. "There you go, sodbuster. We could break the rest of this stuff today, water the hell out of it while the hose still works, and if we get a little rain we can plant by the end of the week."

"What about seeds?" she asked.

"Yeah, we need good ones. High-quality organic stuff. Not Monsanto Frankenseeds. That's our biggest challenge. Farm supply stores. Gotta get on that fast, before everybody else."

The sound of a car engine came from up the street, and they both turned. It was Aubrey's car, Scott behind the wheel. Aubrey watched, frowning, as the car pulled into her driveway, too fast.

She handed the sod lifter back to Phil. "Thank you. Let's talk later today."

"You got it, Aunt Beru."

She was already crossing the street and looked back, confused. "Who?"

"Aunt Beru? Famous moisture farmer?"

"A famous what?"

"The Lars family moisture farm? Where Uncle Owen and Aunt Beru raised Luke?" He waved her off, wishing he'd never gone down that particular path. "It's a *Star Wars* thing. You have a good day."

Yes, Phil was a data analyst, all right. Aubrey smiled, gave him a little wave, and turned back, heading home to deal with Scott. As she drew closer to the driveway, she saw that he wasn't alone in the car.

There was a teenage girl in the front seat.

17.

A hundred feet underground, Ann-Sophie knocked on the door of unit 9A. She waited, holding a bouquet of wildflowers, a cloth grocery bag slung over her right arm. She knocked again, still got no answer, then tried the doorbell, a small, hard-to-see button nestled in the wood paneling of the landing. A few seconds later, Marques opened the door, in jeans and a T-shirt. He smiled, surprised.

"I *thought* I heard somebody knocking. It's so quiet in here I could barely tell."

"I know." Ann-Sophie smiled. "Weird, isn't it? Do you feel your ears popping in the elevator?"

"Yes! Drives me crazy. I've chewed more gum in the past three days than my whole life. Sorry, did you want to come in?"

Ann-Sophie peered behind him. "Are Beth and—I'm sorry, I forgot her little girl's name."

"Kearie."

"Kearie. Are they here?"

"No, Beth took her up to the gym to burn off some energy. But come on in anyway." He opened the door and she stepped inside.

Unit 9A was one of the smaller apartments, a one-bedroom with an alcove in the living room. The pastel palette of the rest of the complex had been continued in here, more shades of light brown than anybody should see in their whole lives, but Thom had read some psychological adaptability test that said beige tones were the most soothing colors. Ann-Sophie hated it.

"You can repaint if you want, you know," she said.

"No, no, it looks great."

"Oh, it does not. I'm Scandinavian. We know about dark. You don't want brown; you want bold colors. Plus candles. I put a couple in the bag. This is for you guys." She set the cloth bag on the small dining room table.

"Wow. That's so nice of you." He meant it. The atmosphere around the facility had been hostile and discontented so far, and her gesture was the first kindness he'd encountered.

"Plus a few spices and sauces, things they don't have in the stock house. Cholula, some spicy mustard, anything with flavor, basically. And the kids picked these flowers for you all."

Marques took them, unsure what to say. "Thank you so much."

Ann-Sophie nodded and looked around, uncomfortable. She'd been putting off coming down here for a few days, and now that she was here, it was harder than she expected. She'd been married to Thom for nearly a decade and had been tidying up the emotional messes he'd made since she'd known him. She was used to sweeping up the broken plates, but now, knowing that she wanted out of the marriage, it was harder to keep doing this particular chore. Thom's inability to hide his narcissism shouldn't have been her daily problem anymore. But if she was going to be living in a bunker with this family, she didn't want there to be any tension whatsoever.

"He can be quite an asshole," she said.

"Sorry?" Marques asked.

"Thom. How long have you worked for him?"

"Four years."

"So you know it's true."

Marques smiled. "No comment."

"I did one of those checklists for borderline personality disorder once and he had seven out of ten. Not enough to make it a diagnosis but definitely enough to qualify as a jerk."

"I wouldn't say that. We took him by surprise. Sort of forced the situation on him. I'm not sure I would have reacted any differently."

Ann-Sophie shrugged and looked around again. Her eyes fell on the alcove, an extra sleeping space in case the occupants of the apartment had a child. The bed there was made but had been slept in. She looked at it twice, feeling something slightly off. She couldn't put her finger on what it was—the lack of stuffed animals and other detritus of childhood, perhaps? She looked away and back at Marques.

He suddenly seemed anxious. "Could I make you a coffee? I think I have it down with the Keurig thing."

"No, thanks. I should be going. The kids are outside, probably playing with a rattlesnake by now."

Marques laughed, a little too hard. "I know, we're not really desert people. Kearie keeps wanting to go for a walk, and Beth's like 'Yeah, girl, if you find me a pair of cowboy boots.'"

Boots. That was it. Ann-Sophie turned her head to the side and looked at the bed again. There was a pair of boots beside the bed, toes neatly tucked underneath the end table. Definitely not children's footwear, they were men's boots, set carefully next to the bed, and that was a man's chunky wristwatch on the bedside table.

That was not Kearie's bed, Ann-Sophie realized. A man was sleeping in that bed, *Marques* was sleeping in that bed, which meant Kearie was in the bedroom with her mother, and why would they settle on that arrangement, unless they were having a fight? But Ann-Sophie had seen Marques and Beth around, and if they were a couple in the midst of a you-will-not-sleep-in-this-bed fight, they sure didn't look like it.

She turned back to Marques, failing to hide the look on her face.

He looked back and forth from her to the bed. "What?"

"Hmm?"

"Sorry."

It was a nonsensical exchange between two people who both knew what the other was thinking.

Marques brightened, suddenly and too much. "Oh, damn. Did it again." He walked over to the bed, bold as he could muster, picked up the boots, and marched them over to the closet. He opened it and tossed them inside, shaking his head and smiling. "I leave my shit everywhere, drives her crazy."

"OK." She was thinking, and he could see she was thinking.

"I snore," he added. "Pretty loud. Kind of a problem."

"We never sent you patio furniture," she said.

"What?"

"I do all the gifts for senior staff. Weddings, bar mitzvahs, housewarming, babies, all of it. Every single one of them, and I do them myself. We never sent anyone patio furniture. I would have remembered."

Marques looked stricken. "That's so weird. Shit, I wonder who it was, then? We owe somebody a thank-you note!"

"I am, literally, the last person on earth who cares if you lied to Thom."

Marques looked around, nodding, buying time while he thought. When he turned back to Ann-Sophie, all pretense was gone. "Thank God. That was exhausting."

"Beth is . . . what then?" Ann-Sophie asked.

"Next-door neighbor."

"Are you a couple?"

"Nope. She's gay."

Ann-Sophie broke into the biggest smile she'd enjoyed in months. "So she just hitched a ride with you?"

"No, no, it wasn't her, it was totally my idea. Everything they were saying on TV that was going to happen? She had no idea what to do. She's on her own, with a little kid. I practically forced them to come with me."

"And what you said about her father being dead?"

"Kearie's father was a donor. Neither one of them ever met him. Goddamn, I feel so much better. I'm sorry, I'm not a natural liar."

"That's a good quality, not a bad one."

"We'll go if you want us to."

"Don't even think about it," she said. "I consider what you did heroic."

"*Fuck*, I feel better. Hey, do you want a drink? Like a drink-drink?"

Ann-Sophie pulled a chair out from the table and sat down. "I would love a drink-drink."

Ninety feet above them, in the communications room on the third subterranean floor, Thom watched their images on one of a bank of control-room monitors. The pin-dot cameras that had been placed in the upper-left corner of the LED screens in the living rooms of all the units were a need-to-know-only feature of the accommodations, and certainly the residents didn't need to know. Thom had intended to use them only in case of medical emergencies and never planned for them to be any kind of surveillance device. But Ann-Sophie had been cold to him for the past several days, barely speaking at all, and when he'd seen her get in the elevator with a bag of food gifts and a bouquet of flowers, his natural curiosity, coupled with years of dating faithless models, had gotten the better of him. He'd come to the comms room and monitored her progress down to level nine, and into Marques's apartment.

Now he could see but not hear them as they poured the good red wine she'd brought and toasted each other on the sofa. What in the name of *sweet Jesus* was that all about?

There was no one else in the communication room at the time, as there wouldn't be from that moment forward. When Thom left that day, he issued clear instructions that from then on no one was to enter the room except at his specific invitation, and even then, only in his company, which would allow him to go in first and turn off any monitors he didn't want seen at that particular moment.

If his wife was going to start fucking his pilot, he'd make goddamn well sure he was the only one who knew about it.

18.

AURORA

Aubrey looked through the windows of the car as she walked up her front steps. The dark-haired teenage girl, her long locks pulled back in a tight ponytail, sat in the front seat with Scott.

Aubrey hid her annoyance and attempted a casual wave, but neither of them noticed her. Scott was talking, gesturing, nodding, putting a hand on the young lady's arm. Finally, some sort of agreement seemed to be reached and they got out of the car. Scott came around to help as the girl reached into the back seat and pulled out a heavily stuffed backpack.

They approached Aubrey on the sidewalk, Scott just behind the girl, holding a hand out to Aubrey, low, a gesture that said both "I can explain" and "Please don't you dare fuck this up."

Aubrey forced a smile. "Hi, I'm Aubrey," she said, figuring that was about as uncontroversial as she could possibly get.

The girl stopped short of her and looked down. Scott stepped in, making the introductions.

"This is Celeste."

Aubrey took a moment, digesting that. She had never met Scott's latest girlfriend in person, nor had she seen pictures, not even online when she'd searched fruitlessly for her on Instagram. There was very little Aubrey knew about her, other than that she was in Scott's grade at school, her home life was unpleasant, and she was Black. Yes, she was certain on all three of those things. She examined Celeste now, noting that this person was not, in fact, Black. Celeste was not Black, Celeste was not Brown, Celeste was not even cream-colored. Celeste's skin was so white it was almost translucent. If Aubrey had to guess her ethnic background, she might have gone with Estonian.

"Hello, Celeste. Nice to finally meet you," Aubrey offered, trying to speak without inflection. "I have to confess, I always get your name mixed up, I keep calling you Caprice. Scott gives me so much shit about it. He's hilarious." She looked at Scott. "You're hilarious."

Scott just stared daggers at her. Celeste tucked her hair behind her ear and looked between them, sensing something was up but not wanting to pick at it. "That's funny," she said, which is what people say when they don't think something is funny. "Thank you for letting me stay with you."

Aubrey didn't even raise an eyebrow at that, just shifted gears like a Formula One driver. "No problem. Why don't you go inside and put your things down? I just need to ask Scott something real quick."

Celeste turned and looked up at Scott. He smiled and gave her an ostentatious kiss on the mouth. She went inside.

Scott spoke before Aubrey could, his tone aggressive. "She's staying in my room with me."

"You don't have to get tough with me, Scott. I don't care."

"I went to her house to check on her. It's shitty there. It's always shitty there, but now it's worse."

"I'm sorry to hear that. How did you guys meet anyway?"

"Rusty works with her dad. Doing what, I don't know, but her dad is an asshole. Rusty's always over there. She can't stay at that house. I'm not kidding."

"I said it's fine. She can totally stay."

"I wasn't asking permission."

"For Christ's sake, would you please stop trying to make a fight where there isn't one? Everything's hard enough right now."

"What did you have to ask me?"

"Why did you tell me she's Black?"

Scott turned and gazed into the distance thoughtfully for a long moment. Finally, he turned back. "I was trying to stimulate a productive conversation about race."

And he went inside. He was, perhaps, the most full-of-shit person Aubrey had ever met.

She remained on the front step, watching as Scott went to Celeste, who was standing awkwardly in the living room. He put his hands on her arms and spoke softly. It was a tender gesture, reassuring without attempting to dominate, and Aubrey teared up, surprising herself. The young man, skinny as a rail and with a gangly body he hadn't fully learned how to control, somehow had picked up the silent language of calm reassurance and was displaying a concern and tenderness she'd never seen in him before. Her eyes shifted to Celeste, who was about Scott's age; she was a girl, not a woman, and she needed all the help she could get. Not a man to tell her what to do, none of that bullshit, but maybe, once in a while, somebody to tell her it wasn't all on her. Someone to look after her, just a little bit.

Aubrey turned and sat down heavily on the front steps. She'd picked up the compact satellite phone from the kitchen, intending to call Thom at some point today. She pulled it out now, turned it on, and waited to see if it had a signal. It did. She picked the most recent of his fourteen unanswered calls and tapped the number.

The phone went through a funny series of clicks, rang once, and her brother's voice answered.

"Please don't ever do that to me again."

"I'm sorry," she said, and she was. "It's been weird."

"I worry about you. It's debilitating."

"I'm fine."

"What's it been like there?"

"Quiet today. There were a lot of sirens the first couple days, and flames in the sky almost every night."

"Those are aurorae."

"No, they were flames. I know what the aurorae look like. Everyone on the planet knows what they look like now. This is different. Power stations keep exploding, a guy down the street said. I don't know, I haven't gone out much."

"Good. You shouldn't. How's Todd?"

She thought. "Scott?"

"Yeah. Rusty's kid."

"He's fine. He brought a girlfriend to stay here."

"There's a lot of that going around," Thom said. "Listen, there's a guy on his way to you from me. His name is Brady. He should be there in"—she could hear the rustling of a sleeve as he made a show of checking his wristwatch—"seventeen hours."

"Wait, who's coming here?"

"He works for me. Former cop. I trust him implicitly."

"*Why* is he coming here?"

"You have no money, Aubrey."

"Oh, for Christ's sake, I'm fine. I have money."

"I've sent enough to handle whatever might come up. I want you to do what I said when I sent money before, but this time really do it. Separate it into four separate stashes and secure them around your house. OK?"

"I don't want a pile of cash in my house." She glanced around involuntarily, to see if anyone had overheard. There were only a couple people out, and they were too far away to notice. She lowered her voice anyway. "I mean, I appreciate it, but we just differ philosophically on this. I think twenty thousand in cash could make more problems than it solves."

"It's more than twenty thousand. Just take it."

"Why are you doing this?"

"I'm trying to help you, for Christ's sake." That came out louder than he intended, and the signal cracked in the middle of his sentence.

He spoke again, softer. "But you will never fucking let me off the hook, will you?"

"Come on. Don't go down that road." But she could hear in his voice that he already had. She could picture him, slumped in a chair, his hand over his eyes, trying to shove the tears back inside where they came from.

"Tell me what's going on with you," she tried.

"Nothing. I'm fine. Everything's fine."

"Are Ann-Sophie and the kids OK?"

"They're great. Everybody's fine. Everything is fine here."

"You're saying *fine* a lot."

"Rosy. Top-notch. What do you want? This is a perfect, high-functioning intentional community. I've been planning this for a decade, and I have a place here for you, if you would just accept it. It's you and me, remember?"

He waited, but she didn't fill in the rest of the line. So he did, morosely. "Because everyone else is dead. Will you please just say you'll call me when Brady gets there with the money?"

"You want to save me. I don't need saving."

"Then fucking send it back!" he shouted, so loud it hurt her ear. She yanked the phone away from her head, and by the time she put it back to her ear, he'd hung up. She stared at the phone for a moment, trying to remember if he had ever hung up on her before, and fairly certain he had not. She had always been the elusive one, the pursued, the one who was called and the one who moved things along with "Well, I should probably let you go." Not this time.

"You guys have a fucked-up relationship."

She turned. Scott was standing in the doorway behind her, having heard the last of the conversation and witnessing its abrupt end.

Aubrey turned the satellite phone off and dropped it on the step beside her. "Where's Celeste?"

"Upstairs. You weirded her out a little bit."

"I was polite and welcoming."

"Yeah, well, she's not used to that."

He came outside and sat down on the step beside her. Aubrey looked away, putting her hand to her mouth. The conversation with Thom had shaken her, and a pointless adolescent argument was the last thing she was interested in at the moment.

Scott stared at her for a long moment, taking her in. "When did your guys' parents die?"

"Could you please just go practice the fucking piano or something?"

"C'mon. When do I *ever* ask about you? Seize the day or whatever. I'm not gonna be interested for that long."

She looked at him and half smiled. He could charm when he wanted. She couldn't decide if she liked that about him or not. "Fifteen years ago. My mom first with cancer, Dad six months later."

"Wow. What'd he die of? Broken heart?"

"You're very sentimental. Suicide."

"Jesus Christ. You never told me that."

"It's the first time you've asked."

He thought about that for a moment. "Fuck. Suicide, after the dude's beloved wife goes. How Rilke can you get?"

"Rilke wasn't married, and he didn't kill himself. He had leukemia. It's not at all Rilke. You can't get any less Rilke."

"Whatever. Your dad died of a broken heart, Aubrey. That's as romantic as a person can possibly be."

"I guess."

Scott nodded and gave it some more thought. He looked back at her. "Is that why you and your brother have such a fucked relationship? Like you both thought your dad killing himself was the other person's fault or something? Should've noticed—that type of shit? 'Cause people think that all the time."

Aubrey turned and looked at him. "You're not going to sell Phil's weed anymore."

"Wait, what? *Whose* weed?" It was terrible acting. Aubrey ignored it.

"Instead, you're going to help Phil plant food we can eat. It's not going to be easy work. We start tomorrow."

Scott turned and looked across the street. Phil was hard at it already, turning the sod in his front yard with a physical energy Scott had never seen in him before. Phil looked up, saw Scott looking at him, and turned away quickly, going back to work.

Scott turned back to Aubrey. "OK," he said.

Aubrey nodded and got up to go back in the house. "Celeste can help, too, if she's going to be staying here."

"Sounds like a plan."

"What's her last name, by the way?"

"Zielinski."

Aubrey hesitated, thinking that sounded familiar. But she couldn't place it.

She went inside, the screen door banging behind her.

19.

AURORA

Brady's goal had been to arrive before dark the day after he left, and the sun was still a half hour from setting when he pulled around the corner onto Cayuga Lane. The drive had gone better than he'd expected. So good, in fact, that he'd stopped and gotten some sleep the night before in Custer County, Nebraska. There weren't a whole lot of places more remote than Custer County, Nebraska, and when he'd turned onto NE-40 just outside Broken Bow, the expanse of long, dark, single-lane road had given him the comfort to pull over, lock the doors, and close his eyes for a while. The incident at the Arco station in Nevada had sharpened him, snapped him back into fighting shape. Four and a half hours later, he'd awakened from a deep and peaceful sleep, his arms cramping, still wrapped around the duffel that held the $250,000. It was the best sleep he'd had in months.

Gassing up along the way had proven to be no problem. The reports he'd gathered before leaving Sanctuary tended toward the dire, but they were more assessments of the state of the country as a whole, not the remote and lightly populated states he'd be driving through—Wyoming, Nebraska, and Iowa. The combination of low population with the sheer vastness of the Great Plains meant the power lines in those states were long, with dozens or hundreds of miles between major transformers, and the damage had been somewhat mitigated by those factors. Albany County, Wyoming, in fact, had looked to Brady's eye to be completely unaffected, and he was shocked to find not one but two open truck stops still pumping gas. The price gouging had been horrible, but Brady had paid happily, both times, and by the time he crossed the Illinois border he still had one full battery charge and five-eighths of a tank of gas.

He slowed to a crawl on Cayuga, checked the street addresses, and turned into Aubrey Wheeler's driveway, careful not to bottom out on the crack in the sidewalk. He'd made it fifteen hundred miles without incident this time, and the last thing he needed was to crack an axle in the last twenty feet. Brady put the car in park, put his hands atop the wheel, and said a quick prayer of thanks to Saint Christopher and the BMW, which had never given him a moment's trouble.

"I have to admit, this is not what I was expecting," he said ten minutes later, sitting in the living room across from Aubrey. The blue duffel was on the coffee table between them, the center of attention and topic of conversation.

"I know," she said. "I'm sorry. You had a very long drive, and I don't imagine it was easy."

"I'm just not exactly sure what to do now," he said. "You saying 'No, thanks' was not something I'd been led to believe was an option."

"I can imagine. I tried to tell Thom, but he didn't want to listen to me. Sometimes my brother can be a little, you know, obstinate."

"Which is, no doubt, how he achieved all that he has," Brady said, without particularly meaning it.

"No doubt," Aubrey echoed. Shit, this one drank the Kool-Aid. "Can you just take the money back to him?" she asked. "I mean, stay here, spend the night, I don't have a guest room, but you're welcome to the couch. Head back whenever you want, and just, you know, return it to him. With my thanks."

"That doesn't seem like something that will be acceptable to Mr. Banning."

"Well, you can't make me keep something I don't want, Mr.— Sorry, it's Brady what?"

"Brady's my last name, not first."

She frowned, confused. "Thom calls you only by your last name?"

"I don't think Mr. Banning knows my first name."

Maybe not *all* of the Kool-Aid. "Can I ask your first name?"

"Patrick."

"OK, look, Patrick. I'm going to propose something else. I want you to hear it all the way through, because you strike me as a certain kind of person, the kind who's not interested in this sort of thing, and that's great, but we're all in the middle of some crazy shit right now and I really want you to consider this."

Brady just looked at her. He had an idea where she was going, and she was right—he was not interested. "I'm not keeping the money," he said.

"Now hang on, just wait. My brother and I are, well, it's complicated, and you don't need to be involved in it. I just don't want his money, that's all. You have a job to do, I can see that you care about it, and what I'm suggesting never has to go any further than just you and me. Keep the money, do what you will with it, and I'll tell him that you gave it to me. That secret goes to our graves with us. Sounds good?"

Brady smiled, immensely uncomfortable. "I am grateful for the offer, but I'm already being paid for this."

"Well, then you'll be paid whatever you're getting plus this much. How much is it, by the way? No, never mind, I don't want to know. Just take it. Nobody will know."

"I can't. It's meant for you."

"OK. I get it. I accept it." She reached out and made a show of pulling the bag a foot closer to her on the table. "Thank you, Patrick, you've delivered the money. Oh, wait a second, I don't need this. I think I'd like to give it to a new friend." She shoved the bag two feet away from her, so it was now squarely in front of him. She shrugged. "How's that?"

"Ma'am, it is a very generous offer, and I do appreciate it. A corny thing is about to come out of my mouth, and I apologize for it in advance, but here it is anyway. You say nobody will know, but I'll know. And my mother would know. I don't know how, because she's in her mid-eighties and doesn't remember my name half the time, but something tells me the next time I saw her she'd take one look in my eyes and say, 'Oh, Patrick, what have you *done*?'"

Aubrey laughed, and Brady smiled. "I'm not kidding, she's like that. I promise you, I'm being paid very well for this job, what's in that bag would just be, well, more, and in my experience, more money doesn't mean more better. It just means more. Sometimes having more even creates a need for more that wasn't there before. So, no, thank you. I'll take you up on the offer of the couch, and if I could trouble you for a bit of dinner, I'd be grateful for that too. But then I'll take the money and go back and do my best to make your brother understand that some people just want to make it under their own steam. Sounds good?"

"Yes. Thank you."

"May I ask a personal question, though?"

"This wasn't personal yet?"

"Why won't you take it? Really."

She took a breath and looked away. "There's only one person in the entire world that Thom owes anything to. Me. I guess I'd like to keep it that way." She looked back at him. "Childish, right?"

Brady shrugged. "Well, you were children together."

"Briefly."

"Still. Things stick. I have a wealthy brother. He sends me a card with a hundred-dollar bill in it every year on my birthday. Drives me nuts. I make my own living."

"Did you tell him to stop?"

"Nah, we don't talk like that. I just give it to the first homeless guy I see. Makes *his* day."

Aubrey gestured to the duffel bag. "If your brother sent you that during a blackout, would you keep it?"

"Well, of *course* I would. I'm not an idiot. No offense."

"Who could possibly take offense at that?"

"I'm leaving early in the morning. Gives you some time. Why don't you think about it overnight? No sweat either way."

She smiled. "Would I freak you out if I said I liked your style, Patrick?"

"You would not."

"Are you hungry?" she asked.

"Starving."

"Peanut butter and jelly OK?"

"Peanut butter and jelly is a dream come true," Brady said, and he meant it.

Half an hour later, the dusky light was shining through the kitchen window as Aubrey, Brady, Scott, and Celeste sat down to a dinner of PBJs, once-frozen peas, and tap water. The teenagers, who'd deigned to come downstairs from Scott's room for the meal, had the clingy, blissed-out look of a young couple who had recently discovered the joys of premarital sex, and Aubrey thought she needed to somehow, someway, find a supply of at least a hundred condoms. It was going to be a long blackout, and she had no intention of taking the Little House thing all the way to giving birth to a step-grandchild on her dining room table.

"Should we do gratitudes?" Celeste asked, just as they started to eat.

The others looked at her. Outside, a car's engine roared as someone came down the street, too fast.

"You know, gratitudes," she tried again. "We go around and everybody has to say one thing they're grateful for, even if it's hard to think of. Especially if it's hard to think of, that's kinda the point. My mom used to have us do it every night during COVID, but then—well, we don't anymore."

Scott's arm moved, and Aubrey could tell he was putting a reassuring hand on her thigh. *Condoms. Gotta get condoms.* Outside, a car door slammed.

Brady brightened, looking at Celeste. "Great idea. Can I go first?" Nobody objected, so he did. "I'm grateful to be here with you all. I realize I busted in, and here you're feeding me and sheltering me, and, well, that means a lot to me."

Celeste slapped him lightly on his bulky arm. "You took mine." She turned to Aubrey. "Thank you for having me here. Very much."

"I'm grateful for bread," Scott said inelegantly, through a mouthful of it. "How much more bread do we have? Is there even gonna *be* bread anymore? When's the—"

"Helloo?"

They all turned, and from the kitchen table they could see all the way down the center hall to the front door, which was open. There was a silhouette in the screen, somebody cupping their hands to block out the light so they could get a look inside the house.

Rusty.

"Hey, you guys, what's up?"

Scott turned, furious, his eyes burning a hole into Aubrey's. "What the fuck, Aubrey? He has to stop just coming here whenever he wants. I thought you fucking talked to him about that."

"Not crazy about the language," Brady said.

"Who asked you?" Scott snapped.

"Nobody. Just voicing an opinion."

"What are you guys *doing* in there?" Rusty yelled, from the doorway. "You gonna let me in or what?"

"I'll handle it," Aubrey said, getting up from the table. Scott turned away, so he couldn't make eye contact with Rusty, and now it was Celeste's turn to try to comfort him. God, Aubrey was going to get sick of that us-two-against-the-world dynamic real quick, but one problem at a time. "Excuse me."

She headed for the front door, making a conscious effort not to force a phony, accommodating smile onto her face. She was done with that shit with Rusty. She reached the door and stopped, pointedly, on the other side of the screen, not opening it. "What's the matter, Rusty?"

He looked at her and frowned, held his hands up in confusion. "What do you mean *what's the matter?* You asked me to knock first. I knocked."

"I mean why are you here?"

He scratched his neck, too hard, and gestured to his truck. "Came to juice you up." Again, he'd backed into the driveway, his truck hanging out into the street this time, since Brady's BMW was already parked beside the house. Aubrey could see the yellow generator in the back.

"Who's Mr. BMW with the California plates?" he asked.

Aubrey was in no mood for his bullshit. "No, thank you."

"What do you mean?" Rusty asked.

"I mean I don't want power right now."

"Yeah, well, I'm not gonna be over this way for another four or five days, so it's kinda now or never, honey."

"That's a chance I'll take." She started to close the front door, but Rusty leaned in, right up against the screen.

"What's your fucking *problem?*"

"Do you need some help here?"

Aubrey turned. Brady, all six foot four and two hundred twenty pounds of him, was standing just behind her, a little to one side.

"Rusty was just leaving."

Brady turned and looked at Rusty, a flat-affect the-lady-says-you're-leaving expression on his face.

Rusty laughed and looked Brady up and down. "Who the fuck are you supposed to be?"

"I'd answer that, but I heard you needed to go."

"Oh, for the love of Christ," Rusty said to Aubrey. "What is this guy, muscle? Jesus, look at this Mick. He's like a ton of corned beef floating in beer." Rusty scratched his neck again, compulsively.

Meth, Brady thought to himself. Everywhere, meth. His brother Terence, those kids in the desert, and now this guy. It felt like it haunted him, stalked him.

Aubrey looked back over her shoulder and saw Scott and Celeste were staring at them. She turned back to Rusty, trying to end the conversation. "He works with Thom. He's here helping us out today." The moment Thom's name was out of her mouth, she wished she could snatch it back out of the air before it reached Rusty's ears. That seemingly innocent and non-specific comment was the first of two calamitous mistakes Aubrey would make.

While Rusty and Aubrey were married, her husband and brother had never gotten along. Rusty was somehow deeply resentful of Thom's attempts to help them financially yet also found his offers totally inadequate. And, of course, the fact that Aubrey continually turned her brother's money down made Rusty crazy.

On dark nights when things were bad, she'd wondered if Rusty had ever loved her, or if it was just her brother's money he'd been after all along.

In the clear light of day, she *knew* that it was. Mentioning Thom at all would mean only one thing to Rusty: money.

In her irritation, Aubrey turned away from Rusty, who was still on the other side of the screen. Her eyes, looking for anywhere else to land besides her ex-husband's rotting teeth, fell on the living room, and on the blue duffel bag that was still sitting in the middle of the coffee table. Her gaze only rested there for a split second before she abruptly looked away, back to the conversation in the doorway.

It was her quick look away that Rusty noticed, and that involuntary reaction was her second, and more grievous, mistake. Rusty, no dummy, picked up the twitch of her head, the way she snapped it back at him, but not just to him, *away* from something. Looking into the living room, his eyes searched for whatever it was she hadn't wanted him to see. The blue duffel bag was the obvious choice, sitting out on the coffee table as if on display.

Rusty's mind, its wiring declining in quality and performance from years of chemical abuse, was still capable of some deductive thought. The bag was upright, brand new with package lines still in it, fully stuffed with something. Obviously, the bag was the new thing here, the variable, along with Brady, and they had come together, those two.

Why did hired security need to personally escort a small, over-stuffed blue duffel bag, except for the obvious reason, and what kind of thing would a billionaire send clear across the country during a massive power outage, except for the obvious thing, and what possible contents of said duffel bag would make his ex-wife so blatantly desperate to conceal them from him, *except for the fucking obvious*?

Whole horizons opened up in Rusty's mind, and he saw that a shift in tactics was advisable.

"I apologize," he said to Aubrey, his voice smooth and placatory. "I won't come again, unless you ask me to. I owe you that courtesy. Scott?" He called out to the kitchen in his best paternal manner. "Take care, son. If you need me, don't hesitate. You know where to find me."

He squinted, noticing the girl next to Scott. "Celeste, is that you? Your daddy's looking for you, sweetie. Better run home."

Celeste didn't answer. She just turned away. Scott bristled, angling his body to block her from his father's view, a gesture more symbolic than effective.

Rusty turned back to Brady. "Sorry about the wisecrack, buddy. Think I heard it in a song once. Stay safe." And with that he headed back to his truck, slid behind the wheel, and drove off at a safe and responsible speed.

Three blocks away, Rusty pulled over at a stop sign and rubbed his face, thinking. This was going to be tricky. But holy *shit* was it going to be worth it. The money piñata was about to burst.

Aubrey closed the door, locked it, and looked at Brady. "My ex-husband."

"I gathered."

"Sorry about that."

Brady shook his head. "I shouldn't have interfered. You had it."

The four of them ate dinner quietly, forgetting to finish their gratitudes.

20.

Things were going wrong, and Thom needed a nap. A nap would fix everything.

The cot was an almost exact replica of Thomas Edison's. Not Edison's nap cot in Florida, which Thom had seen as a child—that one had seemed dinky and uncomfortable even then—but the larger, more commodious cot Edison had kept in the book-lined nook of his library in West Orange, New Jersey. The New Jersey cot was more of a single bed, with sheets, a blanket, and two fluffy pillows awaiting the great man's head at all times. Thom (not Edison) had gone to great trouble to have the whole of Edison's library nook reconstructed in the alcove just off his small office in the main house at Sanctuary. Everything was identical, right down to the titles of the books on the shelves. The world may teeter near its end, but Thom still might get an idea and need to nap it out.

Thom settled himself in the nook, arranging the accoutrements of his nap just so. He had two white-noise generators that he used—one near the office door, to block out distractions from the living areas of the house, and the other on a table beside him, in case any sounds in the room should seek to disrupt his dreamy inspiration. Thom liked four pillows on the bed, two for his head and two longer, king-size pillows he used to form a tent over his face. The pillow bases were kept close to his ears, and the apex of the triangle had to be close enough to block out light but not oxygen. He'd tried a sleep mask earlier in his napping career but found they worked too well, sending him deep into the dark waters of slumber rather than skimming along on the surface. It was there, just over wave top, where Thom's moments of genius fluttered.

He'd taken to the cot today because he knew when a situation was in the early stages of spiraling out of control. Like the Chandler wobble—the unpredictable, irregular rotation of the earth due to its nonspherical nature—the imbalance Thom had detected in his meticulously planned disaster community was difficult to observe and maddening to anticipate. But if anybody could predict the unpredictable, he felt, it was him. He just needed to get himself in the right, deeply concentrated mental state.

He laid back on the cot, sound machines batting away all atmospheric distractions, pillow tent over his face, and he closed his eyes. The first moments of quasi-sleep were the most valuable, and the yellow legal pad was always on the cot beside him, lest he awaken and lose his thoughts in the time it would take him to get out of the nook and over to the desk.

He let his mind drift. What was wrong, and why? Most important, what could be done to correct the course they were on? That was the dream-task at hand.

When Thom was in his mid-twenties and just starting to enjoy the stratospheric success that would come to define the next decade of his life—come to define *him*, if he thought about it—he'd made friends with a data-storage billionaire named Walton Scutter, in the way that rich people tend to do. Hey, you're rich, I'm rich, let's be friends. They'd fallen into conversation at a TechCrunch Disrupt event in San Francisco, back before the word *disrupt* was on the lips of every mindlessly ambitious high-schooler in the country and seemed to stand in as a synonym for *innovate*, which it most certainly was not. Walton

Scutter was fond of tequila, and Thom tried to keep up with him that night, mostly enjoying being seen in his presence.

"Do you know the problem with being a billionaire?" Scutter had asked twenty-six-year-old Thom that night.

"I do not," Thom replied, "but I hope I get to find out."

"I'll save you the wait," Scutter said, knocking back his fourth or fifth shot of 1800 Colección. "The problem is you lose the ability to deal with the unexpected."

"How so?"

"I'll give you an example," the older man said. "A week ago, I got a flat tire. I don't know how, doesn't matter, I was on the freeway, it started to feel funny, then it started to go thumpa-thumpa-thumpa. But I kept driving for a good minute or two, because it just wasn't registering that, yes, that was my car making that noise, and, yes, I had a flat tire. It's not like I've never had a flat tire in my life. I've had plenty. But I hadn't had one since, you know, I got rich. Not rich, but *rich*."

Thom wondered if he would ever speak of being *rich* in such casual tones. He sure the hell hoped so.

"So I pulled over and I called my guy, and I let him have it. I mean, I really laid into him. God, I was pissed off. I *love* cars. I have thirty-six of them. Cars are my incredibly expensive addiction, and I have a full-time staff of five people who have nothing to do except look after them. 'How could this have happened?!' I yelled at the guy, over the phone. 'This can't be! You have nothing else to do!' And on and on. I can't remember exactly what I said, but I'm pretty sure I was an asshole, because I can be an asshole, I'm told. So the guy apologized up and down, and they got a tow truck—*my* tow truck, by the way, from my garage—out to me in about twenty minutes. But while I was sitting by the side of the road, I realized, it's just a flat. That's all. I must have driven over a nail. Or a chunk of metal, or broken glass. Who knows? These things happen. But I couldn't handle it. I couldn't handle the unexpected, because all I could think was, *With the money I pay this should never happen.*"

He tossed back another shot, checked his watch, and took his sport coat off the back of a chair. "I can't handle anything anymore. And the truth is, I'm not interested in trying. That's the problem with being a billionaire. Nice to meet you."

Thom had watched the older man shuffle away. He thought back to Scudder's early, ground-breaking work in data protection, and how out-of-the-box his thinking had been, and now all he could think about was how old, soft, and spoiled he was. Thom vowed never to be like that.

On his nap cot, as his breathing slowed and he drifted into the embrace of midday sleep, Thom wondered if he had become Walton Scutter. Unable to handle the unexpected. But, thank Christ, he was thirty years younger than that guy and wasn't trying to self-medicate his way into an early grave.

The unexpected has occurred, he thought to himself. Not the CME or the blackout—he'd been ready for those. But human behavior, with all its rampant unpredictability, had now kicked into gear, and that, like the earth's wobble, was far more difficult to forecast. One by one, Thom thought of the half dozen unforeseen events that were threatening his planned community. Some were bigger than others, but all were contributing to instability, foretelling a slew of consequences he could not yet imagine. He reviewed them chronologically in his mind:

1. Marques had shown up to the airport with a family.

2. Aubrey had failed to follow all his good advice.

3. His dentist had proven to be a bad hire.

4. Jimmy had asked to bring an unvetted stranger into the complex.

5. Ann-Sophie had returned home yesterday at dinnertime with her cheeks flushed, her speech slurred, and had lied about where she'd been, and,

6. Brady had checked in via SMS from the satellite phone in

Illinois, but in a spare and incomplete manner. "Arrived in Aurora, contact made. Leaving in morning."

When Thom had messaged him back, asking if the money handover had been completed, Brady had failed to respond. So there was more to the story there. What on earth could it possibly be? Was Brady going to prove unreliable as well? *Brady?* The idea was unthinkable, but there were a lot of unimaginable events playing out right now, one after the other, and there were more that could be added to the list.

It was only day five of the crisis, but Thom had noted that the residents of the silo were failing to follow the posted schedules that had been meticulously created for them. Successful communal living thrives on a balanced and rigorously observed schedule that includes exercise, contributive labor, and frequent periods of quiet isolation. That was all pretty much out the window already, as he'd noticed most of the residents preferred to spend their days outside the silo doing fuck-all or, worse, driving around the desert aimlessly, burning gas and "exploring the area."

Chloe had taken to desert meditation and was habitually late for her own yoga classes. Dr. Rahman, their reclusive GP, insisted on Zoom appointments even though he was a hundred feet away. And the Friedmans, the husband-and-wife chef duo, had stopped posting menus and taken to just reheating freeze-dried stuff from the acre-size storage floor, or sometimes just leaving the commissary unlocked, for people to feed themselves.

Ann-Sophie, his own wife and the de facto First Lady of Sanctuary, was the worst offender of all. Just this morning, she'd packed up herself and the kids and told Thom they were spending the day with Marques and Beth and Kearie. She declined to answer further questions, and Thom was pointedly not invited to join.

Disruption. This was how it happened. An oscillation was introduced, which would then become a shimmy, which would quickly accelerate into a wobble before spinning out of control and tearing apart an entire structure. This is how industries were collapsed and rebuilt, this was how fortunes were made, and this was how societies, whether big or small, fell apart.

No, Thom thought. Not here. Disorder, entropy, and vulnerability will not be tolerated. These chaos monkeys will not be released.

He sat up abruptly, the pillows falling away from his face. The nap had, as always, revealed not only the problem but also the answer, and he pawed for the yellow legal pad now, clicking the pen, and writing two words in all capital letters at the top of the page: CREATE ORDER.

And he already knew exactly how to do it.

The simplest way to bind a system is to threaten it.

21.

The black BMW was still in Aubrey's driveway when Rusty approached the house on foot, just after 2 a.m. If the car was there, that meant the big ex-cop-looking guy was still there too. He was in the house, and that made everything more complicated. Part of Rusty had expected the guy to be gone, but another, smarter part of him knew better.

OK. So the guy was still there. Was that a reason to bail on the whole plan, though? No, because it wasn't a plan, he reminded himself. It was a tiny, little unformed scheme that he was noodling around with to see if it would lead to anything.

He didn't *have* to go through with it. He would explore the situation, one step at a time, like a hand of Texas hold 'em, and see how the cards fell. If he got dealt a pair of shit hole cards—if he couldn't get into the house or the money wasn't somewhere he could find it easily—he'd just walk away. There would be numerous chances to get out, he thought, and he was a good-enough poker player to know when the cards demanded that you toss them in and wait for the next opportunity.

In fact, Rusty was the worst kind of poker player, the kind who gives himself credit for skills and wisdom that he does not possess. He was the kind of card player who routinely relied on divine intervention to save his ass; he was a guy who would stay in a hand not just hoping for a queen but hoping for a *red* queen, figuring he was due some good luck. Once an opponent realized that essential truth about him, Rusty was dead. Over the years he'd lost several hundred thousand dollars at poker, a number that was held down only because he didn't have access to more.

Drugs and gambling, Rusty's twin vices, worked in destructive harmony. Either one taken on its own was pricey enough, but putting the two of them together—the clouded judgment of a habitual drug user and the irrational optimism of a compulsive gambler—was like holding a thumb over the end of a money hose.

Rusty needed cash. More than that, his life depended on getting it. Zielinski and Espinoza had made that clear. And there was money here, he could tell. Money that he was probably owed, if he took a minute to try to figure out exactly why and by whom. So he was just going to, you know, *check it out.*

He turned into the driveway and walked softly around to the side of the house, grateful for the light from the dimming green aurorae still visible in the sky. He walked along the narrow strip that bordered the south side of the house, just past the cement apron beneath the kitchen window where he'd hooked up the generator a few days earlier.

The BMW still being there had been a bad deal, but it wasn't enough to make Rusty fold his hand just yet. The true test was the storm-cellar doors. Years ago, when Aubrey's know-it-all brother had deigned to visit their home, he'd told them the flimsy lock on the angled metal doors that led directly into their basement was a security risk and they needed a way to get into the house if they ever lost their keys. Before they even had a chance to agree, Thom went out and bought a biometric lock that must have cost a couple grand—money Rusty and Aubrey really could have used someplace else—and had it installed on the storm doors. It was one of the things Rusty hated about his brother-in-law; he was always buying them things they didn't want, fixing things that weren't broken, instead of just giving them money.

Now, there was only one question. Had Aubrey forgotten to remove Rusty's fingerprint scan from the lock's memory after he moved out?

Rusty edged over to the storm doors. He slid his hand up the vertical line from the bottom, feeling the lip where the doors came together. The flat, square panel of the biometric lock was about three feet up. Rusty took a moment and held his breath. This was the real make-or-break, the flop, the moment when the dealer flipped over the three cards they'd all play from and real betting would begin. If his fingerprint worked and the lock opened, he'd press on, go into the house, and see how long his luck held. But if Aubrey had deleted him, he'd have no choice but to throw in his cards and go home.

He pressed his thumb into the center of the panel.

It lit up green and the lock clicked open.

Rusty was all in.

Inside, he moved quietly across the basement floor, hoping she'd cleaned it up in the years since he'd lived here. It was *black* in the basement, like walking on the bottom of a lake. He slid his feet along on the cheap carpet, figuring that if he kicked something on the floor it was better to nudge it with his toe rather than catch it in full stride. She must have sent a bunch of his old stuff to the dump, because his feet didn't bump anything until he got to the staircase in the middle of the floor.

He crept upstairs, opened the door at the top, and stepped into the back hallway just off the kitchen. He wondered, idly, if at this point his actions qualified as breaking and entering. He hadn't broken anything, he'd just opened a couple doors, but it wasn't his house, and he knew perfectly well he wasn't wanted there. "Unlawful entry," maybe, like that Ray Liotta movie he saw on cable once, but, wait, that guy was a cop and—he stopped, shaking his head at the unwanted thoughts, and tried to center his thinking. This was the sort of undisciplined mental energy that got him in trouble in a card game, spending too much time thinking about what he wanted for dinner or about the tits of the brunette sitting across from him, and losing track of what was out and who had what.

This was a simple plan. Get in the house, see if the money's there, and decide if you can grab it. A one-in-ten shot involving a few simple go-or-no-go decisions along the way. All other thoughts needed to be banished.

He moved slowly across the kitchen floor, trying not to make a sound. When he got to the door on the other side, he caught a glimpse into the living room, which had a greenish glow from the light shining in the window. He'd hoped to see an empty couch and the duffel bag still sitting in the middle of the coffee table but knew that was too much to ask.

He did get the second-best thing, though, which was that the duffel, though not on the table, was still in the living room. He could see the outline of it clearly on the floor beside the couch.

The problem was on the couch itself. The big guy was sleeping there, his arm hanging off the side, and though it wasn't touching the duffel, it might as well have been, his fingertips less than a foot away. Rusty winced, drew a deep breath, and let it out again silently.

This was not a good situation, but it was not an impossible one either. *The bag was there.* Why the bag was still there was another question, but it was irrelevant. The bag of money—and that's what it had to be, he was sure of it—was just ten feet from him, and the guy guarding it was sound asleep.

One tiny adjustment was all that was needed. The couch ran parallel to the wall, about six feet into the living room, and the big guy's head was on the far end, away from the kitchen. If he happened to open his eyes, he'd be looking straight at Rusty. Granted, it was only ten feet from the kitchen doorway to the bag, but that could be a long ten feet, and there was no accounting for the sounds the floorboards might make. Freezing in place was no good if the son of a bitch was going to be looking directly at him.

Simple enough, Rusty thought. He'd go down the short hallway between the kitchen and the front door, re-enter the living room at the other end of the couch, behind the guy's head, and slide the bag out that way. Once he got his fingers on the bag, if worse came to worst, he could just grab it and run, back into the kitchen and out of the house the way he'd gotten in. The big guy wouldn't stand a chance, blundering around in a strange house in total darkness, and he'd be lucky not to run straight into a wall. Rusty would be off, across the basement, out through the storm doors, and into the street before the guy knew what had happened.

The only remaining hitch, of course, was if the bag did not contain cash after all but, instead, the Irish prick's dirty underwear. Rusty had considered and dismissed that—who goes into somebody's house and puts a bag of dirty laundry in the middle of their coffee table?

No. Thom, that smug, entitled asshole, had sent Aubrey a bag of cash to have during the blackout, and he'd sent Paddy McDaniel here to keep an eye on it.

But now the big Mick was asleep, Rusty was wide awake and sober, and this shit was about to get *handled*.

Rusty moved silently down the hallway between the kitchen and front door. It seemed to take forever. Finally, he reached the other end of the living room, the one nearest the front door. He moved slowly, coming around the pillar to where he could see into the room. From this side, he'd be looking over the big guy's head from behind him, and it was just a matter of stealing in, grabbing the bag, and getting the hell out of there.

Except the couch was empty now.

The blanket had been tossed to the side, the pillow had a big melon-size dent in it, and the fucking guy was *gone*.

Rusty stopped, staring for a moment, trying to wrap his head around it, and then heard the click of the gun behind him.

He tried to gasp, but no air came out of his chest. He felt the hard nub of the M&P Scandium, Brady's spare gun, pressing into the base of his skull.

How the hell did he *do* that? The guy was ten feet tall and a thousand pounds—how did he manage to get up, slip into the kitchen, and sneak up behind Rusty without being heard? What kind of scumbag *does* that to a person?

"Raise your arms slowly," Brady said in a quiet voice.

Damn, it was worse than Rusty had even thought, the guy sounded *awake*. Like, not only was he not surprised; he wasn't even asleep. Rusty had been screwed from the moment he walked into the house; he just hadn't known it. He did as he was told, raising his arms 'til his hands were even with his shoulders. He looked down and could see the guy's feet behind him. Fucker even had his *shoes* on.

"Slide your feet forward on the floor, left foot first," Brady whispered.

"Where are we going?" Rusty asked, a bit louder.

"Outside. For a chat. Do not make a sound."

Rusty froze, trying to think.

"Move," Brady said, lifting the barrel of the gun from the back of Rusty's head and tapping it down on the crown of his skull, hard enough to hurt.

Rusty whimpered and moved. He had no plan whatsoever. All the cards were face-up now, and he was looking at garbage, a 2-7 off suit. He'd lost, again, cleaned out, no shot at all. He did as he was told.

When they reached the front door, Brady told him, in that same soft, commanding voice, to unlock and open it. Rusty did. Brady told him to open the screen no more than two feet. Rusty did. Together, they stepped outside, Rusty still with his hands up, staring straight ahead, mindlessly following orders. A beaten dog, once again.

As they stepped outside, he heard the front door close behind them with a click, then the same for the screen. The gun barrel tapped him on the top of his skull again and he winced.

"Could you please fucking stop that?" he said, but he kept moving, no choice but to follow orders at this point. How could he possibly have gone as far as he did with a ridiculously simplistic plan like this? So he was broke, so what? So he owed money and Zielinski might yank one of his teeth, who gives a shit? He had other teeth. Why in Christ's name did he risk everything like this?

"Stop on the grass," Brady said.

Rusty did.

"OK," the big guy told him. "Now we are going to discuss how you will never, *ever* return to this house. Take a step away from me and turn around, slowly."

It was when Rusty started to take an obedient step forward that he saw the lights flash at the corner. It was a sedan, barreling down the cross street at at least sixty miles per hour, with the strobing red lights of a police car just behind it. The fleeing car banged hard on a pothole in the middle of the intersection, scraping and sending sparks flying in all directions.

The next part happened so quickly it was hard for Rusty to remember later, much as he tried. All he knew was that in the moment of the distraction he was stepping away from Brady, hands raised, turning around to face whatever music needed to be faced, and the next second his right hand was stopping at his belt, his fingers closing around the black steel hilt of the fixed-blade Buck GCK hunting knife that hung there, and then he was turning to his left, his hand moving upward, fast.

And then there was the awful slurping sound of the blade finding home in the big guy's abdomen, just beneath his belt line, and the soft, surprised gasp that came from Brady's mouth. His breath, which still smelled faintly of peanut butter, caught Rusty full in the face, and the big man's weight dropped forward. Rusty's reflexes commanded that he catch the guy before he hit the ground, and he did, Brady's full two hundred and some pounds collapsing onto him.

As the fleeing car and the pursuing police vehicle disappeared into the night, intent on one another, Brady and Rusty stood there in the yard for a moment, Brady's mouth opening and closing soundlessly. His eyes swam and then focused on Rusty, confused.

"Terence?" he asked. Then he went into shock.

Rusty's scalp tingled and he felt out of his own body; he could see himself standing there in his ex-wife's front yard, holding up the bleeding body of a guy he'd just stabbed in the gut. He was going to spend the rest of his life in jail.

But then he calmed and forced himself to think. This wasn't over. He hadn't lost. All he needed was for a lifetime of bad luck to turn miraculously at that exact moment, for the gambler's concept of "being due" to prove itself true right when it was needed most.

The first imperative, he knew, was to keep the big guy on his feet. If that 220 pounds went down in the front yard, the game was over. Rusty would never get him back up. He'd be there in the morning, dead from a knife wound, Rusty's knife wound, and there'd be no cleaning *that* mess up.

But if he kept him upright, even just for the ten seconds it might take to reach his car, Rusty still had a chance. He wrapped both arms around the guy, whispering calmly in his ear.

"You're OK, you're OK, hang in there, hang in there."

The words meant nothing, but Rusty hoped that, to a guy who was in shock from a major knife wound, they sounded just reassuring enough to keep him conscious. Rusty brought his left hand back as far as he could and reached into the guy's right front trouser pocket, praying for a bit of luck.

He got it—the keys to the BMW were there. He pulled them out, shifted his grip underneath Brady's armpits, and started backing up across the grass, toward the black car. When they were within a few feet of it, Rusty leaned backwards against the trunk, letting it support both of them for a moment. Brady was rapidly losing consciousness and would soon be dead weight.

Rusty pressed the alarm button on the BMW remote. The doors unlocked with a soft thunk. The lights flashed, but only once, and at 2 a.m. there was no one out to see them. Second piece of good luck: the alarm was not set to chirp.

Rusty threw the car door open, and with one hard twist of his shoulders and hips, he let Brady's weight slide off of him and fall into the back seat. Rusty got behind and shoved him the rest of the way in. He closed the door softly and turned.

Step one was complete. Step two was harder.

He had to go back in the house.

Rusty took a breath and forced his feet to start moving. He hadn't come this far and committed himself this deeply to stop short of his goal. He strode across the yard, opened the front door, crossed the hallway, picked up the duffel bag from the living room, and exited the house again, closing the door softly behind him.

Outside, he retraced his steps across the grass, staring down at it, squinting his eyes in the greenish glow from the sky, looking for blood-stains. He couldn't see any, but that didn't mean they weren't there. On that, he'd have to hope and pray for the best, and he thanked the god-dess of fortune, who usually seemed to hate him, that at least the entire incident had happened over grass, rather than sidewalk. Maybe any blood or footprints would be unnoticeable in the morning.

Rusty kept moving, his plan becoming clearer in his mind.

He came around to the driver's side of the BMW, slipped behind the wheel, and was about to start it when he noticed the EV sticker in the middle of the steering wheel. Another piece of luck: the car was a hybrid and could be started in electric mode. He searched the control panel, found the mode-select button, and made sure it was turned to EV before he started the car. The car turned on, but the gas motor did not fire.

Rusty dropped it in reverse and, silently, the black car glided out of the driveway.

Eight blocks away, Rusty pulled to a stop in a less populated area. While he was trying to work out the next part of his plan, he heard a soft moan from the back seat. His eyes darted up into the rearview and saw a rustle of movement.

Shit. He'd taken for granted Brady would bleed to death; it hadn't occurred to him the guy might recover. Rusty turned, so he could look over the seat, and saw that Brady's eyes were open, his head crammed at an unnatural angle up against the rear driver's-side door. His hands were clutched around the hilt of Rusty's hunting knife, still stuck in his midsection. The fucker was trying to pull it out.

Rusty got out of the car, looked up and down the street in both directions, came around to the rear door, and yanked it open. Brady's head fell out into the open space and he stared at Rusty, blinking. Avoiding Brady's eyes, Rusty leaned in over him, slapped Brady's hands away from the hilt of the knife, pulled it out of the big guy's gut, and stabbed him in the chest.

Rusty repeated the motion four more times, deeper with each thrust, wrenching the knife out of a splintered bone after the last stab. He shoved Brady's head and torso back into the car as far as he could, slammed the rear door on them, and slid back behind the wheel.

East Aurora Medical Center was a massive complex a mile and a half from Cayuga Lane that served three counties. Between staff, patients, and visitors, the main parking garage held seven or eight hundred vehicles on any given day. Rusty cruised, sharklike, through the pitch-black space until he found an empty spot on a crowded floor and backed into it.

He worked quickly, hyper-focused. He popped off the BMW's vehicle ID tag from the front dash, down in the corner where it met the windshield. He pulled off the license plates and dug the wallet and satellite phone out of the dude's pockets. He knew the car could still be identified from the VIN that was etched into the engine block, but really, what were the odds that the cops were going to be trying *that* hard to identify a dead John Doe in the middle of the biggest public emergency the nation had ever seen?

Plus Rusty knew he was on a roll now. Once things started to fall your way, they tended to keep falling your way. This would too. He took the blue duffel bag from the front seat of the car, locked the BMW, chucked the keys into a trash can three levels down, and started the hour-long walk back to his truck.

Halfway there, he got his last and best piece of luck. It started to rain. So much for the bloody grass, Rusty thought. He smiled to himself and shook his head.

After sixteen years of living on Shit Street, Rusty Wheeler had finally drawn a monster hand.

22.

Thom lay in bed, staring up at the ceiling, and counted the minutes. He hadn't wanted to know exactly when it was coming, lest his reaction seem anything less than credible and surprised, but now that he was lying awake at 3:35 a.m., he realized a *window* would have been nice.

He rolled over on his side. Ann-Sophie's cascade of white-blond hair lay across the pillow, visible in the soft blue glow coming from the night-vision light in the bathroom. Thom hated stumbling around in the night; it went back to a fear of sleeping in the dark that he'd developed when he was a teenager, after the accident. For at least a year after it happened, he couldn't close his eyes at night without seeing Kyle Luedtke's face, upside-down, laughing at him. Sleeping with a light on seemed to make it better, if only because when he opened his eyes the light chased the images away. So, at the age of eighteen, a grown-ass man, he'd started going to bed with a night-light again.

Ann-Sophie had been the only one of his girlfriends over the years who'd never questioned it. In the middle of his fumbling cover story the first time she'd spent the night, she'd interrupted him with a shrug and a smile. "It's better that way for some people," she said, and never brought it up again. Sometimes Thom wondered if that was when he fell in love with her. The lust part was easy to pin down; it had come before he'd even met her. He'd seen her picture in a magazine ad and asked to meet her, so obviously the visual portion of his attraction was clear. But the love part, the tenderness, the gratitude, the feeling of being understood by another human being without being questioned—it might have come in that very moment. At the top of his consciousness, he told himself Ann-Sophie understood his aversion to darkness because she was Scandinavian, and light was precious there. But lower down, in the places he didn't go very often, he imagined she probably knew.

Knew what? That he'd gotten away with something and could never, ever be right with it? Maybe. As the years went by and she observed his relationship with Aubrey, Thom wondered if she hadn't intuited that it had something to do with his sister. From there, knowing what she did, it wouldn't have been much of a leap for Ann-Sophie to guess what had really happened. Did his telltale heart beat that loudly? he wondered.

Either way, she'd never said a word, and he loved her for that. He resisted the urge to reach out and stroke her hair now. He didn't want to wake her or have to answer any questions about why he was already awake when—

The gunfire was softer than he'd been expecting. The first few rounds, Thom had to lift his head off the pillow to confirm that he'd actually heard it.

It was louder the second time, two quick series of *brap-brap-braps*, clearly identifiable as an exchange of semiautomatic weapons fire.

Thom sat up abruptly, the reaction coming naturally even though he'd been waiting for it the past two and a half hours. He threw aside the covers and stood, his breath quickening.

Outside, there were two more prolonged bursts of gunfire, but they were still muffled, and goddamn it, why hadn't he considered the thick, soundproof windows of the place? He should have insisted they use higher calibers or something.

Ann-Sophie stirred, not from the noises outside but because she'd been jostled when Thom leapt out of bed.

"What's going on?" she asked, half-asleep.

"I don't know. Stay here!" Thom answered, sounding very much in command. He pulled on a pair of jeans he'd draped over a chair, opened the bedroom door, and hurried down the short hallway into the living room. He went to the big windows, the ones that looked out over the desert expanse to one side, and the concrete guardhouse that was the main entrance to the bunker on the other.

There was another burst of gunfire outside, longer and louder, and this time he could see muzzle flashes. One set of flashes came from far off to his right, twenty or thirty yards down the faux-dirt road that led to the complex, and the other from just below them, near the entrance to the guardhouse.

"We're being attacked!" Thom yelled, and no acting was required at this point. The gunfire, the flashes of light that lit up the surrounding area, the adrenaline in his veins—it was all real. Ann-Sophie jumped out of bed, grabbed her robe, and started to run out toward him.

"Don't come out here!" Thom shouted back. "Get down!"

She did, and almost on cue, there was another round of gunfire outside. Thom noticed the muzzle flashes on the road were drawing closer. He ducked and turned, hissing to Ann-Sophie. "Get the kids and get down to the bunker!"

"What about you?!" she shouted back.

"I'll be right behind you. I need to make sure everything's secure first."

"Thom—"

"*Go!*" he shouted, urgent and convincing.

Ann-Sophie scurried across the floor toward the kids' bedrooms. As she went, Thom stood and turned to look out the window again, assessing the state of things. Just as he reached his full height, he heard the *brap* of another round of semiautomatic weapons fire, followed by a loud thud and a series of interconnected cracks.

Ann-Sophie screamed, Thom shouted, and they both fell backward as the window in front of Thom suddenly bloomed with three side-by-side spiderweb patterns, radiating out directly in front of where he was standing.

"Jesus Christ!" Thom shouted. "What the fuck are they doing?!"

"Get down!" Ann-Sophie shouted. "Get away from there!"

Thom whirled on her, genuinely scared this time, but even angrier than he was frightened. "Get the kids and get to the bunker, right now. I'll handle this."

He turned and went to the door, stepping into a pair of boots. Ann-Sophie shouted after him, but he didn't answer, just headed outside. His behavior seemed to her the height of lunacy, a complete repudiation of all the drills and tiresome conversations they'd had over the years, but there wasn't time to think about it. She ran into the master bedroom, grabbed the nearest clothes she could find, and slipped into them as she stumbled toward the kids' rooms.

Ten minutes later, the A-level residents assembled in the common area on subterranean level four. The place had been modeled on a ski lounge, with two virtual fireplaces, half a dozen comfortable leather sofas, a pool table, a reading corner, and a small kitchen with chunky wooden tables and chairs. The big LED screens placed around the walls like windows had been tuned to alpine vistas, which at this hour meant snowy mountaintops lit by a full moon. There were a dozen people clustered around the room, looking frightened and sleepy. Thom arrived last, having regained his cool, and all heads turned toward him. Chloe was there, bleary and frightened, sitting alone, as well as the Friedmans, Dr. Rahman, and the others, whose names Thom couldn't call to mind immediately. But they all had the desired expression of deep concern on their faces, and he perceived in the room a powerful desire to be led. He was happy to oblige.

"We're fine," he told them. "We're all fine. We were attacked, not sure by who yet, still looking into that, but security was able to repel the assault with no casualties on our side."

Dr. Rahman, who looked more annoyed than anything, spoke first. "Who the hell was it?"

"Who knows?" Thom said. "We might never be certain. Someone who wanted food and water, probably."

"Food and water?" Marques asked. As the pilot and standby driver, he qualified as A-level. Why exactly Beth and Kearie, who were decidedly *not* A-level, had come up here with him was a matter Thom intended to get into later.

"I would imagine," Thom answered him. "What else could it be?"

"What are we—four days into this?" Marques asked.

"Five," Thom replied.

"OK, five. Who attacks an armed installation after five days, looking for food and water?"

"If I was hungry and thirsty, I would," Thom snapped. He turned back to the others, eager to get off this line of questioning from his increasingly insubordinate pilot. "To the matter at hand—is anyone hurt?"

No one was. No one had been above ground.

"Good. All right. Clearly, the situation has deteriorated out in the world, even more rapidly than we assumed it would. I think we need to move things to a more secure footing here. I'd like to propose—"

He stopped, noticing Ann-Sophie was staring at him. Her eyes were slightly narrowed, the way they were when she knew he was up to something but couldn't put her finger on exactly what it was. It was the look she'd given him during the week or so before she'd decided to pay an unscheduled visit to one of his personal training sessions.

Thom forced himself to turn his head away from her. He couldn't imagine what she was thinking, but they had just been attacked, no one could possibly argue with that, and now steps would have to be taken.

Before he could enumerate them, the door to the lounge buzzed and ex-major Jimmy came through. He was sweaty, breathing heavily, and in full battle fatigues. He wore a Kevlar vest and a Ka-Bar knife, and the acrid smell of his recently fired AR-15 practically preceded him into the room. "We all intact down here?" he asked.

There were murmurs of assent and even a few "yes, sirs," people automatically slipping into deference to physical authority. Chloe sat up, moving to one side, making a space beside her, in case Jimmy wanted to sit down. But Jimmy was on duty and stood ramrod-straight.

"Can you illuminate the terrain for us, Jimmy?" Thom asked. He'd managed to get over the rage that had erupted from him five minutes earlier, when he'd come out of the main house ranting and waving his arms, furious with Jimmy for the stray shots that had nearly shattered his living room windows and killed him.

Jimmy had calmed him down after a minute or two—that's three-inch Lexan up there, boss, and you *said* you wanted physical evidence, didn't you?—but for Thom the matter was not settled. He would revisit Jimmy's recklessness later.

"The situation is contained," Jimmy assured the group, "and the assailants have fled. Our lookout in the sniper post watched them retreat through his night vision and reports we wounded two of them."

That was a nice touch, Thom had to admit, a little visual detail to sell the overall picture. Jimmy was a natural.

"Thank you, Jimmy. I'm sure we're all grateful for your efforts, and those of your team." Jimmy nodded and went to Chloe. He bent over, muttering to her and putting a hand on her cheek. *Great*, Thom thought. So that *was* a thing. He couldn't think of why it bothered him, exactly, except that it did. Maybe just because it was more disruption, more unplanned connections and complications. He tried to put it out of his mind and continued to the group.

"We're fine. That's the message here. Our systems worked, and our defenses are strong. But we need to take this for what it is, a wake-up call. We've been extremely lax about our schedules and protocols in these first few days, and I want to say right now, that is *over*. We'll meet about this tomorrow and discuss it in greater detail, but, clearly, we all need to get very, very serious here."

He looked around the room. The Friedmans, who'd been more

temperamental than he'd imagined, were scowling, clearly unhappy with the security arrangements, and perhaps the choice they'd made to get into this community in the first place. But they said nothing. Others looked frightened or suspicious, yet no one was outright disagreeing with him. Good. He continued. "I'd like to start by suggesting that, obviously, the family should move to the underground quarters."

"What family?"

Thom turned, annoyed, to look at the source of the voice. It was Marques. "What?"

"What family? There's a few families here."

"Well, *my* family, obviously."

"Oh, OK," Marques said. "Like, the first family. Like, the president's family." Beside him, Beth put a hand on his arm, silently asking him to stop.

Thom tried to recover. "I'm sorry if that came out wrong. Yes. My family, the only family living above ground. We're moving down here. And there's to be no more outdoor activities without prior—"

"I didn't agree to that."

Thom turned again. Now it was Ann-Sophie.

"Sweetie, we said—"

"No, we didn't say anything," she said. "I don't want to live underground."

"I'm talking about what's reasonable and prudent," Thom said, keeping his voice low.

"Reasonable and prudent would have meant not running outside during gunfire," she said evenly. Eight or nine heads turned away, looked down, or suddenly became interested in the screens of their nonworking cell phones. Mom and Dad were fighting. Dr. Rahman yawned, got up, and headed for the door, walking out on the meeting. Thom noticed he was wearing pajama bottoms and a T-shirt that read, SCIENCE: LIKE MAGIC BUT IT'S REAL. Wonderful.

The image of a rapidly unraveling sweater sleeve flitted through Thom's mind. Mentally, he pulled the loose string and tightened it up again. He turned back to Ann-Sophie. "Darling, can we talk about this later?"

"Why would you do that?" she persisted, pulling the half-sleeping forms of Lukas and Anya closer to her on the sofa. "Run outside and put yourself in danger like that?"

"I was—I wanted to make sure that—" he stammered, unsure where he was going.

"She's right," Jimmy said, firmly. He looked Thom in the eye. "I know the desire to protect your family is powerful and you'd do anything for them, sir, but you've got to leave an open firefight to us. Just let us do our jobs and keep you all alive."

Thom looked at him, grateful, and Ann-Sophie backed off. Marques said nothing more. The flames of suspicion seemed to be doused, at least for the time being.

"All right," Thom said, "I will. Next time, I'll head straight down here."

"Let's hope there isn't a next time," Jimmy replied.

Thom nodded. "That's it for tonight, everybody."

The group dispersed, headed back to their respective quarters.

Thom went to Ann-Sophie, sat down next to her, and stretched out his arms. He wrapped one around each of the kids and pulled the whole family in close. Ann-Sophie, thus encircled, laid her head on his shoulder.

Thom let out a tiny exhale of relief. Aside from a minor deviation, the incident had played out as planned. Order had been restored. The cycle of events would now return to its previous pattern of predictability.

Looking over his shoulder, Ann-Sophie's gaze fell on Marques, Beth, and Kearie. Marques looked at her, and their eyes caught.

Neither looked away.

23.

AURORA

Scott, uncharacteristically, was the first one out of bed. As much as he was thrilled to have Celeste staying in the house with them, her presence did create certain difficulties. Like a lot of teenage boys, Scott was a restless sleeper, accustomed to spreading out, limbs akimbo, over his entire bed. Having to accommodate another person was a new challenge. The two nights they'd spent together the week prior, when Aubrey was out of town, it had been easier to sleep, probably because they were both drunk by the time they closed their eyes. But last night they'd been fully sober, and Scott found Celeste's presence crowding, overly warm, and immensely exciting.

Celeste slept in underwear and a tank top, and the proximity of a nearly naked girl who was interested in cuddling was a distraction Scott found impossible to overcome. Contrary to Aubrey's opinion, they weren't having sex, at least not intercourse, not since their first, awkward attempt at it last week. Both virgins, they'd contented themselves with fooling around for several months. But spending nights in the same bed together left Scott with the unpleasant reality of awakening with a furious erection every few hours. That morning, when he woke at 6 a.m. in his usual discomfort, he'd slipped out of bed, gotten dressed, and gone downstairs.

The chill of the night was still in the house, but the morning was exquisite. Scott couldn't remember the last time he'd seen the sun come up, and so when he saw the light starting to break outside the kitchen windows, he tiptoed down the front hall toward the door to go take a look.

He noticed the empty couch right away. There was something not right about it. The sheet and blanket had been tossed aside and left there, and the pillow too. Brady didn't seem like that kind of a guy; he was a make-your-bed-first type all the way. Maybe he was just in the bathroom.

But, no. The powder room door was half-open, clearly nobody inside. Maybe he'd gone for a walk, Scott thought. Or, more likely, a predawn jog. Yeah, that seemed about right for him.

But the blue duffel bag was gone too. Scott had overheard enough the night before to know it contained cash, and a lot of it. Who takes a big bag of money jogging with them?

Scott opened the front door and went outside. He could see the first rays of light coming through the branches of the trees across the street. As they touched the grass in front of him, it sparkled, heavy and wet from last night's rain. There, he saw a glint so bright he had to blink. A silvery, metallic object was lying in the middle of the front lawn.

The gun was a silver-handled pistol, the kind you had to cock in order to fire, and it looked new and well kept. Scott had handled guns a bit with Rusty, but he'd never liked them much, and had never seen one like this. It looked expensive.

He squatted down over the gun, just staring at it for a moment. He picked up a stick from the nearby grass and, using the thick end of it, flipped the gun over. He looked at the impression it left in the grass. It couldn't have been there very long, maybe just the night.

Scott lifted his gaze and looked around. The BMW was gone from the driveway. He turned and looked back, toward the house. Brady was gone. Not gone on a jog but gone in his car. He'd taken the blue duffel bag with him, and somehow, he'd managed to drop his gun—assuming it was his, but who else's could it be?—on their front lawn in the process.

Put together, it didn't make a great deal of sense. The guy had been in a hurry, obviously, but why?

And somehow, though this *really* made no sense, a thought took up residence in the back of Scott's mind, from which it would never leave.

It occurred to him that his father had something to do with this. He couldn't have said why, but Rusty's presence yesterday, the strange way he'd acted when he left, and his essential *Rusty-ness* made it a possibility he couldn't ignore.

Scott picked up the gun, shoved it into his belt, and went back in the house. He needed to think this through.

An hour later, Aubrey came downstairs and found Scott on the couch, where the blanket and sheet had been neatly folded and stacked on top of the pillow at the far end. She asked about Brady, and he told her. Aubrey was groggy; she'd taken an Ambien and a half the night before, and it took her a while to pull her thoughts together. She and Scott puzzled it through together, searching for any sign of Brady in the house and finding none. Scott didn't mention the gun. Aubrey was anti-gun and would say so, and it was not a conversational opportunity he wanted to give her.

Aubrey was disappointed to hear Brady was gone, and the blue duffel with him. Shortly after retiring the night before, she'd decided to keep the money. Brady's gentle common sense had made it an easy call. She was going to allow her brother to help her for once, and she was going to be grateful. It had not occurred to her that Brady would rise before the sun and leave without saying goodbye, taking the cash with him. She'd never even found out how much it actually was.

It was coming up on 8 a.m. now, not quite seven in Utah, but Thom was an early riser. If she called him maybe he could contact Brady, turn him around, and send him back with the money. It would be mildly embarrassing, but that was a small price to pay for security.

Aubrey dug out the satellite phone and dialed his number. Thom answered on the second ring. She explained the situation.

"I don't understand," Thom said.

"I just hadn't thought things all the way through, that's all. Can you reach him?"

"No. I can't. I tried three or four times last night, and again about fifteen minutes ago. He's not answering."

Aubrey's brow furrowed. "What do you mean he's not answering?"

"He does not pick up his phone. He is avoiding me. And now you're telling me he left without saying anything, and the money is gone?"

"What do you think happened?" she asked.

"I think Brady stole my fucking money is what I think."

"That's not possible. He wouldn't do that."

"Yeah? You know him that well, Aubrey? From your several hours together?"

"You want to tone down the aggression, or am I hanging up?"

"I'm sorry," he said. "I'm under a lot of pressure here."

"I think I do know him a bit, yes. He's a very dignified person. Kind of formal, even. He has rules about things, you can tell."

"Current evidence would suggest those rules were flexible."

"I *offered* him the money. Twice. And he refused it. I told him he could have it; he could have just picked it up and walked away with it, no strings attached, and you never would have known. But he refused. He kept saying he was being well paid for this, and that his mother would know, and—"

"You offered him *my* money?" Thom asked.

"It was about to be mine, wasn't it?"

"You never learned how to accept help. That's your problem."

"Is that what it is? Thank you."

"Yes. It's pride. It's a sin, it's as bad as never *giving* help. You've got no humility, none, zero."

"I think this phone call is over."

"This guy that you liked so much, with the moral code? *He just stole a quarter of a million dollars from me, Aubrey.*"

She paused. "Why in God's name did you send a quarter of a million dollars?"

"I demand that you come here," Thom tried, his tone firm.

She laughed. "Do you?"

"Yes."

"Why?"

"Because you're not safe! And I need to look out for you."

"Since when?"

"Oh, *fuck* you!" he said, but then caught himself. "Wait. I'm sorry." He sounded desperate. "I'm under a lot of stress. We had some trouble here last night."

"You always manage to land on your feet. Good luck, Thom."

She hung up, tossed the phone on the couch, and looked around. She was mildly surprised to see Scott, whom she'd forgotten was still sitting on the other side of the room.

"Wow."

"Give me a minute, OK?" she asked, putting a hand over her eyes.

"Seriously," Scott said. "What the fuck happened to you two?"

He was staring at her openly. Scott had a tendency not to look away from emotion or discomfort; it was one of the things she'd always liked best about him. For a flicker of a moment, Aubrey thought about actually answering his question.

Instead, she covered her eyes again and said nothing.

After a moment, Scott gave up and went back upstairs. She didn't notice when he paused at the couch, taking something from beneath a pillow and concealing it behind him.

When Celeste woke an hour later, Scott was sitting on the far side of the room. He told her what had happened and showed her the gun.

"Are you going to tell Aubrey?" she asked.

"No. She wouldn't want it in the house."

"Is she right about that?"

Scott looked at her, then back down at the gun. "Shit's gonna get worse before it gets better. I'd rather know we have this."

"Have you ever fired one?"

"Plenty of times."

"That specific kind of gun?"

"Mostly shotguns. My dad used to make me go hunting with him, 'til I was about twelve, when I shot this duck and I thought it was dead, but then I heard it flopping around in the skiff and—"

"Scott, that gun you're holding in your hand. Do you know how to fire it?"

"No."

"OK." Celeste thought. "How many shots does it hold?"

"There's a clip."

"Yes, they have clips. How many shots are in the clip?" Scott was shaken, she could see, and she tried not to let irritation show as she walked him through the conversation.

He pressed a button on the side of the gun and the clip popped out. He counted the exposed gold nubs of the bullets.

"Sixteen."

She thought for a moment. "OK. Here's what we'll do. Get Aubrey to let us borrow the car, and we'll drive out to the old dump site. We'll each fire off two rounds, so we know what we're doing, and still have a dozen rounds left. Then we'll agree on a place to hide it, and we'll never bring it up again, unless we need it, which I hope we won't."

Scott looked at her. He knew two things for sure—he was going to marry her one day, and they would definitely need that gun.

In his apartment over the hardware store on Stolp Island, Rusty slept late. He'd been so juiced with success when he'd come home at five-thirty in the morning that it had taken an entire six pack to calm him down. Finally, boozy, bloated, and *unbelievably fucking rich*—the contents of the duffel bag had exceeded his wildest expectations— he'd gone to sleep, making plans for the next day.

First, he'd pay off his debt to Zielinski, who really was a loathsome human being and had made his life extremely stressful for the past six months. That monkey off his back, he'd pick up some choice comestibles, both inhalants and beverages, and have himself a little party, to which he alone would be invited.

Then he'd head over to the Lucky Star, which, as he'd predicted, had so far made a strong and noble commitment to its customers and stayed open, under generator power.

And finally, if he had the energy, he'd see if prostitution was still a viable enterprise in these parts. He imagined it was, what with the end of the world here and all.

Or maybe that one would have to wait 'til the next day. No sense rushing things.

Rusty had money now, and all the time in the world.

Outside Jericho, Thom again watched Ann-Sophie while she slept. She was, after ten years and two children, virtually unchanged since he'd first seen her picture in the magazine. The only difference was that, before, she'd had no opinion about him whatsoever. And today, after a decade of getting to know him, she hated and mistrusted him.

But things were going to get better now. They would move, the four of them, into the tighter, safer quarters in their burrow underground. There were to be no more missing days, no more loosey-goosey stuff, no more mixing at will with whoever they damn well pleased.

They were all in grave danger, and they would come together, coalescing behind the one person who'd seen it all coming, who had planned for and was now executing their future.

They would love him. And if they couldn't do that, they would at least respect him. And if they couldn't manage even that, they were welcome to be afraid of him.

There was nothing, he decided, that he wouldn't do to keep them safe.

Ten miles outside Iowa City, Perry St. John's parents were surprised and delighted to see their only child and welcomed him tearfully. Like everyone, they'd been terrified by the events of the past few days, both by the reality they understood and, more so, by the near-total lack of information about what lay ahead. Perry's radio and the larger, more extensive setup he'd left behind in their basement when he moved out were now vital. What had once been a quirky hobby was suddenly an indispensable resource.

After settling in that first day, Perry ventured out to have a look at the night skies from the West Overlook, high above the Iowa River. It had been a favorite spot of his as a kid, unpopulated and far from the light pollution of the city. But that night, as he sat on the roof of his car and tried to appreciate the heavenly glory, he couldn't help but look down instead.

Black smoke and small blazes dotted the landscape below, some controlled, some not. The occasional gunshot echoed in the cool night air. He could see a faint glow coming from Cedar Rapids, twenty-some miles in the distance. It wasn't the halogen glow of man-made light but, instead, the orange-and-yellow tongues of fires, big enough to be seen here.

Perry tried hard to look up at the wonders above him. But, for the first time in his memory, he was unable to lift his gaze.

The cosmos would always be there. Humanity might be another story.

PART III

BEFORE

24.

Listen:

The morning after Brady was killed, in the brief moment that Aubrey had held Scott's eyes as they sat in the living room of the house, in the fleeting instant in which she'd contemplated telling him what she'd never told anyone before, this was what she'd thought about saying:

"Kyle Luedtke was Thom's best friend in high school and the most beautiful person I'd ever seen in my life. When I was fifteen and a half—I remember it distinctly, because I had taken the written test for my learner's permit a few days before—I took every opportunity I could to hang around with him and Thom. Kyle was seventeen, Thom had just turned eighteen, and they were both graduating seniors, but I was a lowly sophomore. Still, I was pretty cute, if I do say so, and older guys liked me. I'd developed a bit early and always got a lot of attention, so I was used to it and knew how to handle it. It made middle school a drag, because the boys were older than me and it took me a while to catch on to what their looks meant, but it also made me smarter, and better-equipped to deal with that stuff when I got to high school. Some girls don't survive that, but I did.

"I forgot where I was. Oh, right, Kyle Luedtke was beautiful. Oh, my God, he sure was. He was just sort of this perfectly put-together human being, he was maybe five foot ten, had skin that darkened and tanned beautifully, a full head of wavy hair, and the most brilliant white teeth I'd ever seen. For some reason, I was obsessed with his teeth. I don't know, I like teeth, what can I say?

"The thing that everyone knew about him, of course, was that he was a shit. My parents and most other adults loathed him, because he was such an obvious liar and two-faced, and the only times Thom ever got in trouble were when he was with Kyle. But in Thom's case the good-looking smarmy boy wasn't just one of those bad-influence types that you wait for your kid to outgrow; he was an active menace, and a threat to our family's master plan.

"Because Thom was a genius. Everyone knew that. From as far back as I have memories, I remember sitting on the couch, between my parents, while Thom gave 'lectures' to us about meteorology, chemistry, bagpiping, you know, whatever happened to be his fascination that particular week. And he had a *lot* of fascinations, every single one of which my parents allowed and encouraged him to pursue, even if it meant pulling him out of school and taking him somewhere expensive and inconvenient. The Galapagos? No problem. Stanford, for a spring-break program? Absolutely. Looking back, I'm sure it was an incredible drain on their finances and energy, but they never seemed to think twice about it. The schools would get on board with it, too, because it was so obvious to everyone that Thom was this incredibly brilliant kid, and one day we would all be able to bask in the reflected glow of his genius.

"I know this should have made me incredibly jealous and resentful, and I guess maybe at times it did, but since I was younger and it was such a dominant theme in our family life, I just sort of accepted it. There are things you just know as a kid, things that can never be disputed: we love this sports team, Grandpa is a drunk, and Tommy is a genius. None of that can be questioned, and nothing but *nothing* can get in the way of it.

"Which was why Kyle Luedtke was a huge problem and, looking back, probably goes a long way toward explaining my violent, uncontrollable crush on him. He was beautiful *and* he was a danger to Thom's predetermined path to greatness? Sign me up!

"June 2nd of that year was the first really hot day of the summer, and as evening came it turned into one of those bathwater-humid midwestern nights, when you feel drunk just breathing the air. Kyle and Thom were headed out for the night, to the movies on Highway 100 they said, but I knew that was a bunch of bullshit. They were just going out to drive my dad's old Chevy Caprice Classic around town all night. For a teenager in a boring-ass town like this, an available car with a full tank of gas is, as I know you know, the gateway to all evil. Drinking, drugs, sex—there was really nothing that couldn't be done in a moving vehicle at night in the summertime. This, please understand, was not wise. I am not recommending this type of behavior. I am telling you how it was, Scott, and you will no doubt recognize it as how it still is today. But very bad shit was going to go down that night, so please don't romanticize what I'm saying. At all. It is my step-parental duty to tell you that.

"Anyway. I'd had a particularly awful day, full of the sorts of things that normally would be forgotten by the following week, but given the events of that night, I remember every single one in vivid detail. Trust me when I tell you they are all exceptionally boring. Something about so-and-so saying something shitty about me to what's-her-name and bullshit like that. Point is, I was really sad and depressed and had locked myself in my bedroom when I saw Thom and Kyle headed out to the car, and I yelled to them, out the open window, that they should take me with them. Thom didn't even respond, but Kyle stopped, looked up, and said something to Thom, so I knew there was hope.

"Kyle and I had made out before. Twice. Maybe a little grinding. I'm sorry, too much detail? OK, well, we'd made out twice, and he never tried to touch my breasts or anything. OK, I'm *sorry*, Scott, but this is how the story goes and you asked, so do you want to hear it or not? My point is, he was seventeen, I was fifteen, and he'd been sweet and tender with me and never tried anything I didn't want him to. Which only made my crush worse. I remember the second time we made out

I'd tried to push things further than I should have, and he suddenly remembered he had to be somewhere. And he *left*. This guy may have been a liar and a troublemaker, but he knew how to behave himself with someone younger than him. Fine, I was in love with him. Or maybe I just remember it that way. Memories can be fucked sometimes.

"So they let me go with them. And we all three drank and those two smoked weed, and at some point after midnight, somebody had the bright idea that we rock mailboxes. It's sort of an antiquated custom, you may have never heard of it, OK, wait, I can see by the look on your face that you have, so, fine, you know the drill. Find a good-size boulder, not so big that you can't hold it comfortably, then look for a mailbox that's on a long, straight stretch of road, get the car up to at least forty miles an hour, and drop the rock on the mailbox as you go past.

"It's actually way more of a skill than it sounds, particularly if you've been drinking, and those guys were at least seven or eight beers into the night at that point. I'd had maybe two at the most, because I really couldn't handle drinking at that age. That, as they say, is an acquired skill, and as you know I am much more fond of the occasional pharmaceutical than I am a booze buzz. Gives me headaches.

"So we hit some mailboxes. We discovered early on that if you drop the rock from the front seat you are in serious danger of the rock bouncing back into the door or rear quarter panel, so Kyle and I had ended up in the back seat together, taking turns, one of us leaning out the window and dropping the rock while the other held onto you. We were trying to be careful, because you had to get a pretty good lean out the window going in order to get the right angle on the mailbox, and, you know, we didn't want anybody to get hurt or anything.

"I'll skip the next part, because I can see that you're uncomfortable with the realities of teenage hormones and sexual desires, but I guess it can be summed up by saying that I was attempting to misbehave, and Kyle was attempting to not fool around with his best friend's little sister right in front of him while on a vandalism spree. But that happened, and I can't really tell the story without it. My hands were where they should not have been.

"Kyle asked me to stop, but I couldn't tell how much he meant it, and, as I said, I'd had two beers. That was a lot of liquor for me. Kyle, I remember, moved my hand away from him, and shoved me across the back seat. I thought it was pretty funny and, like a kid that doesn't know when to stop a game, which is exactly what I was, I slid right back up against him. And he shoved me back again.

"Thom yelled something at us from the front seat, but I was laughing so hard I couldn't hear him. I sat forward—of course nobody was wearing a seat belt—and I yelled at him to mind his own business, and he yelled back at me, and I called him something awful, and it went back and forth like that for a while. We could really fight in those days. After a bit of that, I sat back, determined to continue this increasingly fun and physical shoving match with Kyle, because I knew I was *safe* with him, you know what I mean? It was the greatest feeling in the world—I could explore things, I could push things, I could take it too far, because I knew I was with someone who would always pull me back before I went over the edge of the cliff. Isn't that sort of exactly the type of person you need to know when you're a teenager?

"But when I turned back, Kyle was gone.

"Like, not in the car anymore. I was alone in the back seat, and the car was moving at fifty miles an hour, and the guy I had just been fooling around with was *gone*.

"I didn't scream, because it was too confusing. One minute he'd been there, I was kissing and touching and shoving him, and the next minute I was alone, the back windows wide open and the balmy summer air whipping around inside the car.

"I shouted to Thom what had happened, but I'm sure I didn't make much sense, I probably just kept yelling 'He's gone!' over and over, and when Thom finally looked into the back seat, he saw the situation for himself. But then I saw something that made me scream and I pointed, and Thom turned, eyes wide, and he saw it too.

"It was Kyle's face, upside down, looking in at us through the windshield. He was on the roof of the car, and he was screaming like a maniac, but there was no question that he was perfectly fine and that he thought this was all perfectly hilarious. That crazy son of a bitch, that *beautiful* son of a bitch, had crawled out the open window, grabbed hold of the cross-country ski rack on the top of my dad's car, and climbed out onto the roof while we were driving at fifty miles an hour.

"I never saw the deer, myself. I was looking at Kyle. But Thom saw it and locked up the brakes. It was, you know, one of those involuntary movements, the kind of reflex your body completes before your brain has a chance to weigh in on things.

"So Thom braked, the car skidded hard, and all at once Kyle was gone again. I can see the image of his face, upside down in the windshield, and then it just kind of . . . wiped away. There was a dark blur as his body flew off the roof and landed in front of the car, then a horrible, kind of muted thud as we hit him.

"And that was it. We killed him.

"Fuck. I'm sorry. I haven't said all that out loud before. Ever, to anyone.

"Give me a second.

"OK. So. The rest. I've thought a lot about why I did what I did next, and Thom and I tried to talk about it a few times after it all happened. But then we stopped bringing it up, because there didn't seem any point in it, and I guess I could never explain it anyway.

"Did I tell the cops I was the one driving because I wanted to save Thom? Because he was already eighteen and drunk, and it would have ruined his life forever? Maybe. Once you dip a toe in the criminal justice system, who knows what'll happen? There's no question it went better for me, at fifteen, than it would have for him, a legal adult who was legally drunk.

"Or did I say it was me because I felt guilty? Because if I hadn't been fucking around in the back seat Kyle never would have had the idea to escape out the window, even as a joke?

"Or did I lie for my brother because our family mythology demanded it? Because Thom was a genius and was going places, and I was a pretty girl who would marry somebody and be fine, and nothing must be allowed to interfere with our destinies?

"I guess, if I had to answer all those questions right now, I would just say, 'Yes.'

"You were right, Scott. My dad died of a broken heart. But you could say my mom did too, because what is cancer if not the body giving up, because it can't take it anymore? Neither one of my parents ever got over what happened, because I think they both suspected the truth about who'd been driving—Thom has always been a terrible liar, still is—and they both just let it all happen anyway. They let a fifteen-year-old girl ruin her life so her brother could go design apps in Silicon Valley.

"I'll say this for my parents, they got me an excellent lawyer. The judge gave me five years' probation for reckless endangerment and driving without a license. I stuck around Aurora and tried to pick up the pieces. I escorted both of my parents out of this world over the next ten years and made a series of very dumb choices in men, culminating in your father, whom I think we can both agree is the dumbest choice anyone could possibly make.

"And my big brother moved away and made four billion dollars, which at some twisted level he probably thinks he owes me. And I admit, I've never gone out of my way to convince him otherwise.

"So, yeah, Scott. You're right. Thom and I have a fucked-up relationship."

That was what Aubrey had thought about saying. But she didn't. She had never told a soul all that, and she never would.

Aubrey took care of everyone.

PART IV

COLLAPSE

25.

AURORA
Four months later

The goats were back, and it was about time. Mrs. Chen had seen them wandering over on Stratton, and she and her boys herded them to Cayuga Lane, where they were sorely needed. The sod had all been turned months ago, the front yards replanted as community fields, but there was a ton of invasive, weedy growth all around the driveways and the edges of the sidewalks. It was coming out of cracks in the road, dripping from the trees, and anywhere else nature had possibly been able to get a toehold.

And then there was the garbage. Store-bought waste had dropped dramatically in the past four months, but food scraps were everywhere, as not everyone on the block was scrupulous about getting their refuse to the compost heap. The goats, about a dozen in all, had broken free of the barriers of a petting zoo about a mile away and had been on a leisurely circuit of the area since that time. No one, it seemed, was too interested in goat meat, and so the animals had come to serve a greater purpose, as agents of community cleanup. They were exceptionally good at their job.

The only problem was keeping them out of the Cayuga crops, which, by late August, were in full, ripe maturity. The neighbors all worked a rotating shift of harvesting schedules and so someone was usually there to keep the animals out of the produce, but the goats were quick and relentless. You couldn't so much as glance away. Someone had to be on the job full-time. Norman Levy, though noticeably slower and frailer than four months ago, seemed to have found a new calling in life, which was goatherd.

He'd started, as was his way, by getting on his radio setup and asking questions. Connecting with a farmer in Sudan, he'd learned a number of valuable tips, and after two or three sessions with the goats, they started behaving exactly as he wanted them to. Throwing rocks to steer their course was a popular method of control, but in the opinion of the Sudanese goat farmer, it tended to make the goats skittish, and therefore slower at their jobs. Using a stick was fine, never to hit the animals—talk about making them jumpy—but instead to lightly tap the ground beside them, ushering them away from the things you didn't want them to eat. By late June, the goats had become accustomed to seeing Norman as their leader, and he found that tapping the stick was no longer even necessary, just carrying a large one was enough to do the job. Norman loved his new profession and always met the return of the goats with joy and enthusiasm.

Scott had gone from avoiding Norman to joining him, helping the old man with the more arduous parts of the physical work and learning everything he could about Norman's radio setup, which had become their only real source of information about the outside world. Aubrey could tell Scott was still leery of spending too much time with Norman, but at least she'd begun to understand why. Norman was going to die at some point, probably soon, and the boy didn't want to suffer another loss. As a result, he wasn't very communicative.

"Talk to me," Norman would implore him. "You've got to talk to people."

"Why?" Scott had asked.

"Because there is nothing more worth doing."

Scott had shrugged and said he'd think about it, and for now he just took quiet pleasure in the work time with the old man. The fields, as a result, were beautifully maintained all around.

The cul-de-sac had been completely transformed. Rock gardens, perennial flowers, shrubs, and any other ornamental horticulture had been stripped out, yard by yard, during the second and third weeks of the blackout. After initially seeking and not finding consensus among the residents, Aubrey and Phil had simply turned their own yards and begun planting. Soon enough, curious neighbors wandered out to see what they were up to, and as food supplies diminished and visits to the government distribution events became more frightening and less productive, every house on the block had eventually signed on.

Now the real problem wasn't animals—they'd fenced adequately— but thieves in the night. The most popular items to steal had been the tomatoes, which had come in first and most bountifully. It was Phil who'd suggested overplanting them and anticipating a certain amount of pilferage, and he'd been right. They were the easiest to spot for ripeness, he'd said, required the least amount of effort to pluck, and a person can only carry so many, especially if you're trying to be sneaky about it. Let's just plant more than we think we need and write the rest off. So they did.

In normal times, mid-August was the season when garden-minded people started pushing their excess produce at each other. By late summer, you usually couldn't give away a cucumber. Not this year. Everything grown was harvested, and everything harvested was eaten, stored, or given to the hungry stragglers who were stopping by the neighborhood in growing numbers. There was not a shred of waste, there couldn't be, and everyone knew perfectly well why without having to say it.

Winter was only three months away.

Aubrey came out of the house around 10 a.m. the morning of August 26th, already exhausted. It was day 137 of the black-sky event, for those who were still counting, but Aubrey had stopped a long time ago. Far more important than numbers was that today was a Thursday.

Mondays and Thursdays were water days, when the City of Aurora would turn the pumps on just after sunup and let them run for about two hours. Aubrey typically spent the entirety of that time in motion, moving between her kitchen sink, the downstairs bathroom, and her basement.

In the kitchen and bathroom, she'd run short lengths of hose from the faucets, which she kept running as long as the water was on, making sure the ends of the hoses stayed in the five-gallon water jugs on the floor. The first few weeks of the drastically limited water schedule had been brutal for everyone on Cayuga. They improvised as best they could to catch the water with hundreds of empty jelly jars, mixing bowls, and full bathtubs, which invariably spilled, sloshed, and ran out too soon. But then Scott and Celeste, on one of their daily foraging trips around the area, had found an abandoned Arrowhead water truck filled with empty jugs. After their initial disappointment, they'd seen the real value—it wasn't in the water they'd hoped would be in the jugs but in the containers themselves. Aubrey, who was water marshal for the block, now owned sixty-two plastic five-gallon jugs that, when full, managed to meet the water needs of the whole cul-de-sac for up to five days at a time.

Back in the kitchen, she topped off and capped a nearly filled bottle, switched the hose to the next empty one, and carried the full jug down to the basement storage area. She put it in its spot with the others along the cool exterior wall of the basement and went back upstairs to get the next one from the bathroom. By staggering their fill times, she could use just about the entire two-hour water supply without a pause or a spill. The killer thing was her arms.

Sixty-two jugs, at about forty pounds each, was over two thousand pounds of water to carry down the stairs, and Aubrey's biceps burned every time she was on duty. Her arms were different, she could tell, but not in the way of the ripped, angry arms of Madonna or Michelle Obama, the kind of arms the world had been telling her she was supposed to want her whole life. These new arms had *strength*. Her whole body had changed in the past four months. It was a body built not so it would look good in a swimsuit but so that it could fulfill a purpose—getting things done. She'd lost weight, didn't know how much, and didn't particularly care. All that mattered was that she felt in the best mental and physical shape of her life.

Running out of medications had helped. She and Scott had finished off the painkillers within days of the power going out, and Aubrey had toggled between Ativan and Ambien for the first few weeks after that. But then she started to run low and knew she'd be unable to refill them—pharmacies had limited hours, were under heavy guard, and filled only prescriptions deemed essential. So she'd decided to kill the suspense one night, to stop the countdown by flushing the rest of her pill supplies down the toilet. Of course, she'd forgotten the water pumps weren't on at that hour, and in the humiliating moment when she'd dropped to her knees and attempted to fish the soggy pills out of the dirty toilet water, she'd realized this was about as low as she cared to sink, pharmaceutically speaking. She left the pills there to dissolve and hadn't thought about them since.

The water stayed on for close to three hours that morning, and once she ran out of plastic jugs Aubrey ran around the house like in the early days, filling whatever containers were handy. She even stopped up the bathtubs and let them fill to the rims. Not for pathetic sessions where she, Scott, and Celeste would fill cups and drink from them morosely, staring at each other in the waning light, as they had at first, but this time for actual *baths*. They wouldn't be hot-water baths—the water heater hadn't worked since April—but it felt like it was going to hit ninety degrees outside again today, and if she left the blinds open in the bathroom and kept the door shut, she thought the water in the tub might creep up to the mid-seventies by late afternoon. The day was off to a good start.

Her morning chores done, Aubrey went outside. She looked up and down the block, which was busy with the early shift. Mrs. Chen and the boys were in the zucchini patch, Derek and Janelle had drawn the hard work of picking the cabbage worms from the cauliflower and blanching every head to protect it from the sun, and the Sunderlands were turning and harvesting the orange watermelons, which were, as Phil promised, the sweetest fruit Aubrey had ever tasted in her life.

She blinked and rubbed her eyes, stung by the acrid haze of cooking smoke, which had become a permanent feature of the atmosphere. Natural-gas service had come and gone since it first went out in late May, but unlike the water there was never any telling when it would be on. They'd tried various pit ovens and solar ovens, but none of them worked nearly so well as an old-fashioned campfire, so cooking fires dotted the whole of the city every night. It was a shame, Aubrey thought, because the skies for the first month of the event had been the clearest and cleanest she'd ever seen in Aurora. But uncooked food for every meal was more than any of them could bear.

Wincing, she squinted across the street and saw Norman, walking among his goats like Moses. "What do you hear, Norman?" she asked.

"Promising news from the hinterlands," Norman called back, which in no way meant there was promising news from anywhere. It was just what he always said. How an eighty-eight-year-old man who'd begun his life fleeing Nazi Germany with his parents and was ending it in a global blackout managed to have an optimistic viewpoint about anything was beyond Aubrey, but that was what made Norman Norman.

"Yeah? Like what?" she replied, reaching the far side of the street and stopping to pet one of the goats. It was the black one, her favorite, the one who always seemed like he was trying to cut in line in front of you. He didn't know where he had to be; he just knew he had to get there before you did.

Norman knew better by now than to give bad news. In the early months, he'd talked a lot about death counts and food riots in various eastern cities, but he soon realized he was doing nothing but depressing the shit out of his neighbors. It didn't matter, anyway, at least not to them. The news needed to be either local or upbeat. Nothing else was useful or welcome.

"My former student in Bethesda, you know, the one who was with NOAA?"

"Perry something, right?"

"Highest marks for memory." He paused, taking a breath. Norman's breathing was more labored lately, and she knew to just wait in the moments when he struggled. He continued. "Perry's outside Iowa City now, at his parents' place for the past few months. He's got the hand-cranked 32G Brennan shortwave, very spicy little piece of equipment."

"What did he say, Norman?"

"As of last night, Perry reports they've had two separate instances of intermittent power there."

Aubrey looked at him, stunned. "You're kidding."

"I kid about funny things, not this."

"How long did they last?"

"Less than a minute. If that. Perry said it was the rough equivalent of a six-month-old baby suddenly finding himself standing up, realizing he has no business doing that yet, and collapsing right back onto his ass. But it happened."

"I won't get my hopes up," Aubrey said, continuing on toward Phil's house.

"Never understood that expression," Norman said after her. "What else do we have except hope, and the capacity to wait? Only things that separate us from the goats."

"That's insightful."

Norman shrugged. "Dumas. Not me."

Aubrey smiled back over her shoulder at him and walked down the narrow path in front of Phil's house, between the tightly packed rows of edamame, fava, lima, and snap beans. She climbed the steps, opened his front door without knocking, and went inside.

She looked around the room, which was mostly closed off against the sun, since Phil's front windows faced south. There were shafts of light coming through the slats of the blinds though, illuminating the dust that floated in the air. Phil didn't keep a very tidy house, but he could be forgiven that. None of them did, not anymore. There was too much other work to be done.

"Phil?"

She didn't hear an answer, but some clunking sounds came from the basement, and she walked over to the open doorway and looked down the stairs. She could see him down there, working at the canning station they'd built where his hydroponic beds had once been. He was lost in work, and hadn't heard her come in, so she modulated her voice, careful not to scare him. Phil could spook easily.

"I don't have all day, mister."

Phil turned, looked up at her, and smiled. She put her hands on her hips and stared down at him, feigning impatience.

"I'm quite sure I don't know what you're talking about," he said, but Phil wasn't a very good actor, and he knew exactly what she meant. Aubrey turned and walked off. Phil came up the stairs and followed her, as she knew he would.

Phil had a poster of Yoda over his bed, which at first had been a bit of a turnoff, until Aubrey realized that of *course* Phil had a poster of Yoda over his bed. Anything else would have been un-Phil-like. She'd tried to convince him that, perhaps, having the line "There is no try, only do" over one's *bed* carried certain other connotations and perhaps suggested just a hint of erectile disfunction, but that had only made him like the poster more.

She pulled her shirt off as she came into the room, tossed it over the chair, and unsnapped her bra. Phil watched from the doorway as she unbuckled her shorts and pushed them off. Naked, she moved toward the bed and stopped, realizing he was staring at her. She feigned offense. "Uh, excuse me, sir, can I help you?"

Phil shook his head. "What do you think, I'm some kind of machine? That you can just come over here and demand sex anytime you want?"

"Yes." She pulled back the covers on the unmade bed and lay down.

"Yeah, you're probably right." He slipped out of his clothes and joined her on the bed. Aubrey wasn't the only one who had lost weight, and Phil didn't so much take his pants off as undo his belt and release them, to fall to the floor.

"I've been doing water jugs all morning. I kinda stink," Aubrey said as he slid up beside her.

"Once again, you are the most romantic person I've ever met," he said, kissing her neck.

She rolled toward him, reaching down to his crotch. If Phil had ever had a problem in bed, it wasn't an issue anymore. He hadn't smoked pot, to her knowledge, since his supply had run out in late June, and she could tell the difference.

She moved on top of him.

An hour later, Aubrey came back out on the street. Scott and Celeste had, as usual, spent the morning foraging in the surrounding area. Today's emphasis had been on firewood. Buddy Lomax's open-bed pickup, which they all took turns using for wood collection, was parked in the middle of the block, and residents were busy unloading. The few wooded lots around Aurora had given up their supplies early on in the event, and Phil had pointed out that moving into the parks was difficult and relatively fruitless—the trees there were healthy and green. They'd be an enormous amount of work to bring down, even with chain saws, and their sap-filled wood wasn't likely to burn well anyway.

Cannibalizing the abandoned house on Sycamore was Celeste's idea. It was an old two-story on a tiny lot whose owners had defaulted on the loan, and the bank had been unable to resell it after the real estate crash of 2008. It had sat, derelict, for the past dozen years, and had fallen into such disrepair that even the COVID-based buying boom was unable to move it off the market. Since it was bank-owned and needed to come down eventually, Celeste had pointed out, why shouldn't they help things along a bit? Take it apart, pieces at a time, until there's nothing left that can be burned. The idea had worked like a charm, and when the skeleton of the house stopped giving up burnable fuel, in late July, the young couple had just cruised around until they found another house in similar disrepair.

It wasn't the only good idea Celeste had come up with. Aubrey had decided that the initial impression Celeste gave, that of a slightly beaten dog, was either an act or a bad habit or both, because it bore no relation to the actual young woman she'd come to know. Celeste had ingenuity, guile, and reserves of strength that were sometimes almost frightening to Aubrey. Whatever she'd been through at home—and Aubrey knew better than to ask—it had put steel in her spine. She was a survivor and knew how to make difficult decisions. Tearing down houses she didn't own was only one of her suggestions, and if there was a community strategy meeting, it was usually Celeste who would propose taking a step the rest of them weren't entirely comfortable with. Like when she said they should loot the Best Buy, even though all its goods would be useless, and in fact *because* all its goods would be useless—they'd have the place to themselves and could stock up for the day when the power came back on, ready to cash in. The others had demurred on that one, and Celeste had just shrugged. She had more where that came from, and she was happy to wait.

Today, though, as Aubrey came out of Phil's house and went to the truck, Celeste looked rattled, more like the wild-eyed young thing that had shown up at her house back in April. Scott had an arm around her shoulders and was holding her tightly.

"What's going on?" Aubrey asked.

Celeste turned away, now attracting attention she didn't want. Aubrey saw her wipe a few tears from her eyes, more in irritation than sadness.

"It's OK," Scott said. "Just a little run-in, that's all."

"With who?"

"It doesn't matter. She's—"

She took a step around him, to see Celeste directly. "Celeste, what's up?"

"I'm fine."

"Where did you have a run-in? At the firewood house?"

"Yeah. There were more people there this time. It's happened before, usually we all just agree on parts of the house and divide it up and leave each other alone, but I noticed somebody kept staring at me. He kept looking away whenever I turned—" She stopped, shaking her head.

Scott was unable to contain himself any longer. "It was Rusty."

"What?"

"He tried to grab her," Scott said. "I was around the back, and I heard her screaming, and when I came running that fucking asshole had his hand on the back of her neck and he was dragging her toward his car."

"What? What happened?" It was Phil, who'd come outside and overheard the last bit. Norman and one or two others were joining the conversation now too, exactly what Celeste had been trying to avoid.

"Rusty tried to *kidnap* you?" Aubrey asked.

Celeste straightened, getting angry. "Could everybody just stop? I'm fine. He kept saying something about my dad, and that he was taking me home."

"I'm going to kill him," Scott said. "I am literally going to go back over there and kill him."

Aubrey held a hand out, trying to keep him calm while she talked to Celeste. "Why does Rusty care if you go home or not?"

"He doesn't," Scott said. "He's just trying to get in good with her dad. They have a very sick relationship, drugs and scams and shit like that. Rusty's always sucking up to him."

"My dad's an asshole and a criminal," Celeste said. "He can't stand that I left, he can't take it if anybody gets away from him, and he's probably been pissed off about it since the day I got here."

"How'd you stop Rusty?" Aubrey asked.

Celeste shrugged. "I stomped on his foot, elbowed him in the balls, then turned around and punched him in the throat."

There was a moment of silence as the others digested that summary.

"Where'd you learn that?" Aubrey asked.

"YouTube." She looked around. They were all staring at her. "What? That's what we're supposed to do. Right?"

"Yes," Aubrey said. "It's exactly what you're supposed to do."

"So maybe everybody could stop staring at me?"

They did. Aubrey turned to Scott. "What about you? What were you doing?"

"Watching her in awe."

"OK. Do you guys think anybody followed you back here?"

"No," Scott said. "Rusty was on his hands and knees barfing, I don't think he followed anybody anywhere."

"OK." She looked at the open end of the block, where Cayuga met the cross street. The two SUVs they kept parked nose to nose there had been moved back into place after Scott and Celeste had returned in the pickup. The Witzky brothers were sitting in the beds of the trucks on folding lawn chairs, taking their turns on guard duty. "Let's move another row of cars out, and maybe the Witzkys can stay out there after dusk for a few hours. Just to make sure."

"He's not coming," Celeste said. "My dad's not coming here." She shook her head, but it felt like a gesture that was more to convince herself than anyone else.

At sunset, after Aubrey had made sure Frank and Johnny Witzky were still in their lawn chairs at the end of the cul-de-sac with their twelve-gauges across their laps, she hurried home. She was eager to get to the upstairs bathroom before the sun went off the window.

Opening the door, she was happy to find the room had retained an intense amount of heat from the late-afternoon sunlight. With the window shut and the door closed, it had approached sauna-like temperatures, and as she ran a hand through the water in the tub, she thought it was easily over eighty degrees.

She undressed, feeling a twinge in her right calf, which had slipped on a step to the basement while carrying one of the water jugs earlier. She thought that, if she could find a Ziploc bag later that was near enough to the end of its life cycle, she'd make a gel pack with rubbing alcohol and water and see if it helped. It usually did.

Aubrey stepped into the tub, settled back, and closed her eyes. Downstairs, she could hear Scott noodling on the piano. Sounded like a show tune of some kind, mournful and melodic. She hadn't heard him practice this one before. It must have been something new he'd picked up from the neighbor over on Third. After years of trying and failing to get him to practice the piano, Scott's overwhelming boredom had finally won the battle for her. He'd gone door to door around the neighborhood in late June, asking if anyone knew how to play the piano and if they might be interested in teaching him. Mrs. Papadopoulos, nearing eighty and alone, had been happy to oblige.

Aubrey's breathing became regular as she listened to the music drifting up the open stairwell. She was tired and satisfied. She'd harvested three hundred gallons of water. She'd had satisfying sex with Phil, who in the past few months had revealed himself to be much more substantial than she'd ever thought. She'd been given a sliver of hope by Norman, though she refused to let herself dwell on it. And the neighbors had come together to protect Celeste, who'd shown every sign of not needing protection at all.

The kid had even punched Aubrey's ex-husband in the throat.

It was, Aubrey thought, a nearly perfect day.

26.

Thom sat on the edge of the bed, staring down into the drawer, and wondered if Ann-Sophie expected him to take his glasses too. There were eleven pairs of them, after all; the felt-lined drawer had been custom-built to hold them, and the cases had long since been thrown away. It wasn't as if he could just bring the nightstand with him, either. It had been molded into the wall in their bedroom. What was he supposed to do, throw a dozen pairs of thousand-dollar eyeglasses into a brown paper bag and take them downstairs? That would be a little ridiculous, wouldn't it? Then again, the whole situation was ridiculous. Did his things really bother her *that* much, that she couldn't bear to lay eyes upon them, even by accident?

Thom had never been thrown out of anything in his life, and, he quickly reminded himself, he wasn't being thrown out now. No, no, not at all. He'd been politely asked to leave, and, by mutual consent, he and Ann-Sophie had agreed his departure from the big house was for the best. They'd returned to it back in April, after only a week in the subterranean apartment following the "attack" on Sanctuary. Thom's nightmare scenarios about the risks of the outside world did nothing to persuade his wife and children, and the truth was, he missed the space, light, and creature comforts of the big house above ground anyway. So he had graciously acceded to their request, and they'd all moved back upstairs.

The problem was his wife hadn't really wanted him to join them. Her behavior deteriorated over the subsequent weeks; she stopped speaking to him or feeling any responsibility to account for her whereabouts, even overnight. By mid May, Thom found himself neatly rotated back to the underground bunker. Alone, this time. Ann-Sophie had insisted it was for a "cooling-off period," a time for them to give each other some space before coming back together to work on the relationship, but Thom wondered if this hadn't been her plan all along and she'd simply maneuvered him, in her passive-aggressive way, back into the basement so she could have the house to herself.

Things got worse in the weeks that followed. The whole equilibrium of the community, such as it was, seemed thrown off by the change in domestic circumstances of the First Family. It wasn't as though it could be kept secret in such tight quarters, and Thom had gone from acting as though it were all perfectly normal, at first, to shooting harsh glares at anyone who looked at him askance when he got in the elevator to go down to his apartment alone.

By the sixth week of the event, defections had begun to pick up. Over the course of two months, the community lost two of the custodial staff, the nutritionist, Dr. Rahman, and, most painfully, the married chefs, the Friedmans. None of them had bothered to go to Thom to explain their reasons for leaving or ask permission; they just got in their cars one day and drove away.

Worse, some of them had returned within a week, apparently finding the outside world unappealing, and they brought family members with them.

These days, Thom never knew who was there, who was gone, or who half the people he saw on the property over the course of any given day were. He might as well have been living in a hotel. Routines were abandoned, rules were forgotten, and there was no hierarchy whatsoever. Or, if there was, Thom knew for goddamn sure he wasn't at the top of it.

That had been evident a few weeks earlier, when Jimmy and the other three militia members, their sole protection out here in the middle of nowhere, came to see him one Friday morning and "resigned." Their much-less-than-believable reason for having to slink away in shame was their own "inexcusable lapse in security:" they claimed masked marauders had broken into the facility in the middle of the night, found the interlocking vault rooms on sub-level twelve, and drilled open enough safety-deposit boxes to steal $3 million in cash. Yeah, right.

Thom assumed Jimmy had been planning the heist for some time. Unable to come up with a convincing cover story, it seemed the ex-major had decided on just looking his boss in the eye and telling him an almost laughable lie. His expression practically dared Thom to question him, and Thom did not accept the dare.

Jimmy and his men left, presumably taking the $3 million with them. Thom comforted himself with the knowledge that they hadn't managed to get into the subsequent rooms and steal the other $12 million, but, really, who gave a shit? He'd been robbed, by his own people, and they didn't care if he knew it or not. Chloe, unsurprisingly, went with Jimmy. So much for yoga sessions, decent haircuts, and what was left of Thom's faith in the durability of a personal-services contract. Nobody seemed to give a shit about anything anymore.

And now here he was, finding a new low point once again. Ann-Sophie had gone downstairs to see him that morning and, silly him, his heart had skipped a beat when he opened the door and saw that it was her. Maybe this was the start of the reconciliation he'd been hoping for. But, no, far from it. She was there to ask him to come upstairs and get the rest of his shit. Why this was a sudden and timely issue was beyond him, but he had sullenly agreed, and so here he was.

Fuck the eyeglasses. He decided to leave them exactly where they were. He slammed the drawer of the nightstand, grabbed the big suitcase that contained as many of his things as he cared to pack up, and headed for the door.

Halfway down the short hallway to the elevator, he stopped in his tracks. There was someone else at the other end of the corridor, someone who'd just gotten off the elevator and was walking this way, also with a suitcase in hand.

Marques.

He looked like the mirror image of Thom, one of them coming and the other going, two men of about the same age, carrying their things in a bag, one moving out and the other—what, *moving in?*

Thom turned his head, like the RCA dog, trying to understand the strange image at the other end of the hallway.

"Shit," Marques said.

"What the fuck?" Thom asked.

Marques sighed. He set his black canvas suitcase down gently and drew himself up to his full height.

"Awkward conversation we're about to have, boss."

"Awkward conver— What the fuck are you talking about, Marques? What are you doing? What is that next to you? What the fuck is going on?"

Thom had been proud of the fact that, other than a few days back when it had all started, he'd stopped tracking Ann-Sophie's movements on the surveillance monitors in the communication room. Somehow, he had even convinced himself that he'd been wrong about it all, that she *wasn't* sleeping with Marques, that she never had been, and the days and nights when she was gone had been mental health breaks, a case of her giving herself some needed space so that she could then devote time and energy to repair the marriage and *oh, fuck her, she's been screwing my pilot the whole goddamn time.* That's why she wanted his stuff out, to make room for Marques's goddamn epaulets.

"Obviously, I was under the impression you weren't here right now," Marques said calmly.

"'Obviously, I was under the impression you weren't here,'" Thom said, automatically, in a pinched, high-pitched voice. His own ears couldn't believe what had just come out of his mouth. He had imitated Marques in the exact manner of a fifth grader.

"I'll come back later," Marques said. He picked up his suitcase and turned.

"Don't bother," Thom said. "It's all yours. *She's* all yours. Good fucking luck." He picked up his own suitcase and felt a tiny muscle in his back give way. That's what fucking happens when you can't do fucking yoga, he thought. It hurt a little but enraged him a lot, so with a roar of anger, he lifted his half-zipped suitcase with both hands and slammed it against the wall. Unsatisfied, he slammed it again, and again, and continued to do so until it sprayed clothes and books and toiletries in all directions. With a final scream of rage, he hurled the empty suitcase at Marques, who ducked it.

Thom turned on his heel and walked back the other way, into the house again and out the front door. His dentist, his pilot, his yoga teacher, and now his goddamn wife. Who the fuck *else* was going to disappoint him?

He didn't know where he was going, but he sure as fuck was going *somewhere*, at least for a few hours. In front of the main building, he went to the untended guardhouse and banged through the unlocked door. The key box was hanging open like at a bad valet stand, and he ran his hands over the keys, looking for anything fast and loud. The key fobs were all basically identical, so he grabbed the first one his fingers closed around and stormed outside with it.

He walked down the row of cars just behind the fence line, pressing the button on the badass-looking black remote. He was hoping for one of the Jeep Wranglers or Toyota Landcruisers, but instead the lights flashed on a silver Volvo XC60 sport wagon. Jesus Christ, I'm not fucking storming off into the desert in a rage in a goddamn *Volvo*, he thought, and turned back to get a different set.

As he turned, though, he saw Ann-Sophie coming out of the main house, calling to him, Marques just behind her, and *that* was a scene he had no intention of playing anytime soon. His humiliation was complete enough already without her sympathy and under-fucking-standing. God in heaven, one fucking blowjob from my trainer, and I've been paying for it ever since. OK, not one, but whatever.

He got in the Volvo, started it up, and roared, to the best of the electric battery's ability, the hell out of Sanctuary.

27.

STOLP ISLAND, AURORA

Rusty screamed, his knuckle snapped, and his left pinkie finger pointed straight up into the air. He looked up in shock at Espinoza, whose clammy hand had made the break in one clean, sharp move. Espinoza winced in sympathy and took a step back from the table.

"Don't look at me like that, Rusty. You know I hate this shit."

"Through the nose," Zielinski advised, sitting in the chair across from Rusty, legs crossed, fanning himself with his white straw summer hat. "Breathe through your nose, nice and slow. It'll help."

Zielinski, once dapper, was a dishwater-gray copy of his former self. Four months ago, he'd prided himself on the crisp, clean white of his shirts; now they were dingy and unpressed. It bothered him.

Rusty picked up his hand and looked at it, horrified, tears rolling down his cheek. His balls and throat still throbbed from where Zielinski's bitch daughter had attacked him that afternoon, and now his finger was sticking up from his hand at a hideous, unnatural angle. If his stomach wasn't already empty, he would have vomited.

He turned, sucking air in and out through his nose as told, and looked out the open window of his hotbox apartment.

Stolp Island had deteriorated sharply in the four months the power had been out. The tiny downtown apartments were always over-crowded, stores and services were hard to find even in good times, and the homeless or drug-addicted population had already been an intrac-table problem. But now, it was like something out of a zombie movie. The water-pumping schedule was more erratic than in the higher-tax parts of the city, to the point that residents here had pretty much given up on water for any purpose other than drinking. Dumping fresh water into the toilets to make them work seemed a hideous waste, so most people resorted to throwing buckets of human waste out their open windows.

The streets, therefore, reeked at all times. No one went out with-out a mouth and nose covering that had been heavily doused with any kind of scent, even if it was unpleasant. Pets had been abandoned since week three, and skeletal dogs ran through the streets, scavenging from the piles of stinking garbage. The lucky ones were able to revert to some form of predatory pack behavior, and in the hours just after dusk, the high-pitched screams of unlucky housecats in their death throes echoed off the stone walls of the old buildings.

Even the Lucky Star had surrendered, boarding up its doors and windows after six weeks of intrepid, gas-guzzling service to the gaming community.

Rusty turned, the pain subsiding somewhat, and looked at Zielinski, his eyes pleading. "Why are you doing this to me?" he whined.

"*Why?* I don't fucking know *why*. Why did the power go out, Rusty?"

"The thing from the sun?" Rusty asked. He wanted to understand but truly didn't.

Zielinski shook his head, impatient. "I wasn't actually asking. I know why the power went out. Look, your thinking is wrong. You're thinking like it's last year, but it isn't, Rusty. It's this year. You gotta hurry up and get your head around that." Zielinski leaned in, a born explainer. "See, last year, things made sense. Last year, you walked into the gro-cery store, you paid a fair price, and you came out with your dinner. This year, you beg somebody to sell you a week's worth of groceries for a thousand dollars. If you're lucky, they say yes, and you eat. If you're not, they beat you to death, *take* your money, and *they* eat. There's no cops to call, there's no phone to call them on. And if you do see a cop and manage to flag him down, what happens?"

He turned to Espinoza. "What happened to that lady on Elmhurst? That cop she let in her house?"

"Raped her and killed her."

"He raped her and killed her," Zielinski repeated. "So they say. Broad daylight, in her own house. Is it true? I don't fucking know. Nobody knows. Nobody knows *anything* anymore, except that you never walk too close to an apartment building, unless you want to get a bucket of shit dumped on your head. And that if the Illinois Guard rolls up on your block for a few days you better keep your head down and keep walking so you don't get shot in the face." He gestured to his left—"*Last*-year thinking"—and to his right—"*This*-year thinking. You get it? You see the difference?"

Rusty held his throbbing hand, choking back tears. "We were partners. I treated you decent. Always. I tried to bring Celeste back home, didn't I?"

Zielinski sat forward, livid. "Did I ask you to do that? Did I? No, I did not! I did not ask you to interfere in my family. *Never once* did I ask that. All you did, Rusty, was fucking *remind* me of you. I told you exactly what I wanted a week ago, and you have *not done what I asked*."

Rusty drew in his breath, shaky, and tried not to sob. "I paid you back. I don't deserve this."

"Me neither!" Zielinski shouted. He took a breath, calming himself. "I followed the rules. Most of 'em. I buy and sell things; I don't kill people. We used to all get to live that way. Now we don't have that luxury."

"What did I do wrong?" Rusty asked, plaintive.

"You had money. That's what you did wrong. You had a *lot* of money, Rusty, a quarter of a mil, and you flashed it around at the Star and you let me see it. I watched you piss huge amounts of it away. And what did I do?"

Rusty just looked at him.

"No, this time it's an actual question. What did I do?"

"You took it from me."

"Yes! I took it from you, before you could lose the rest of it. I took it because I am stronger than you. Don't look for morality here. I took it from you, and I ate. And my wife and my four kids ate, and Espinoza's family ate. And now it's gone, and we're hungry again. But you had that money once, and that means you can get more. I don't know exactly where you got it, but I got a pretty good guess. Everybody knows about your brother-in-law."

"He's not my brother-in-law."

"Well, he sure the fuck used to be."

"I haven't talked to him in years."

"Then he'll be happy to hear from you."

"I don't have a phone. There's no phones."

"I bet you'll figure it out. See, I think you're a smart guy, Rusty. Your problem is nobody ever counted on you to be smart. To figure things out. I'm counting on you."

"I'm telling you, Z, there's no way to—"

Zielinski gestured to Espinoza, turned to look out the window, and listened to the sharp crack of Rusty's other pinkie finger as Espinoza broke that one too. Rusty screamed, a thin, high-pitched shriek that bounced off the walls of the dirty room. Zielinski turned back.

"Please stop screaming." He waited. After a bit, Rusty's screams turned to whimpers, and Zielinski continued. "Do you know how much of the earth had electric power before this happened?"

Rusty shook his head no.

"Eighty-seven percent. I remember it from the Discovery Channel. That means seven billion people have never lived any other way except with electricity. Neither have their parents, their grandparents, or their great-grandparents. And then, whoosh—it's gone. All gone. And nobody knows shit about how to live without it. So what have a lot of us been doing?"

Rusty shrugged. He'd given up.

"*Dying*, that's what they're doing. But that's not going to be me, my friend." He stood up and put a hand on Rusty's shoulder. "Put your hands on the table."

Rusty, cradling both hands in front of him, shook his head, fearing whatever torture was about to come next.

"Put your hands on the table. I'm not going to fuck with you."

Quivering, Rusty laid his palms on the table. Both pinkies stuck up at grotesque angles.

Zielinski tried not to laugh. "You gotta admit, that looks pretty comical." He went to the far side of the room, searching the shelves. "Do you own a book, Rusty?"

"A what?"

"Yeah, that's what I thought. Nothing. Look at this. Look at these shelves."

"Here's one." Espinoza had ducked his head into the bathroom and came out with a large hardbound *Guinness Book of World Records* from 2004.

Rusty started to hyperventilate. Zielinski waved him off, irritated. "Don't be a baby. What are you gonna do, walk around with your hands like that? Like you think you're at some kind of fucking tea party or something?"

He nodded to Espinoza, who came around behind Rusty, bent over, and wrapped a bearlike arm around his torso, holding his arms in place. The big man averted his eyes.

Zielinski raised the book high over his head and smacked it down on Rusty's right hand. Rusty screamed, Zielinski lifted the book, and slammed it down on the other hand.

He tossed it aside and stepped back, admiring his work while Rusty howled in pain.

"See? I fixed you."

Rusty looked down through watery eyes. His pinkies had been broken in new places, more or less straightening them out. He lifted his gnarled hands and pulled them close to his belly, moaning in pain.

"His phone," he moaned, almost to himself.

Zielinski looked at Espinoza, questioning. He looked back at Rusty. "Whose phone?"

"The Irish prick. I got his phone."

Zielinski smiled. "I don't know what that means," he said, "but it sounds like this-year thinking."

28.

Eight or ten miles west of Sanctuary, Thom was just about ready to turn the Volvo around, head back, and say some scathing shit to certain people when he felt the bulky satellite phone buzzing in his pocket. He pulled over and looked at the screen.

Brady?

Brady was picking *now*, of all possible moments, to resurface? After four months, and with a lame-ass explanation of his whereabouts and what had happened to the quarter of a million dollars meant for Aubrey? Sure, why not? Why not today, why not Brady too, why not just pile everything on top of me and light me on fire?

He pressed the green button and put the phone to his ear. "I can't wait to hear this."

"Tommmmy," said the voice from the other end.

Thom hadn't heard Rusty's voice for five years, but there was no mistaking the midwestern twang and the slightly mocking, above-it-all tone that he'd always used with Thom.

"Hello?" Thom said, to buy a little time while he tried to think this through. His ex-brother-in-law, calling on Brady's phone?

"Yeah, hey, buddy. It's Rusty."

"Is Aubrey all right?"

Rusty sighed. "I'm fine, Thom, thank you so much for asking. How are you?"

"Come on, Rusty, what the hell is going on? Why are you calling me? And where did you get this phone? Is everything all right with Aubrey?"

"That's a lot of questions. Which one do you want me to start with?"

Thom held his tongue. Rusty's voice sounded a little shaky. He asked again, calmly. "Is Aubrey OK?"

"Well, Tommy, that's the thing."

"What? *What* is the thing, Rusty?"

"Take it easy, brother."

"I'm not your brother. We were related for a little while, and we're not anymore."

"Still got the touch with the common man, don't you, big guy?"

Thom closed his eyes, trying to will himself to be patient. Rusty had always enjoyed fucking with him, but this was the first time Thom could remember that he'd actually held the upper hand. Clearly, he was sitting on some information that he knew Thom wanted desperately, and he was playing it out for as long as he could. But there was something else, and Thom couldn't put his finger on what it was.

"I'm sorry. I hope you're well, Rusty."

"You guys got power there?" Rusty asked.

"No, we don't have power. Nobody has power."

"Oh, come on. *You* don't have power? The master of the universe?" Rusty said, and Thom could feel him warming up a little into the conversation. Thom heard the slosh of liquid, and it made more sense. Rusty was drinking.

Thom kept his tone measured. "Generator power, yes. At the facility. I thought you meant this part of the country. What's the story, Rusty? I haven't spoken to Aubrey in months. I'm worried about her. Could you please tell me what's going on with her?"

Rusty let out a long, slow breath. "I was hoping you could tell me. But you haven't talked to her?"

"No. Not since April."

"Do you have any way to get a hold of her?"

"I'd given her a satellite phone, but it's been off since then. How did you get Brady's phone? What the fuck is going on, Rusty?" Thom was almost pleading at this point.

"Aubrey's in trouble, buddy. Big trouble."

"What kind of trouble?"

Rusty sighed heavily. "It's a long story. You gotta hang with me."

"OK."

"She was just here. I've seen her pretty bad, you know, one too many pills, one too many drinks, but never like this. Like, strung out or something. She was scared shitless. Wouldn't tell me why at first, just said she needed money, bad."

Thom narrowed his eyes, thinking, trying to make sense of it. "Aubrey wanted money from you?" He tried hard not to put the emphasis on *you*.

"Yeah, that's what I thought, too," Rusty said, picking up on it anyway. "She's in trouble, Tommy. And I'm really sorry to have to say this, but it's kind of your fault."

"What's my fault?"

"This bad character you sent." Thom could hear the slosh of liquid as Rusty took another drink. He picked up the pace, as if warming into the story. "The guy you sent, with the bag of money."

"How do you know about that?"

"She told me, man. So this guy shows up back in April, right, and he scares the shit out of her. I was there for dinner the night the guy came; I could tell right away there was something off about him. So he shows her the money you sent, but then, on the spot, he like changes his mind. He tells her no, *he's* gonna keep it. And that if she ever tells you about it, he'll come back and kill her."

"Doesn't sound like Brady," Thom said.

"Look, I didn't know the man, but it's weird times. People will do anything. Have you heard from him since he left with your money?"

"No. I haven't."

"Well, I think that says a lot, don't you? Anyway, Aubrey lets him take it, she figures that's the way it goes, but the other day this guy Brady, he shows up in town again. He busts through her front door; he grabs her by the throat and tells her he wants more. Like, he blew through it all already or something. She tells him she doesn't have anymore, but he doesn't give a shit, he says, 'You know where you can get it as well as I do, and if you *don't* get it, you're gonna wake up with a knife in your neck some night.'"

"Jesus Christ," Thom said, believing not one word of this. "And how did you end up with his phone?"

"Huh?"

"His phone, Rusty. You're calling me on Brady's phone."

"Yeah, I know. That was Scott." Rusty chuckled and took the last slurp of his drink. Thom could practically hear him thinking. "Scotty got in a fight with the fucker, they're rolling around on the floor, the guy drops his phone. And then the fucker split. That kid of mine, man. He is for sure his old man's son."

"I see," Thom said.

"I warned you about shit like this, Tommy, over the years. Your money can't fix everything. Sometimes it just makes things a whole lot fucking worse."

"I don't remember that particular advice from you, Rusty."

"Anyway, that's the deal, man. This guy, this Brady fucker you sent, he wants another quarter mil or him and his friends are gonna come back and put some hair on the walls. That's what he said. Exact words, Tommy. Aubrey's in trouble, brother. I don't see any other way but to pay him. Can you send more cash?"

Thom took a breath. This was going to require some serious acting skills. "Yeah. Yeah, of course, yes, I can, and I will. God, Rusty, thank you so much for calling me."

"Dude, it's the least I could do. We go back."

"Is Aubrey still there? Can I talk to her?"

"No, she went home. She's pretty shook up."

"Could I ask you to go over there? Give the phone to her, so I can talk to her?"

"She was pretty clear she didn't want to talk to you," Rusty said. "I don't know what fight you guys had this time . . . ."

"I totally get it," Thom said. "OK, let me get on this. I can get the cash and be there in twenty-four hours."

Rusty let out a long sigh of relief. "I am so glad to hear you say that, Thom. I mean, I cannot *tell* you how glad I am to hear you say that. Because I still love her, you know? But I know you two have had your share of troubles over the years, you and Aubs, and I wasn't sure how you were going to react."

Thom hadn't even needed a nap to figure this one out. Brady was dead. Rusty had screwed up: "I didn't know the man." *Didn't.* Past tense. Brady hadn't stolen the money. Rusty had. Brady hadn't returned for more. Rusty had. Aubrey was in trouble, all right.

"I'll be there as soon as I can," Thom said. "I have to get the money first."

"As much as you can. Whatever it takes to make this guy go away for good. No offense, Tommy, but you sent him, so you gotta get him off her back."

"I understand completely. Keep this phone on."

Thom hit the off button and thought for a moment. He checked the fuel gauge. The car's tank was full. He pulled out his wallet and opened it. There were eight hundred dollars there. Other than that, he had only the clothes on his back.

The hell with it. Aubrey needed him.

He dropped the car in gear, cranked a big, sweeping U-turn across the desert highway, and headed back to Aurora.

29.

AURORA

It had taken Scott and Celeste an hour to get to the outlet mall off Highway 59 and even longer to get back, which meant they'd burned an unconscionable amount of gas. Aubrey had reminded Scott of this, repeatedly, both before he left and after they got back, but Scott had been adamant. He wanted *that* candy, and no other. They didn't use much gas these days anyway, he'd said, and it wasn't like there weren't ample parking garages around town that they'd been able to methodically work their way through, siphoning what they needed as they needed it.

Besides, Scott had said, it's for Norman. He might as well have started with that, because Aubrey knew that if it was something for Norman, there was no point in discussing it with him. Scott's devotion to Norman had increased in the recent weeks, in direct proportion to Norman's decline. Aubrey stopped fighting, Scott and Celeste braved the wilds of North Aurora, and they came back with the goods, telling only mildly horrifying tales of what the inside of the once-bustling mall had looked like. Looted stores, the rank stench of raw waste, and vast, dark, windowless spaces were what they'd expected, and they'd found them in abundance. But in their quixotic mission, they'd been successful.

Aubrey headed across the street to Norman's house with the small white box in hand. She'd asked Scott to come with her, but he'd re-fused, and she didn't press.

She knocked, waited, knocked again, and opened Norman's door, calling out.

"You decent?" she asked, as was her custom.

"Not remotely," he replied from the living room, as was his.

She smiled and walked inside, closing and locking the door be-hind her.

Aubrey had to make an effort to control her expression when she saw Norman. It had only been a few days, but the difference was strik-ing. He was seated in the beat-up leather club chair that was his favor-ite, which he had long since pulled around so that it looked out at the neighborhood through his big picture window. He'd sit there for hours at a time, watching the hive of steady activity in the former front yards, which were now lush and productive fields, colored in rich yellows, reds, greens, and browns by the late summer harvest. "It's like looking at a Manet," he'd told her, "except it moves."

Today he looked frailer than ever, a marked decline since Aubrey had seen him last. "Brought you a surprise," she said, pulling a chair from the dining room table and sitting down next to him.

"Did you now?" he asked, smiling. He looked down at the package in her hand and furrowed his brow, recognizing the logo on the top. "What in the name of heavenly glory have you done?"

"Wasn't me, it was Scott." She smiled and opened the box, turning it around so he could see the contents.

Norman leaned forward, the fraying old blanket spilling off his chest. "Fanny Farmer Candies?!"

"Well, they're Fannie May, now. Or since about ten years ago. I think they bought them out. You like the fruit slices, right?"

"No, ma'am, I do not like the fruit slices. I *adore* the fruit slices. The orange ones, above all else. How in God's name did you know?" He reached into the box with his long, bony fingers, picked out an orange, half-moon-shaped jellied candy, and held it up, regarding it with sur-prise and delight.

"Scott knew. He went and got them."

"Well, how about that?" He kept staring at the orange slice, turning it this way and that in the light that streamed through the open window.

"Why don't you try it?"

He turned and looked at her. Her gaze was steady and unblinking. He knew what she meant, and why they'd sent his favorite candy.

"I look forward to it, dear." He set the slice down on the table and looked back up at her, his entire face creasing in a grateful smile. "Please give that thoughtful young man my thanks."

Aubrey persisted. "If you don't eat, Norman, you're going to die."

"Aubrey takes care of everyone. Who takes care of Aubrey?"

"This isn't about me. Everyone's noticed. You can't not eat."

"I beg to differ. It's quite easy not to eat."

"Would you mind telling me why you're not eating?"

He looked at her and dropped the smile. "Because I am a human being, Aubrey. Because I'm eighty-eight years old, because I have been through wars and plagues, and I have decided that the time and place of my death are going to be of my own choosing. I have picked here, and I've picked now. Ish."

She looked at him. She'd expected him to fudge, to lie or hedge, but he'd just come out with it. For that, she had not prepared herself. She didn't know what to say.

"Don't look so sad," he said.

"Will you please just take a bite? For me?"

Norman looked at her for a long moment, weighing her request. He picked up the orange slice, gave it a delicate sniff, and closed his eyes, trying to concentrate on the aroma. Finally, he opened his eyes and nibbled off a corner. He looked at her and smiled, chewing.

"Happy?"

"Ecstatic." She sat back in her chair, looking out the window at the neighborhood. "Hell of a view you got here."

"Isn't it gorgeous? I've lived here thirty-seven years and I've never seen the neighborhood look halfway so beautiful."

"We're taking the squashes, figs, and chard in the next few days. Pumpkins and kale the week after. I'll bring you some."

"Please do," he said.

Aubrey glanced to her right, into the den just off his living room, where Norman kept his radio equipment. "What have you heard lately?"

He waved an old-man hand at her, dismissing the subject. "Not much."

She turned and looked at him, not buying the brush-off. "What have you heard?"

"You said not to bother with bad news."

Aubrey nodded, turning and looking out the window again. She shook her head. "Some days I feel so incredibly good. Better than I have in years. And then other times—it can be the next day or the next minute—it all turns, and I just don't know how much more of this shit I can take."

Norman set down the orange slice, reached out, and put his hand on top of hers, on the arm of her chair.

She looked up at him. "What have you heard, Norman?"

"That things are going to get worse before they get better."

"What do you mean?"

"If I told you, if you knew exactly what was going on in San Jose and Capetown and Budapest, would you do a single thing differently today? Here? On the street where you live?"

She shook her head no. She looked down. Against her will, her eyes filled with tears and overflowed. Her shoulders heaved, and she choked out a sob.

Norman didn't try to make it better. He let her cry for a while, and when he spoke again, his voice was soft and tired.

"'He who has a *why* to live for can bear almost any *how*.'"

"I don't believe that."

"Then you're a fucking idiot."

She laughed, wiping away tears with the back of her hand.

"I have seen the best of humanity," he said, "and I have seen the worst. I have seen friends suffer the loss of their fortunes, their spouses, their children. I have said, 'There but for the grace of God go I,' and then I turned around and suffered every single one of those same unimaginable losses myself. And somehow never saw it coming. I have seen the hopes of whole generations crash against reality and collapse, I have watched the horrors of the last century—and really, historically speaking, you could pick a better century out of a *hat*—and through all of it I've noticed one thing. Life is worth living only when it has meaning. That is our biggest task and our greatest challenge."

"What kind of meaning?"

"Viktor Frankl says there are only three that matter. To do work that matters to you, to care for others, and to rise to the challenge of difficult times. Work, love, courage. That's it. Any other human pursuit is horseshit."

"OK, Norman."

"Don't fucking do that." He leaned forward and shook his head emphatically. "Do not blow past this. Look out the window. Look at what you've done."

She looked up, through the window. The neighborhood was alive with activity. Phil and Scott and Celeste and Mrs. Chen and her boys, Derek and Janelle, Frank and Johnny Witzky, and half a dozen others were all sweating in the late-afternoon sun, working with a common purpose.

"I know you consider yourself a failure," Norman said. "I know that's hardwired into your brain for some unfathomable reason, but your life is not without meaning. Love, work, courage—you have it all. Your life is goddamn *rich* with meaning."

She started to cry again. It wasn't hopelessness this time but exhaustion.

"I love you, Norman."

"Right back at you, kiddo." He looked out the window, to where Phil was harvesting tomatoes. "What are you gonna do about your fella, once the lights go back on?"

"I don't know. I don't expect it to last."

Norman shrugged. "Sometimes those are the ones that do."

"I wouldn't know. Guess it'd be nice to find out."

"Well, he cleaned up nice, anyway."

Aubrey smiled. She looked down at the orange slice, on the table between them, only a tiny bite taken from one corner, not enough to feed a mouse. Norman followed her gaze, then looked up at her and shrugged. "It went stale, sweetie. It happens."

"Scott wanted to bring them himself, but—"

He saw through that and waved her off. "Don't get mad at him. Dying isn't a spectator sport."

She leaned forward, wrapped both her arms around the old man's bony shoulders, and squeezed him tight.

"Please don't go."

"I still don't believe that I will," he said. "Isn't that just like a human? Even in the face of overwhelming evidence, and the experience of the billions who came before us, it's still hard to get our heads around the idea that we are going to die."

She pulled back and looked into his watery, brown eyes.

Norman smiled. "Now that's what I call a hopeful species."

Half an hour later, Aubrey walked back home as the sun set. She and Norman had eventually switched the conversation to lighter topics— how little they missed talking about politics, the quality of the sunlight through the woodsmoke, and the surprising deliciousness of unripened plums. Then he'd grown tired and drifted off. Aubrey kissed him lightly on the forehead and left him to his late-afternoon nap.

As she crossed the street, Phil looked up from where he was working and came to her, putting an arm around her shoulders and pulling her in close. She laid her head on his shoulder.

"You OK?" he asked.

She nodded, and her tears flowed again.

He held her for a while, letting her cry. When she stopped, he spoke softly. "You want some company tonight?"

"I'll be fine." She lifted her head. "I got your shirt wet."

"And I *just* had this dry-cleaned."

She smiled and looked up at him. He kissed her on the lips. "I'm around if you need me."

"Has there ever been a lovelier sentence?" she asked. She turned, waved to one or two other neighbors, and climbed the steps of her front porch. She looked up at the hundred-year-old heap, her fixer-upper that had only ever gotten halfway fixed up, and she said a silent gratitude to the house for serving them well, for sheltering them through all the shitstorms of the past few months, the past few years. She went inside and closed the door.

By the same time tomorrow, her living room walls would be splashed with blood.

30.

IOWA CITY, IOWA

Thom had learned more about government cheese in an hour than he'd ever known in his life.

The hunger pangs had started five or six hours into the drive. He'd done enough intermittent fasting to know they'd pass in a while, and he attempted to direct his thoughts elsewhere. The emptiness and nausea were familiar, and as long as dizziness and confusion didn't start up, he saw no reason why he couldn't make it through a twenty-four-hour drive without eating. Gas hadn't been a problem so far. Lisa, his assistant, was back in San Francisco, on generator power at the Vida offices, and in her relentless monitoring of satellite-phone and emergency-radio frequencies, she'd found him a temporary fuel station in western Nebraska. A tanker truck was parked in front of a Mobil station that was going to be open for a six-hour window, under heavy guard. Thom got there before most people knew about it and lost only an hour in line before heading back out with a full tank, ahead of his already ambitious arrival schedule.

But then his hunger turned ferocious, angry and gnawing. He was having trouble thinking straight, and he had no intention of rolling into whatever steaming mess Rusty had created with anything but a clear head. Lisa, again, had saved the day, this time finding a report on a FEMA frequency of a newly scheduled government food-distribution event, supervised by the Iowa National Guard. It was only thirty miles off his route. A couple hundred people were in line ahead of him when he got there, but there were still plenty of the processed cheese logs left when he reached the front. While he waited, he'd asked a lot of questions. Turns out government cheese isn't so much one certain kind of cheese as all cheese. Cheddar, Colby, curd, and granular cheese all went into the vat, then they dumped in a load of emulsifiers and a few other things it was better not to think about, and it was melted, poured into footlong rectangular blocks, and cooled. The government had been making them since World War II, storing them in a hundred and fifty warehouses across the country and distributing them to schools, welfare recipients, and now victims of the nationwide food shortage.

The cheese was one of the most delicious things Thom had ever eaten. As soon as he was handed his, he'd stepped away from the line and slunk over to a grassy hillside with it, finding a spot away from the crowd. He sat down and was a good five or six mouthfuls into it, reminding himself not to hit it too hard—it was processed cheese, after all, and he was operating on an empty stomach—when he noticed a guy ten feet away staring at him.

Thom squinted. Had the guy recognized him? Was he some sort of starstruck tech geek?

The guy gestured, waving Thom over.

Thom looked behind him. Nope, the guy meant him. Thom waved in a "no, thanks" way, but the guy gestured again, insistent, and spoke softly. "You won't regret it." He held up a small brown bag, wrinkled and grease-stained, indicating its contents. He bounced his eyebrows suggestively.

Intrigued, Thom got up and moved closer. The guy, a Black man in his mid-thirties, looked up at him and smiled. "I don't know any cheese that isn't better with bread."

He reached into the bag, tore off a large crust from an unsliced loaf of bread, and held it out to Thom discreetly. Thom looked both ways, sat down, and took the bread, grateful. He broke off a chunk of cheese, put it on the bread, and ate it. It was heavenly.

The guy smiled, pleased. "Actual bread. My mom bakes it in a stone oven in the back of the house. How long's it been since you've had *bread*, right?"

Thom moaned, chewing, to indicate it had been a very long time. He did not mention that in fact it had been just a day and a half. But that was factory bread, full of chemicals, pre-sliced and frozen for eight months, and this—*this* was in a whole different category.

He finished chewing. "Incredible. Thank you."

"You looked hungry."

"I was."

"You from here?" the guy asked.

Thom shook his head. "California."

"Long way from home. Where'd you get the gas?"

"There's still places."

The guy looked at him, trying to figure him out. "What are you doing here?"

"Passing through on my way to Illinois."

"Well, you're not far now. What's in Illinois?"

"My sister, outside Chicago. She's got—well, there might be some problems."

"Sorry to hear that."

"Me too," Thom said.

"How'd you know about cheese day?"

Thom shrugged. "Just got lucky." Best not to mention his assistant back at corporate headquarters in Silicon Valley, slavishly poring over the nation's emergency-radio frequencies to find him food.

The guy shook his head. "I'm not sure *lucky* is a word I'd use to describe any of us right now. But if you were hungry and you found food, I'm glad for you." The guy thought about it for a minute, then turned back to Thom, trying to phrase this delicately. "You didn't maybe want to bring some food with you on a long car trip during a five-month blackout?"

"In retrospect, sure," Thom said. "Would have been a great idea. I would have brought a whole bunch of things with me. But I left in kind of a hurry. I was, um—I was a little upset, and I was trying to do things differently. For once." He laughed, running a hand through his hair, the food in his stomach giving him a bit more strength and clarity of thought. "Now that I think about it, I've never been as unprepared for something in my entire life as I am for this."

"Ah, don't be hard on yourself. Nobody was prepared for it."

"I don't mean the blackout. I was prepared for that; I was *a hundred percent* prepared. I saw it coming, I took steps, and the day it happened I put everything into flawless motion."

The guy looked at him, skeptical. "Did you?"

"Oh, yes. Most definitely."

"Then I'd imagine everything has turned out fine for you?"

"It has not. It has turned out the opposite of fine."

The guy nodded and shrugged. "Not surprising, I guess. There's a fundamental limit to the precision with which the behavior of particles in phase space can be predicted."

Thom looked at him and smiled. "You laying some dynamical system theory on me there, my friend?"

The guy smiled back. "Don't get a chance to slip it into conversation very often."

Thom took a deep breath and let it out. "I don't know what's going on. I guess I'm trying to do things in a new way because the old way wasn't working out anymore. I believe I'm on what's called a voyage of self-discovery. You?"

"Getting cheese for my parents."

Thom looked at him, assessing him differently now. "What do you do for a living?"

"I work for the National Oceanic and Atmospheric Administration. I monitor satellites for solar flare activity."

Thom laughed, knowing when he was being put on. "You should have worked harder."

The guy shrugged. "Tried my best."

Thom wrapped the plastic around the remainder of his brick of cheese and stood, wiping his hands on his trousers. "Thank you for the bread. That was generous of you."

"Not a problem. Good luck on your voyage."

Thom held out his hand and they shook, but he and Perry St. John didn't exchange names. "What do you think?" Thom asked. "Power coming back anytime soon?"

"Depends who you believe," Perry said. "People are out there working their butts off. 'Bout eighteen hundred transformers have already been replaced. Mostly the smaller ones, in rural parts of the country. But the cities are still pretty fucked and will be for a while."

"I hear that. Well, nice to meet you."

"You too." Thom started to go, but Perry called him back. "Hey." Thom turned around. "How far outside Chicago you gonna be?"

"About an hour."

Perry nodded, thinking. "Everything I've heard is things get worse east of here. A lot worse. I get your whole voyage-of-discovery thing. I do, I understand trying to let things play out, to not be a control freak. But don't take it too far."

"How do you mean?"

Perry glanced around, then looked back at him. "If you don't have a gun, get one."

31.

AURORA

Scott had developed some pretty solid knife skills in the past four months, and when he was really feeling his chopping groove Celeste said it was like being at Benihana. Aubrey could have lived without some of the blade twirling, but still, she found it fun to watch. It wasn't just that he was good, or the obvious joy he took in it, or the intense level of concentration that creased his face when he was at work in the kitchen. The real delight, for Aubrey, was that he was doing it at all. That this diffident fifteen-year-old boy, who for years had fought like a son of a bitch whenever she insisted he be a functional part of a household, was not only now a part of things; he was a vital cog. Given their largely vegetable diet, cleaning and chopping was the most important job in the house, after harvesting. And no one was as fast as Scott. He was the best at something, he took pride in it, he scheduled it himself, and he was usually done with his work in the kitchen long before the other two.

Celeste, for her part, had taken an early and intense interest in the art of fire creation and maintenance. For the high-heat, low-flame cooking fire they'd need that night, she'd had to get things started early and proceed with great patience. Back in May, Celeste had dug her first fire pit out back, but it was too deep, too big, too exposed to wind, basically too everything. She'd refined and refocused her efforts over the weeks that followed and had spent four or five days choosing rocks alone. At first, she'd started with sandstone and limestone chunks, which were the easiest to find in the holes she dug in the back yard. She was operating on the theory that they were lighter and more permeable, and therefore would conduct heat better. It was a theory she'd been disabused of after the first couple fires. They were light and permeable, all right, but that meant they filled with moisture easily and were prone to bursting at high temperatures. Exploding rocks will put a damper on any chef's work.

Undeterred, Celeste regrouped, asking around the neighborhood for advice, and learned that hard, dense rocks like granite, marble, or slate were safer and more effective. Those were impossible to find in the area without serious mining, but she'd hit upon something even better at the first abandoned house they'd torn down: fire-rate brick. Once the house's skeleton had been revealed, she found an ample supply of brick in some of the exterior walls. With it, she built a restaurant-grade fire pit in Aubrey's backyard. They used it almost every night.

Tonight, the kitchen table was set, the salad had been tossed, and Aubrey had a moment to herself. From where she sat, she could watch Scott, working away at the cutting board, and with just a turn of her head she could look out the window and see Celeste, fussing over the fire pit. They both worked quietly, without complaint, and without having to be asked. They knew their roles and took pleasure in playing them. They'd become an impressive young couple, good at sharing work, full of energy and an eagerness to please, and so far unburdened by resentment.

Normally, in these moments of quiet, Aubrey would have let her fears and anxieties play out. She usually went to the same ones: Norman's health, their food supply, the potential for violent social upheaval. In her darker moments, she'd think about the coming winter. The inevitable and brutal Chicago cold was a frequent subject of discussion on the block, but no one had any genius ideas about how to survive it. Aubrey had considered heading south, or west, to try to find her brother's place if she could, but any plans were still amorphous and overwhelming to contemplate.

Tonight, watching the teenagers work, Aubrey felt none of those concerns. Instead, she had an unfamiliar and welcome sense of peace. Tonight, the house was warm and safe, tonight, they would eat well, and tonight, the three of them, this odd and pleasant unofficial family, would be tranquil. Aubrey closed her eyes, listening to the sound of Scott's knife on the cutting board and smelling the sweet pine of the burning wood as it drifted through the open window.

She was content. Her entire life, she'd been told to be happy, either by herself or with her family or her friends or the whole goddamn world, but she knew now it had been impossible to achieve all along. It was an absurd goal. You can't find happiness; happiness finds you. We are completely passive in the act of our own contentment because it *isn't* an act. It's a result. For the first time in years, she was living an uncomplicated life, and happiness had resulted.

The evening sunlight slanted across the kitchen table, adding another visual to her sensory delights. Aubrey squinted out the window and guessed it was around six-thirty, based on the angle of the light. She figured she'd wander over to Phil's house for the cake in a few minutes. Phil had a gas oven and had somehow lucked into service that morning. He'd told Aubrey about it immediately, thrilled, because today was Celeste's sixteenth birthday. Mrs. Chen had flour and sugar, and if they could scare up a few eggs from anywhere in the neighborhood, that had meant they could bake her an actual cake. Aubrey and Phil had set off as on a scavenger hunt and come up with the necessary ingredients, and the smell of the cake had wafted out onto the street about an hour ago. Butter for icing had proven to be an ingredient too far, but Aubrey was certain Celeste would be delighted, nonetheless.

Now, Aubrey figured, it was time to go get it. She pushed her chair back from the table.

There are some events in life that mark the dividing line between "before" and "after." That's the bombing of Pearl Harbor for one generation, 9/11 for another, COVID for nearly everyone alive on the planet today. They are the moment or event that defines the boundary between life as you used to know it and life as you came to know it. For better or worse, but usually worse, people come to regard themselves as separate beings, judging everything they did "before" in one light and every action they took "after" in a different one.

For Scott, Celeste, and Aubrey, "before" meant the time prior to the knock on the door that came at that moment.

Aubrey, already turning in her chair, stopped. She hoped Phil hadn't misunderstood and brought the cake over early, despite their fairly explicit plans for the surprise. If so, she'd better head him off before Celeste saw anything.

"I'll get it," she said.

Scott kept chopping, Celeste fed the fire, and Aubrey went to the door.

She opened it. Rusty smiled, and she could smell the rot of his teeth through the screen.

From the back of the house, Celeste screamed.

32.

Thom had decided on a new personal credo, which was "If a stranger gives you bread and says get a gun, you must eat the bread and find a gun."

The first part of that philosophy had proven substantially easier than the second. Even Lisa's exhaustive radio searches and satellite phone calls had failed to turn up a credible source for the purchase of a firearm during a worldwide emergency. It likely wouldn't have mattered if she had, since Thom was down to his last several hundred dollars in cash and handguns were sure to be selling for a high multiple of that amount.

Had it not been for the BMW 7-series that cut him off as he exited the interstate, he never would have remembered Brady's car at all. But as the aggressive asshole going at least ninety on an off-ramp blared past him, the thought had flashed across Thom's frontal lobes. There wasn't just one gun in Thom's go-car, the one Brady had chosen to drive here; there were *two*. The chances that Brady left one or both of the guns behind were slim, but they were not zero, and it was the only idea he had. Plus he knew exactly where the BMW was parked.

The Linxup tracker had been the first thing Thom had checked after

Brady went off the radar. It showed the car was in a garage at the local hospital in Aurora, somewhere between the third and seventh floors, based on its elevation. It hadn't moved since late April. Thom's assumption had been that Brady, aware of the multiple tracking systems in the car, had ditched it there after he'd stolen the money. It made sense that Brady, rather than driving around in a stolen car whose enraged owner had great wealth and power at his command, had left it behind. Thom would have abandoned the car himself, if he were Brady.

But since Rusty's call, he was now certain Brady had been the victim of something nefarious. If he was right, that meant the car was, perhaps, not, uh, empty. Maybe, he thought, it wasn't just the car that was ditched but Brady as well.

He pulled into the parking structure a little before 6 p.m. that day, exhausted, but with his adrenaline pumping. The garage looked as it might have on any busy day, full of cars, and it wasn't unless you looked closely that you saw most of them had the doors of their gas tanks jacked open or wrenched off their hinges to facilitate siphoning. Thom cruised the lower floors slowly, working his way upward, his mind concocting ever more vivid mental images of what might await him inside the BMW once he found it.

The reality turned out to be worse than anything he'd been able to picture. The car was there, on the sixth floor, backed into the space Rusty had picked out back in April. It had been undisturbed, as had most of the cars on this level. Gas thieves, it seemed, didn't like to climb that many flights of stairs. Thom knew the BMW by its front grille and didn't need to confirm the license plate number. That car had been in his garage for a year. He'd walked past it a hundred times and driven it half a dozen. He'd obsessed over its battery and gasoline capacity, and he'd supervised the installation of the two gun compartments. That was his BMW, all right.

The windows of the car were oddly fogged, not with condensation, but with a greenish mist of some sort, like a slime mold. Thom sat in the Volvo for a second, just staring at the BMW's windshield, wondering what the green murk meant but knowing perfectly well. It was Brady. He hadn't taken off on the highway (Thom's first hope, for Brady's sake), he wasn't stuffed into the trunk (his second hope, for his own sake), but he was inside the car. Thom just prayed it wasn't the front seat.

The doors were locked, and Thom couldn't make out any more through the windows up close than he'd been able to from a distance. He tried kicking the driver's side glass a few times, but it showed no signs of give. He pulled a tire iron from the Volvo's trunk and gave it a few half-hearted swings and then several vicious blows, 'til finally the glass spiderwebbed and he was able to wrench it out of its frame.

The stench that was released from the BMW's passenger compartment nearly knocked him over. Thom recoiled and covered his mouth and nose with his arm, but still, the smell seemed to grab hold of him and shove its dirty fingers into his nostrils. He fell to his hands and knees, gasping, but the heavy odors were dropping too, and they found him on the cement floor. Thom scrambled back up onto his feet and backed away from the car a good ten yards, gagging.

He stood there for a moment, chest heaving, staring at the BMW as it vented its noxious fumes into the parking garage. His eyes were stung and watering, and the dense smell of offal leaving the car seemed almost visible. The BMW shuddered in his vision, as if it was relieved to at last be expelling the odious stink.

After he'd contained his urge to wretch, Thom went back to the Volvo, opened the glove compartment, and took an N95 mask from a box stashed there. Sucking air through the two-ply cloth, he headed back to the BMW. Turning his head away, he reached through the broken driver's window, found the door handle, and pulled it open. He staggered back again, to let as much foul air out of the car as possible. Satisfied that he would never be satisfied, he walked toward it.

As he drew closer, the dark outline of the shape on the back seat was gradually revealed. Thom remembered his college biology class and noted with some interest that the body had been spared the maggot stage, as blowflies apparently hadn't been able to penetrate the sealed glass and steel environment of the car. That was one thing, at least: the corpse didn't seem to seethe. But what the maggots had missed only left more for the bacteria to attack, and four months was an awfully long time.

Thom forced his eyes away from the remains and sat down in the driver's seat, moving quickly to the task at hand. He turned to the arm rest, slid both hands alongside it, and pushed at the two spots that Brady had shown him, one under the front lip and the other along the exposed edge. Thom's greatest fear had been that he'd remembered incorrectly how to open the magic-box gizmo. He'd figured if it came to it, he'd rip the thing apart with a crowbar, but that wasn't necessary. The box clicked smartly under his grip, and he flipped it open on the first try.

It was empty. That had been his second concern. So the Scandium, the gun he'd been most familiar with, was gone. Maybe it was somehow still on Brady's person, but, please, God, let's pray it didn't come to that. There was still one other possibility.

Thom turned to the center console of the car, trying not to let his eyes flick up to the rearview mirror, eager to avoid even an accidental glance into the back seat. He lifted the armrest and slid back the recessed panel, revealing the tumblers of the lock. He spun them around a few times, pleased to find they moved easily, still in good repair. He stared at them for a long moment.

He didn't know the combination. Goddamn it, he wished he'd paid better attention when Brady was briefing him on this. Had Brady picked a code and not told him? That seemed like an awfully big hole in the disaster plan. He couldn't imagine he would have allowed something like that, not in a million years. He must have chosen the combination himself, there was no other sensible way to have done this.

He tried his birthday: 1-1-8. Nope.

He tried Aubrey's: 2-2-3. Nope.

He tried both his parents', no luck. He tried Ann-Sophie's and each of his kids', nope, nope, nope, and then, just as panic was beginning to take hold, a nonsense question flitted through his brain, unbidden—"Do I feel lucky?"—and all at once he remembered that he *did* know the combination, he'd picked it carefully, and he'd even created a mnemonic to remember in case he was ever in this very situation. *Magnum Force* was one of Thom's favorite movies, in particular the oft-quoted Eastwood monologue where he stares down the punk, extolling the destructive virtues of his possibly empty .44 Magnum, and delivers his famous line, which was what went through Thom's mind now.

"Do I feel lucky?"

He sure did. Thom spun the tumblers, stopping on 0-4-4, squeezed the handle on the front of the MicroVault gun safe, and flipped it open. The Glock was still there.

Thom exhaled, pulled the gun out, and popped the clip, the way Brady had taught him. There were thirty-two rounds inside it. He snapped it back in and turned to get out of the car. As he moved, a glint of light caught his eye. He looked up, not into the rearview mirror itself but at something dangling from it.

It was a Saint Christopher medal. Thom realized, in that moment, that he'd seen it before, that in fact he'd been looking at it for the past four years, from the back seat of the customized Suburban in which Brady had always driven him. In that car, Brady had kept it wound tightly around the post of the rearview mirror, so the medallion portion just barely peeked out from underneath. He must have thought Thom wouldn't notice it that way. But Thom had seen it often and several times had been on the verge of asking Brady to please keep his religious iconography to himself. But Thom had always stopped short, meaning to check in with HR first. The last thing he wanted to do was face some bullshit religious-rights lawsuit and end up looking like an abusive jerk in the press, even though it was his goddamn car.

But that was then. Now Thom looked up at the medal, dangling freely from the rearview mirror, unabashedly displayed by a man no longer worried about his boss's opinion but who had been very much worried about his life and limb as he headed out on a perilous cross-country mission that he never should have been sent on in the first place. Thom felt a vibrant rush of shame rise inside him, color creeping up his neck and into his cheeks.

Setting the Glock on the seat, he reached up, unhooked the medallion's chain from the mirror, and looked at it. There was a carved image of Christopher, slogging across rough terrain with a walking stick, and a tiny, floating infant Jesus above his head, to whom Christopher's head was turned, gazing upward beseechingly. The words SAINT CHRISTOPHER were etched into the medallion across the top, and at the bottom the simple request PROTECT US.

Thom got out of the car, opened the rear door, and regarded Brady's remains. His faithful employee's head was crammed against the back seat at an unnatural angle. Rigor had set it firmly in that position, and Brady's distorted posture was fixed in time now.

Nobody had protected Brady.

Thom spread the chain wide, bent into the car, looped it over Brady's head, and arranged the medallion so it hung neatly over the remains of the dead man's chest.

"I was an asshole, Brady. I'm sorry. Thank you for everything."

He closed the door, picked up the Glock off the front seat, and headed to Aubrey's house.

33.

Aubrey turned at the sound of Celeste's scream and Rusty pushed through the front door, shoving her into the room. Aubrey shouted, but Rusty was quicker. He had a plan and the element of surprise going for him. Before she could fully react, he'd clamped a strong hand over her mouth and nose, stepped inside, and kicked the door shut behind him.

"I'm *protecting* you. Don't fight!" he hissed in her ear, pulling her body tight against his and dragging her farther into the room.

Aubrey tried to scream but realized she couldn't even breathe, with Rusty's clammy fingers covering her nostrils. She sucked air hard and made as loud a noise as she could in her throat, hoping he'd get the message.

At the back of the house, she saw Celeste's body slam up against the door frame outside, shoved by someone she couldn't see. Celeste turned to object, more angry than frightened, but a man's hand flashed into view and smacked her hard, across the face. Celeste shrieked and fell back again. Zielinski, her father, now rushed toward her, got a hand up under her arm like a vice-principal with a truant, kicked the back screen door open, and marched her into the house.

Scott, hearing the commotion, shouted from the kitchen and came running out, chopping knife in hand. "Get the fuck away from her!" he shouted, brandishing the knife toward Zielinski, but then he caught sight of Rusty, his hand suffocating Aubrey as he dragged her into the living room. Scott stared, wild-eyed, uncomprehending. "Rusty, what the *fuck*?!"

But no one had time to answer, as there was another bulky shape moving through the rear door. Espinoza took in the room quickly, eyes falling on the only exposed weapon, which was the knife in Scott's hand. He swept toward him and Scott whirled, blade in front of him. Espinoza caught the boy's wrist between his thumb and first two fingers and gave it a sharp twist.

Scott screamed, Aubrey heard his wrist snap, and the knife clattered to the floor.

One after another, Scott, Aubrey, and Celeste were thrown down on the couch, stunned and in pain. Aubrey gulped air and turned to the other two, to see if they were OK, while Rusty stood over them, shouting at them to calm down. It didn't help.

Espinoza picked up the kitchen knife and moved quickly, closing curtains and locking the front door. The room turned dark.

Zielinski took a chair from the dining room table, set it across the coffee table from the sofa, and sat down opposite them.

Rusty, near the window, tried not to hyperventilate.

For a long, weird moment, nobody said anything.

Finally, Aubrey turned to Rusty and spoke in a low, angry voice. "What the fuck have you done now?"

Rusty looked away. Zielinski laughed, then turned back to the couch, his eyes falling on Celeste.

"Happy birthday, baby. Did you think I'd forget?"

Celeste spat in his direction. It fell short, but the message landed.

Zielinski shook his head and looked at the others. "Daughters."

Aubrey, regaining her composure, sized up the three intruders, one after the other.

As calmly as she could muster, she asked the only question that mattered. "What do you want?"

Zielinski looked at her. A direct question deserved a straight answer. "Your brother's money."

Aubrey furrowed her brow. She looked back and forth from Rusty to Zielinski, but Rusty wouldn't hold her eye. "I don't have any money. And my brother isn't here."

"He will be. Let's give him a minute." He looked at Rusty. "He said twenty-four hours?"

Rusty nodded, furtively, not meeting anyone's eye. Aubrey just looked at him, disgusted and enraged. She turned to Scott, who was holding his wrist in agony, his face white as paper. She looked up at Espinoza. "You broke his wrist. A teenager. You proud of yourself?"

Espinoza looked away, and Zielinski rolled his eyes.

"Let's not play the blame game, OK?" he said. "This is very simple. We need money. You've got some on the way. You may not know it, but you do. When it gets here, we will take it and we will go. Celeste is going to come home with me where she belongs, and you'll never see any of us again."

Scott's face flushed with anger, and he looked up. "She's not going fucking anywhere with you, you piece of shit!"

For a short, fat man, Zielinski moved with remarkable speed. One second he was in his chair, across the coffee table from Scott, and the next he was on his feet, over the table, and had a knee in Scott's chest. He punched down, cracking his fist into the boy's face two, three, four times.

Celeste screamed and lunged to protect Scott. Zielinski turned on her, backhanding her away from him. He would have done more damage had Espinoza not run over and pulled him off.

Rusty stood inertly by the window, his back half-turned.

There was a knock at the door, and they all froze.

Zielinski, breathing hard, turned to the room and spoke in a hushed, urgent voice. "Not a fucking word, not one of you." He turned to Rusty.

He nodded toward the window, where there was a narrow crack in the drapes that Espinoza had pulled a few moments ago. "See if that's him," he said.

Rusty edged toward the crack in the drapes, peered outside, and stepped carefully back again. He shook his head from side to side and whispered. "Some asshole with a cake."

Aubrey's eyes whipped toward the door, praying that Phil would not take it upon himself to open the door.

He didn't. He waited. He knocked again.

Zielinski held a hand out to all of them, palm down, warning them to stay exactly where they were. They waited. Phil knocked one or two more times, then called out, puzzled. After another agonizing sixty seconds, they heard him set something down and walk away, down the stone steps.

Zielinski sat again, rubbing his sore right hand and flexing his fingers. Scott moaned in pain, Celeste choked back sobs, and Aubrey breathed hard, full of rage and unable to do anything about it.

Zielinski picked up a box of kitchen matches from a side table, struck one, and lit the two candles that were there.

He spoke quietly to Aubrey. "I'm going to tell you exactly what you need to say to your brother when he gets here, and you are going to say it. Word for word. After he leaves the money, me and Celeste are gonna take it and go. But until he gets here, we are all just going to sit here and wait. Silently. Anybody says anything I don't like"—he nodded toward Espinoza—"I'll put the barrel of his gun between their teeth and pull the trigger."

He looked around the room. "Are there any questions?"

34.

CAYUGA LANE

The first thing that gave Thom pause was the two SUVs, parked nose to nose, that were stationed at the end of Cayuga Lane. It made sense, he supposed, given the condition of some of the neighborhoods he'd driven through on the way here, but it wasn't reassuring. Neither was the fact that the two lawn chairs in the beds of the trucks were empty. If this was a guard post, it was unmanned tonight.

His fears were somewhat allayed by the Edenic nature of Aubrey's block itself, which looked like it was out of a Utopian future. It was dusk, so some of the vibrant colors of the fields were dimmed, but he could see, as far as the light allowed in both directions, the rich, verdant plantings that had been carefully sown, tended, and harvested over the past several months. He kicked himself for never having considered this, in even one of the dozens of think-tanking, brain-dating, and strategic-planning sessions he'd held over the past ten years.

Had he actually picked the desert? Live in the *desert* and eat freeze-dried food? What had been the matter with him? Eat what you can grow, grow everything you can. Nothing else would work. Why had he never seen that? He was so concerned with continuing to live life as it was that he'd never thought about living it as it might be.

The street was quiet as he approached Aubrey's house. He'd been there only once, but remembered it because it was the oldest one on the block, and he'd thought she was crazy to buy it. It sat near the end of the street on the left, or *loomed* there, he'd thought at the time, like the scary old money pit it was. There were no lights on, of course, but there was a wavering glow visible through a tiny part in the curtains of the front windows.

He reached the bottom of the steps and stopped, noticing the second odd thing.

It was a cake.

Or it looked like a cake, anyway, a thick, brown, round thing on a wire cooling rack, sitting at the top of the front steps. He climbed the steps and stopped near the top, bending down to take a closer look. Yes, it was a cake, a homely-looking one, no icing, but someone had clearly baked a chocolate sponge cake and left it here, on Aubrey's front step.

Thom looked around. Nobody out on the block.

He looked back at the cake. He reached down, laying a finger on the side of it. Still warm.

He moved it carefully to the side, stepped up to the mat, and opened the screen door. He thought he detected a flash of movement through the sliver in the living room curtains, and he snapped his head that way. There was light inside, maybe the flickering of a candle.

Thom shifted, adjusting the jacket he was wearing. It was too hot for the sultry evening, but he'd put it on to cover the Glock, which he'd shoved into the back of his pants. He'd had to tighten his belt an extra notch to keep it there, and it was uncomfortable as hell. With any luck, about thirty seconds from now he'd realize he didn't need it. That this had all been a big overreaction.

He knocked on the door.

A long moment went by. He thought he heard movement inside, but no one answered.

He was about to knock again when the door opened, leaving his hand hanging in midair.

Aubrey looked at him for a long moment, then forced a strained smile. "Hello, Thom."

"Hey, Aubs."

"Thank you for coming," she said. But she didn't move to admit him, just stayed standing in the two-foot gap of the open door, her body blocking the entrance to the house.

"Least I could do," he said. He tried to look past her, into the house, but she didn't move.

"I know Rusty called you. He didn't have to do that, but I'm glad he did."

He looked back at her. If he had suspected something was wrong before, he *knew* it now, and not just from her stilted tone. She was *glad* Rusty called him? She hadn't been glad about anything Rusty had done for years.

Thom thought he heard a footfall inside. His eyes flicked toward the living room, but he couldn't see into it from this angle.

"Is that Todd?" he asked.

"Who?"

"Scott. I'm kidding, you know, I always get his name wrong?"

"Right. Yeah. Scott's here."

"Can I say hi?"

"Not right now," she said. "He's in kind of a mood."

Thom nodded. "Teenagers. Always trouble."

"Exactly." She looked at him, holding eye contact. "Trouble."

"I heard Brady came back and threatened you," he said.

"Yes. Three or four days ago."

"I'm sorry that happened," Thom said. He shifted his eyes toward the living room and inclined his chin, silently asking her if there were others inside.

Aubrey nodded in answer. But out loud, she continued their conversation. "I'm pretty pissed at you, Thom," Aubrey said. "You never should have sent him, and you probably never should have sent so much money in the first place."

"I'm sorry."

"Did you bring the money Rusty asked for?"

"I did." He held up a single finger to her, mouthing a silent question: *one?*

Aubrey shook her head no. He held up two fingers, another question. She shook her head no again and looked him up and down. "Where is it?"

"I had to keep it somewhere safe," Thom said. "It's nearby."

He held up three fingers and, finally, Aubrey nodded.

"Well, then you'd better go get it," she said. "He could come back at any time."

"OK. I can be back in a couple hours."

"Please hurry," Aubrey said, and stepped back. She swung the door, holding eye contact with him until the last possible moment.

The door clicked shut, and he heard the dead bolt turn.

Thom hesitated, listening, but heard nothing more from inside. He turned, walked down the steps, and moved off down the sidewalk.

He thought, as he rounded the corner at the end of the block, that nothing in his life had even remotely prepared him for what he was going to do next.

Forty-five minutes later, night had fallen. There was a half-moon, enough to see by, but barely. Thom was grateful for the lack of street or house lights as he crept back around the corner and moved toward Aubrey's house. He stayed out of the street, crossing as close to the other houses as he dared. Far enough away to not be seen from a window but close enough to be lost in the shadows.

The last light of day had seemed to take forever to fade. Thom had sat in his car the whole time, running through numerous scenarios in his head, all of them unacceptable. He thought first of the police, but even if he'd been able to get a call through to them, the chances they'd actually show up were slim. There was too much real chaos and bloodshed taking place for them to bother with his suspicions, no matter how well founded they were. And even if they'd agreed to come, from what Thom had heard over the past few months, law enforcement was as much a threat risk as a protector. True or not, it was a chance he couldn't take. Private security, even if he'd been able to find it, couldn't be trusted either. He didn't know them here, they didn't know him, and the promise of a substantial payday was as likely to incite bad behavior as good.

This was one problem he couldn't outsource. This was something he'd have to solve himself.

He'd practiced four or five shots with the Glock back on the second level of the parking garage, where he'd been seized with the sudden knowledge that he'd skipped the firearms training courses Brady had arranged for him. It was simple enough, once he found the manual safety release near the upper rear of the gun and learned he needed to chamber a round before the gun would fire. After that, he could pull the trigger as many times as he wanted to shoot. If there were three intruders in the house, that may be a lot. Or maybe, he hoped, the mere presence of the gun, coming in suddenly and from an unexpected part of the house, would be enough for Rusty and whatever lowlife friends of his were with him. Thom would, after all, have the advantage of surprise.

He reached Aubrey's driveway and ducked low, to avoid being seen through her kitchen window. He slid over to the side of the house and duck-walked beneath the sill. He could see wavering candlelight, faintly, coming from the living room.

He reached the storm doors on the side of the house, slid his hands across them to the middle, and found the biometric lock he'd had installed five years ago. One of the selling points of this unit, he remembered, was the shelf life of the wafer-thin lithium-ion battery inside it, which was guaranteed for ten years at an average temperature of seventy degrees. Given the winters in this part of the country, Thom had cut that estimate in half, which took the battery life down to about five years. He figured the chances it was still live at fifty-fifty.

When he had set up the lock, Thom had programmed in his own fingerprint as the system administrator. His concern, in those days, had been not for a home-invasion scenario but that Rusty, who was already starting to be lost to substances, would become a true threat of some kind. In that situation, Thom wanted to know that he could fly there and get into the house if he needed to.

He'd never shared that detail with Aubrey. Part of being a guardian angel, he'd told himself, is being invisible.

He pressed his thumb on the panel, the screen lit up green, and the lock buzzed. He lifted the door, an inch at a time, desperate not to make a sound. But the hinges squeaked. Thom froze. He held in place until the muscles in his arms started to burn, then lifted the door another two feet, slipped inside the house, and lowered it again.

The walk across the darkened kitchen was excruciating. Thom's eyes had partially adjusted in the blacked-out basement, but when he reached the top of the stairs and came out into the kitchen, he realized he had almost no memory of the layout of the house. He regretted intensely that he hadn't visited his sister in her home more than once. He hoped he'd get a chance to correct that one day.

He stood still for a full minute and let his eyes gather whatever bits of light there were in the house. The thin candlelight in the living room became visible around the edges of the kitchen door, which looked as if it swung both ways, like in a restaurant. He moved toward it.

Thom was sweating abundantly. The jacket he'd worn to conceal the gun in his belt was denim, and he'd started to perspire in the humid August night before he'd even stepped out of his car. Now, as he moved across the kitchen, his body tense and stiff, sweat was pouring out of him. He could feel it trickling down the back of his neck, out of his armpits, down his sides, on the backs of his knees, everywhere. He paused at the sink, wondering if he dared to slip the coat off. The real danger, he thought, was his hands—if his palms were wet and his grip on the Glock turned slick, he was afraid he'd drop it or, worse, fire it by accident.

But he'd have to set the gun down to take the coat off, and that was out of the question. He'd live with the sweat. He kept moving to the door to the living room, thinking that this sort of decision had never come up in his planning sessions. He wondered if, rather than spend so much time worrying over the right yoga instructor, he might not have been better off hiring a few former FBI agents to help him with infiltration training drills.

A voice from the living room snapped him back into the moment. It was a man's voice, soft and deep, and was followed by footsteps. Thom stiffened, the gun in front of him, and pointed it at the door, ready for it to swing open. He didn't know if he'd have the nerve to fire, if it came to that.

But it didn't. The voice stopped, so did the footsteps, and the living room was quiet again.

Thom moved forward, covering the last few feet to the swinging door. He stood there, listening for more sounds from the other side. There weren't any. He bent his right arm in an L-shape, holding the gun pointed at the ceiling, pressed his left palm against the swinging door, and pushed it open an inch and a half.

He turned his head, putting his left eye in the crack in the door. He could see into the living room and had a relatively high degree of confidence that he was not visible, given that the kitchen behind him was completely dark. His vantage point was from behind the sofa, which was about six feet away from him. He counted heads.

There were three people on the couch. On his far left, he could see the side of Aubrey's face, lit by candlelight from the table. She was one. On the other end of the couch was a teenager he assumed was Rusty's kid, Scott. His left cheek, dimly visible, looked as though it had taken a recent beating. There was someone seated between them, a bit shorter than Scott, or maybe slumped low on the couch. Thom didn't know who that was.

Across the room, there were two more people. Rusty was standing at the mantel, leaning back against it. He looked as if he'd aged a decade since Thom saw him last. Seated in a chair in front of the fireplace, facing the couch, was a stout, bald man in a stained white shirt. Thom didn't know who he was, but from his domineering posture, he guessed he was the ultimate source of the problem here.

No one in the room spoke. They were waiting. For him, Thom supposed.

He counted heads in the room again. Five people total. Aubrey had said there were three intruders. Take away Scott and Aubrey, that left Rusty, the bald man in the chair, and the mystery figure on the couch between Aubrey and Scott. Keeping an eye on them, Thom supposed.

All five were accounted for.

The only weapon in evidence was a kitchen knife, on a side table next to the bald guy in the chair.

Thom took a deep breath. He'd practiced his entrance and what he would say in his mind a hundred times. There were three motions he'd need to make before entering the room, and he had to do them all within the space of a second or two. He reviewed them one last time in his mind. Nothing left now but to do it.

Go.

He flicked the gun's safety off with his right thumb, racked the slide on the top of the Glock with his left hand, and put his shoulder into the kitchen door, swinging it open wide.

All heads turned.

"Stay exactly where you are," he said, his voice only quavering slightly.

So far, Thom felt, things had gone exceptionally well. He'd driven across the country, found food and gas on his own, armed himself, detected danger when he spoke to Aubrey, snuck into the house after dark, and come through the door and into the room with a loaded weapon, completely surprising everyone in the place. Really, it could not have gone better.

Except he'd counted wrong. He knew it the moment the three heads on the couch turned to look at him—Aubrey, Scott, and whoever-the-fuck-that-is in the middle. Far from being some criminal mastermind, the third figure, whom he'd assumed was one of the intruders, was a teenage girl. She too looked like she'd taken a couple punches to the face, her eyes showed fear, and her right hand, Thom could now see, was on the cushion, holding Scott's tightly, their fingers interlaced.

All at once, Thom realized

1. The girl was not an intruder but a captive,

2. She was Scott's girlfriend, who had come to stay with them, which Aubrey had told him about, and, shit, he really needed to listen more carefully when he talked to people,

3. That left a person unaccounted for,

4. Which explained the low voice and the footsteps he'd heard moments ago, as if moving across the room,

5. The swinging dining room door he'd shoved open blocked his view toward the back of the house, which, he remembered now, was where the bathroom was, and

6. That door was now moving again, fast, straight toward him.

Thom oofed as the door slammed into his left side, knocking him off his feet. Espinoza, who'd gone to relieve himself, reclaimed the room with a vengeance, banging through the door the rest of the way, sending it swinging into the kitchen.

But Espinoza continued on, catching Thom as he bounced off the wall and knocking the Glock out of his hand. He grabbed Thom by the neck with a hand like a catcher's mitt, lifted him off his feet, and hurled him across the room.

Thom landed hard on his right side and felt a white-hot flash of pain in his shoulder as his arm flattened beneath him and his collarbone snapped. He knew, as the pain cut into him, that he had failed. He had not controlled the situation, he had not dictated the course of events, all he'd managed to do was unleash a climate of mayhem, and whatever happened in the next forty-five seconds would be on his conscience forever.

Should any of them survive.

Celeste screamed, Zielinski leaped to his feet, and Scott bolted up from the couch, racing out of the room, and thundering up the stairs.

Espinoza reached into his belt and pulled out a nine-millimeter as Zielinski shouted at him. "Shoot that motherfucker! Shoot him!"

Aubrey lurched forward, reached under the coffee table, and flipped it over, into Zielinski's knees. Zielinski shouted, more in surprise than pain, and Aubrey jumped up, diving toward Thom's gun, which was on the floor between the couch and the front hall.

Celeste moved too, lunging for the kitchen knife on the end table next to Zielinski. Her father caught her by the wrist, spun her around, and pulled her close to him, raging in her ear as he held her with one bearlike arm.

Rusty, who spent the first few seconds sitting the conflict out entirely, saw Aubrey nearing Thom's gun, on the floor. He pounced, grabbing her by the hair and hauling her to her feet. He moved to throw her across the room, but Aubrey resisted, finding strength in her legs and core that wasn't there four months ago. She snapped her head back, shaking off Rusty's weak grip, and turned on him. She was stronger than him and smarter than him, and he could see it in her eyes. He froze, and she shoved him hard, both hands slamming into the middle of his chest. He flew back, into the mantel, the wind knocked out of him.

Thom, the broken bone in his shoulder searing, crawled toward the Glock.

Zielinski shouted at Espinoza again. "*Shoot* the son of a bitch, god-damn—"

But he cut off in the middle of his sentence as Celeste stomped down on his foot as hard as she could. He howled in pain and lost his grip on her. She whirled around, brought her knee up into his balls, and, as he started to double over, punched him in the throat.

"That's for you, *naruszyciel prawa*."

Zielinski, in pain but livid, stood and drew back his meaty right hand, to backhand her across the face. Celeste stood her ground, ready to take the blow.

From the bottom of the stairs, a thunderous gunshot exploded, shaking the walls of the house. Aubrey and Celeste winced, Thom flinched, and Rusty covered his ears and backed away.

The back of Zielinski's head burst open, spattering the wall behind him with gore.

At the base of the stairs, Scott stood still, Brady's M&P Scandium in his right hand, its barrel smoking. The gun suddenly heavy in his hand, Scott's arm dropped to his side. He stared at the dead body, in shock at what he had just done.

Behind him, Espinoza spoke softly. "Don't raise your arm, kid. Keep it exactly where it is."

They all turned and looked at him, too terrified to move. Espinoza, who'd been forgotten in his spot against the wall, held his gun on them with one hand. He held the other hand up, signaling they should not move.

He turned and looked at Thom, still down on the floor. "You got the money?"

"No."

"He's lying!" Rusty shouted.

"Shut up, Rusty." Espinoza didn't bother to glance at him. "Did you bring any money at all?"

"No," Thom said.

"Didn't think so. I wouldn't have either."

"He's full of shit!" Rusty shouted, taking a menacing step forward. Espinoza turned and looked at him with an expression of severe annoyance.

Rusty's face was reddening with rage. "He's got the money, he's got the fucking money, *he's got the fucking—*"

Espinoza swung the gun from Scott to Rusty and fired three shots. The first hit Rusty in the right shoulder, spinning him half to the side. He regained himself and staggered toward the back door, to flee. But the next two shots hit him squarely in the back, propelling him into a post on the small back deck, where he bounced and turned, looking back at the others in disbelief.

He fell to the ground just outside the door, dead.

Espinoza stared at him for a moment, then looked up at the others.

"He never would have left you alone. Or me." He looked around the room, at the two bodies on the floor and the blood on the walls. "For the record, I hate this shit."

No one spoke.

Espinoza backed away, toward the rear of the house, never taking his gun or eyes off them. He reached the screen door, pushed it open, and walked away into the night.

Thom dragged himself up off the floor. He looked at Scott, still standing there, gun in his hand, too stunned to speak or move.

Thom looked over at Aubrey, breathing hard, streaked with Zielinski's blood. "Anybody hit?" he asked.

They all muttered no.

Thom looked back at Scott, still holding on to the gun he and Celeste had practiced with months earlier. Thom looked at Zielinski's body. He turned his head, hearing sounds from outside—voices, shouts, people on their way.

Some decisions take forever. Others are instantaneous. Thom felt like this one had been made before he even knew it. He went to Scott, took the gun gently from his hand, and turned the boy to face him. "Listen to me and do exactly as I say."

Scott looked at him.

"Go into the bathroom right now and wash your hands. Thoroughly. Don't ask why. Just do it."

Scott stared, uncomprehending, but Thom didn't have time to explain. The shouts from outside were getting closer. "Go." He gave Scott a push in that direction, and the boy went.

Thom looked down at the gun he was holding, still warm from the shot Scott had fired. "Cover your ears," he said to the room. He raised the gun, pointing it in the direction Espinoza had fled, and fired three shots out the open back door. Aubrey and Celeste turned and looked at him, trying to understand.

"I shot them," he said. "Both of them. Got it?"

Aubrey looked at him, quizzical. Thom turned to Celeste. "Go tell Scott. Make sure he gets it right. Don't let him come out 'til he's got it. I shot them. Me. Not him."

Celeste nodded, understanding, and ran after Scott.

Aubrey looked at Thom. "You don't have to do this. It was self-defense."

"There's two dead bodies, Aubrey, and the gun that killed one of them just ran out the back door. It's not gonna look right."

"We can explain."

"Whatever happens, let it happen to me. Not him. He's only fifteen years old."

The shouts from outside were in front now; hands pounded on Aubrey's front door.

Thom looked at his sister, his eyes welling with tears.

"Fifteen years old."

35.

AURORA

Sometime after 7 a.m. on October 6th of that year, Aubrey was on her front step drinking a morning glass of water when she heard a familiar sound. It was a sizzling, like a piece of bacon dropped in a hot pan, coming from somewhere just above her. She looked up.

The light over the front stoop was flickering.

Aubrey stared at it. She furrowed her brow and worked to make her brain register what was happening. The light, which had been switched on the night that it all began, back in April, was once again receiving a trickle of electrical power and was trying its goddamnedest to do what it had been made to do.

As abruptly as it started, the sizzling stopped, and the light flickered off again. For a long while, Aubrey just stared at the darkened light-bulb, trying to decide if she felt relief, excitement, or even, God help her, a faint tinge of disappointment.

The power was restored, not all at once, but bit by agonizing bit over the course of the next eight weeks. By early November, ninety percent of the country was electrified again. Since it happened much faster than had been expected, it was widely considered a triumph of recovery and ingenuity. Those who had managed to keep their spirit and virtue intact when things were dark wept and prayed. Those who had not, also wept, and they also prayed.

The official death toll for event-related fatalities of all causes in the United States was somewhere over a million three hundred thousand, though exact numbers were impossible to calculate. Of those, normally preventable medical emergencies took something over half, starvation claimed about one-quarter, and the remainder were estimated to be victims of violent crime. The general consensus among the scientific and medical communities was that, all things considered, we got off easy. Had powerlessness persisted into winter, there was no telling how widespread the loss of life might have been.

Norman Levy hadn't lived long enough to see the return of normalcy, which he would have insisted was not so normal at all. Things and people had been changed forever by the experience, and some aspects of life would never be the same. That, Norman would have said, was the good news. Fingers crossed they were the right things, the ones that had needed to go anyway.

Scott, who had successfully avoided Norman until his death and then angrily regretted his choice, had gone quiet for weeks after the old man's passing.

Aubrey unlocked the front door of Norman's house just after eleven on a morning in mid-November. She was wearing the dark blue dress with the bright yellow stripe she'd last worn three years earlier, the day her fledgling conference business had its formal launch and her PR person had managed to wrangle a local television interview. It seemed so long ago now it might as well have been the Cretaceous Period; before COVID, before Black Sky, as the world had taken to calling it, before she'd seen and done things she never would have dreamed she would say or do. But she remembered, as she went through her closet that morning, that she'd always felt good in that dress, so she picked it. She spent half an hour putting on makeup, the first time in at least six months, and it now seemed like one of the more useless things she'd ever done. She couldn't for the life of her imagine why anyone had ever bothered with it, until she came downstairs and Scott said, "What the fuck? You look great."

Then she remembered.

Now, standing in the open doorway of Norman's empty house, she fought the reflexive urge to call out "You decent?" and set about her gloomy business. She went first to his bedroom and scanned the few books on his night table, but none of them seemed appropriate. The couple stacks on the floor near the bed were likewise unpromising, so she headed for his study, which was where she'd thought she would find it anyway. She glanced at her phone and cursed; she was already late and getting later. She never should have put it off this long, but, really, there had been no reason to think she wouldn't have been able to find the quote on the internet that morning unless, of course, the internet chose today, of all days, to go down again. The massive infrastructure of the web was still a rickety, unstable thing, and she should have known better than to count on it in a situation like this.

Norman's memorial, postponed until mid-November, figured to be well attended, as befit a man who seemed to know everybody and had always behaved as if he had time for them all. Norman had chosen his own eulogists, and Aubrey had been mortified to hear that she was to be one of them. He hadn't left many instructions regarding his service, but who was to speak and how long they were allotted had been important to him, and Aubrey knew he would expect wit, depth, and, above all else, brevity. She'd written and torn up half a dozen efforts over the past week, none of her words seeming good enough to her, until she remembered what he'd said about human meaning. She didn't want to paraphrase the quote. She wanted to get it exactly right—Norman deserved that—and if she couldn't find it on the internet, she'd have to find the book he pulled it from in his extensive stacks.

Now, in the study, she ran her hand over one shelf after another, searching and not finding, and, really, this was hopeless. She didn't even know the title of the damn thing, much less where in God's name the quote would be found even if she did come up with it. She was about to give up when her eyes fell on his desk, covered in a sheet she'd thrown there the day after she'd found his body, because she didn't want his things to go to ruin from dust and disuse. In her upset, she realized she'd never properly gone through the papers and effluvia on top of the desk, and maybe it would be there, on a Post-it or in a stack of well-thumbed texts. She threw the sheet aside, revealing a time capsule of the last days of Norman's life.

There were no books on top of the desk, but Aubrey noticed something she hadn't seen that day, in her sorrow and upset. Underneath the desk was a large cardboard box, about two feet square, heavily trussed and wrapped, with a pile of eight or nine manila envelopes neatly stacked atop it. The box had been pushed back a bit, so Norman still had legroom, and the effect was to have kept it just out of sight to a person standing beside the desk.

Aubrey bent down, closed her hands around the side of the box, and slid it out from under the desk, careful not to spill the stack of envelopes. They were addressed, each of them, in his careful hand—names, addresses, and the right amount of postage for each. The box itself had no address, just a neatly lettered name. Aubrey teared up when she read it.

She covered her mouth, upset with herself. Here were Norman's last communications, his postmortem wishes and goodbyes, all carefully chosen and set aside, put in a place where someone—he must have figured it would be her—would be sure to discover them and see them safely on their way, once life as we knew it resumed. Except she hadn't seen them at all. They were the proverbial letters lost in the storm.

She thumbed through the stack of envelopes. The first few names were unfamiliar to her, but she stopped when she reached the fourth one. It was addressed to her. She tore the manila envelope open with a shaking hand, reached inside, and pulled out a weathered paperback. It happened—it just so fucking happened, as Norman would have said—that it was the very book she'd come here to find. There was a three-by-five note card paper-clipped to the cover, its few neat lines typed on a real typewriter, his 1967 turquoise Olivetti Lettera:

```
To my Star Student,

No long goodbye letter for you, because we got
to say it all. Is anyone ever so lucky?
   Here's seventy-five years of underlining and
dog-earing instead.
                                Yours always,
                                    Norman
```

She wiped away a tear as she flipped through the book. *Man's Search for Meaning* was written in 1946, and it looked to Aubrey like this one had been bought that very year. It was yellowed, cracked, and smelled faintly of mildew. She flipped through the book and, as promised, found page after page of dog-ears, underlines, and exclamation points. She would be able to quote the very book she'd hoped to reference at Norman's memorial, and the choice of quotes wouldn't even be hers. It would be his.

Is anyone ever so lucky? she wondered.

Thom, mindful of the significance of his sister's loss, had flown back for her friend's memorial. He'd brought Anya and Lukas with him, as it fell on one of his weekends with the kids. He had a final police interview the next week as well, and Thom and the kids were, at Aubrey's suggestion, staying with her while in town. When she asked about his legal situation, he'd say it was intense but not serious. The cops were inquisitive and persistent, but they had four months of mayhem to sort out, and the file on a clear case of home invasion would eventually be closed. Aubrey was grateful he'd kept Scott out of it.

After Norman's service, they sat on the front steps of her house and watched the neighborhood as it prepared for the coming winter. Enthusiasm for the community garden had remained high, even after the food chain was restored. Phil was hard at work, as November was a busy time in the vegetable patches. Scott and Celeste were with him, lifting parsnips, which were at their sweetest after the early frosts, and seeding the perennial bed with rhubarb and asparagus crowns. They'd missed the window for autumn garlic, a mistake all of Cayuga Lane had vowed not to repeat next year.

Lukas and Anya had been recruited to help in the fields as well, but they were still in their funeral clothes and seemed more interested in pelting each other with manure from the waiting pile. Aubrey watched them, smiling, and wondered how it was that the sight of her niece and nephew throwing shit at each other made her feel so oddly at peace. Then again, she was by now used to that sort of feeling showing up unannounced. Happiness came when it came.

Thom nodded toward Scott and Celeste, who were goofing around while they worked, grabbing each other, laughing.

"They still say they're gonna get married?"

"Yep."

"How's that going to work?" he asked.

"Well, emancipation turned out to be too much paperwork," Aubrey said, "but Celeste is sixteen, so she only needs her mom's permission, which she already got. And when Scott has his birthday next month, I'll help him track down his mother and try to get her to say yes too. She can't really object. She hasn't seen him in years."

"You're going to *let* them get married?"

"What possible difference could it make, after everything they've been through?"

"I guess."

"It's not the sort of mistake that'll cripple them forever. They start talking about having a kid, that I'll stop."

Thom nodded. "How's he doing with—you know, the rest?"

"OK, I guess. Pretty quiet."

"Therapy?"

"Doesn't want to go. I haven't pushed it yet."

Thom looked out at the street again. Lukas and Anya were still tormenting each other, moving on from dirt clods to pushing and shoving, and their voices had gone up in pitch, the early, rising tones of an argument. Thom tensed, watching them, but when Anya fell, as she invariably did—she was the clumsiest kid he'd ever seen—Lukas's tone shifted from hectoring to gentle, and he reached out to help his sister to her feet. To Thom's surprise, the volatile little girl accepted it.

Thom turned back to Aubrey. Her cheeks were pink in the chill autumn air. He thought she looked twenty years younger. He stared. She noticed. She put a hand on his back and felt his shoulders twitch as he began to cry. She put an arm around him and pulled him close.

He spoke, his voice weaker than she'd ever heard it. "I never should have let you do it."

"I like my life, Thom. It didn't ruin me."

"No. But I think it ruined me."

He put his head on her shoulder, and they watched the children play in the fading light.

"We're OK, Tommy. We're OK now."

Later, when Scott came back into the house, he found a two-foot cardboard box sitting on the dining room table. He let out a little gasp of surprise, seeing his name written in handwriting he'd never expected to see again.

He picked up the box—much heavier than it looked—took it to his bedroom, and unwrapped its elaborate packaging. Packing peanuts, bubble wrap, and wadded-up year-old newspaper had done their job for the past several months. Inside was cradled Norman's beautiful, meticulously preserved 1957 Zenith Trans-Oceanic shortwave radio, complete with a pristine copy of its original owner's manual. THE ROYALTY OF RADIOS, its cover boasted.

There was a note clipped to the manual, typewritten on an index card:

Kiddo,

Talk to people. I promise you there is
absolutely nothing more worth doing.

Yours,
Norman

P.S. Watch the skies.

ACKNOWLEDGMENTS

The notion of extraordinary global events that deprive us of power—in ways both literal and figurative—is something I've explored in the past. But it was fascinating to shift my focus from the global to the hyperlocal, and the ways in which tiny communities might come together or split apart during hardship.

For any insights or inspirations I might have had along those lines, I want to thank the residents of the Street Where I Live, in Amagansett, New York. Lucy and Joe Kazickas, Tracy and Matt McQuade, and all your delightful kids, both full-grown and teeny-tiny, you were the best pandemic neighbors we could have possibly hoped for during those frightening, isolating months of 2020 and 2021. When I think about a safe place to shelter in a storm, I think of our street.

The science in the book regarding the sun and power grid is, for the most part, accurate. I'm grateful to Professor Lucie Green of the Mullard Space Science Laboratory at University College of London, and Dr. Sara Seager of MIT, who were enormously helpful in that regard. Anything I got right was with their help; anything that's wrong is entirely my fault.

Likewise, everything good I know about sibling relationships I learned from my brothers, Steve and Jeff, and my sister, Cathy. Everything bad I made up out of whole cloth. Sibs—I love you.

Thank you also to my invaluable early readers—Howard Franklin, the tirelessly supportive Gavin Polone ("Why don't you write fifty pages and see how you feel then?"), Susan Lehman, Brian DePalma, Andrew Waller, the enigmatic John Kamps, and, of course, my immortal beloved, Melissa Thomas, without whom our whole traveling circus would fall apart.

In matters of business, I am forever grateful to my brilliant agents, Mollie Glick, Brian Kend, and Richard Lovett of CAA, and the ever-savvy and levelheaded problem solver David Fox, the best attorney a boy could ask for. The writer Will Reichel, who moonlights as my assistant, is unflappable and constant. If we were a football team, Will would be the kicker who makes the fifty-six-yard field goal, even after they ice him. My editor, Noah Eaker of HarperCollins, was consistently insightful and encouraging, and, Noah, I thank you for shepherding movie boy through the world of novel writing. Also, continuing thanks to Zachary Wagman, without whom I likely wouldn't be typing these words at all.

Like Don Corleone, I am sentimental about my children. Unlike him, I have never introduced them to a life of crime. Ben, Nick, Henry, and Grace, thank you for enriching my life in all ways. You have, each of you, been my greatest adventures.

ABOUT THE AUTHOR

David Koepp is a celebrated American screenwriter who has written more than two dozen feature films in a wide variety of genres, including the first two Jurassic Park films, *Death Becomes Her*, *Carlito's Way*, *The Paper*, *Mission: Impossible*, *Spider-Man*, *Panic Room*, *War of the Worlds*, *Angels and Demons*, *Inferno*, and *Kimi*. Some of the films he has both written and directed are *Stir of Echoes*, *Secret Window*, *Ghost Town*, and *Premium Rush*, the latter two cowritten with John Kamps. Koepp is also the author of the novel *Cold Storage*.